C A N D L E L I G H T
Ecstasy Supreme

"ARE YOU PLANNING A REPEAT PERFORMANCE OF TONIGHT?" KEITH DEMANDED.

"Well, of course I am," Lita answered. "I'll be singing here every night until I finish my contract."

"Not that," he said sharply. "I mean, do you plan once again to personally entertain all the stray men who frequent this nightclub?"

"I don't see where that's any business of yours," she replied heatedly.

"Oh, no? That kind of activity can be dangerous, and I'd hate to see you get involved in something you couldn't handle."

"Look . . . I've been taking care of myself and everybody else in my life since I was big enough to walk. So don't worry about me!"

Keith grabbed her shoulders and pushed her inside the doorway. "You may be an expert in taking care of yourself, but as long as you're working in my club, you'll avoid encouraging men to hang all over you. Is that understood?"

TORCH SONG

Lee Magner

A CANDLELIGHT ECSTASY SUPREME

Published by
Dell Publishing Co., Inc.
1 Dag Hammarskjold Plaza
New York, New York 10017

Dell ® TM 681510, Dell Publishing Co., Inc.

Candlelight Ecstasy Supreme is a trademark
of Dell Publishing Co., Inc.

Candlelight Ecstasy Romance®, 1,203,540, is a registered
trademark of Dell Publishing Co., Inc.

ISBN: 0-440-18718-4

Printed in the United States of America

May 1986

10 9 8 7 6 5 4 3 2 1

WFH

To Our Readers:

We are pleased and excited by your overwhelmingly positive response to our Candlelight Ecstasy Supremes. Unlike all the other series, the Supremes are filled with more passion, adventure, and intrigue and are obviously the stories you like best.

In months to come we will continue to publish books by many of your favorite authors as well as the very finest work from new authors of romantic fiction. As always, we are striving to present unique, absorbing love stories —the very best love has to offer.

Breathtaking and unforgettable, Ecstasy Supremes follow in the great romantic tradition you've come to expect *only* from Candlelight Ecstasy.

Your suggestions and comments are always welcome. Please let us hear from you.

Sincerely,

The Editors
Candlelight Romances
1 Dag Hammarskjold Plaza
New York, New York 10017

CHAPTER ONE

The raucous notes of a western gull pierced the peaceful late afternoon.

Lita Winslow shielded her eyes from the sun and turned to watch the bird dive and land gracefully on a rock not too far below her. "Don't despair!" she called to the bird. "That's not the only fish in the sea! You'll get the next one if you try hard enough."

The wind swirled around her, twisting the dark brunet hair cascading down her shoulders into a cloud of tangled strands. She gathered it in one hand and held it close to the back of her neck as she turned to climb the stone path back up the cliffside.

"This is just great," she muttered in cynical amusement. "Now you're talking to sea gulls! You've been out here too long, Lita! Too long!"

The deep, clear blue Pacific crashed into the rocky northern California coastline, sending surges of white froth pouring into every nook and cranny it could find.

Another gull cried.

Lita smiled sympathetically. She'd felt like screaming herself lately. Frustration could do that, she thought with a grin. "I guess I should take my own advice," she said aloud, casting a last glance at the small colony of gulls scattered across the rocky seacoast. "When at first you don't succeed, try, try again!"

She'd been stuck on the first line of her newest song for

weeks. No matter what she did, it wouldn't come. Hard work, relaxed work, no work. It all ended the same. It just wasn't ready to be born yet.

Lita was ready for the song, however. She knew it was there. She wanted to get it out on paper and hear it in her head, from start to finish. Every day she'd become more and more frustrated when she couldn't coax it into the light of day.

She reached the rustic stone terrace at the back of her seaside home and sat down to dust off her bare feet before going inside. In spite of her professional and creative frustrations, she loved living here. This was the only place where she truly felt at home. It was a feeling she treasured.

Considering how she'd grown up, it was not a great surprise, she admitted. But she didn't want to further darken her afternoon by raking up old wounds, and she pushed the memories out of her mind.

The sound of a car's engine brought her up sharp.

"Now, who would be driving out here?" she wondered aloud, rather surprised.

Hers was a private home, well off the road. Scenic Route 1 drew tourists with an eye for beautiful country-side, but they never strayed onto her driveway. In addition to being an awkward turn to make from the high-way, it was clearly marked Private. You had to be looking for it or know it was there.

She walked to the corner of the terrace that curved onto the driveway at the side of the house. She watched the small American-made compact pull up in front of the gate. A man got out, leaving the engine running.

"Jack Connery!" she exclaimed in surprise, waving as she recognized him. "What brings you out here?"

Before she could take a step in his direction, the phone rang inside the house.

"Just let yourself in, Jack!" she called out to him. "I've got to get the phone."

"Wait!" shouted her visitor, with unexpected urgency.

Lita hesitated. The phone shrilled insistently. "Come into the kitchen!" she shouted as she ran inside. She never could stand an unanswered phone. Panting, she picked up the phone. "Hello," she said.

"Lita, it's Mom," said the voice at the other end.

Lita slumped against the kitchen table and twirled the cord around her finger. Conversations with her mother were rarely brief. "How've you been, Mom?"

Jack Connery raced into the kitchen, pulling up short when he saw Lita already talking.

"You'll never guess who's dropped in for a visit," Lita said, giving him an engaging smile. He was waving a hand at her as if to stop her conversation, but Lita had already started to answer her own question. "No, it's not Daddy. It's Jack Connery! Yes . . . Isn't that a surprise?"

Jack seemed to be at a loss and looked at her strangely as she chatted with her mother for a few minutes.

"Since I'm sure Jack hasn't flown from one coast to the other to stand in my kitchen and listen to me talk to you, maybe you should get to the point, Mom," Lita prodded lightly. She frowned as she heard her mother's question. "No, I haven't talked to Melanie for several weeks. Why? Is something wrong?" When Lita heard her mother's response, she paled and sat down on one of the breakfast-bar stools. "Now, don't get upset yet, Mother. Just because there's been no answer at her apartment is no reason to believe the worst."

Lita had immediately thought of some very unpleasant possibilities herself, however. The last time Melanie had disappeared, they almost hadn't gotten her back at all. Lita refused to think about it. There had to be a reasonable explanation. There *had* to be.

"Look, Mother, I'm sure Melanie is all right. If it will make you feel better, I'll fly out tomorrow and look her up. I have some business to take care of out there, anyway." Lita looked at Jack. "I don't know if he knows anything about it, but if he does I'll let you know. Okay?"

Jack was Melanie's agent. The fact that he had appeared on Lita's doorstep at the very time her mother called to say Melanie was not answering calls at her apartment was too much of a coincidence to suit Lita. But she didn't want to pass on any bad news to her mother without having had a chance to grill Jack. Mother didn't take bad news well.

"Yes, Mom . . . I promise!" Lita swore, her exasperation growing. "Go fix yourself a nice cup of tea. I'll fill you in as soon as I know something. Bye." As soon as she dropped the phone in its cradle, Lita turned fully toward Jack. "Has something happened to Melanie again?" she asked, holding her breath and praying he'd say no.

He sighed and looked gravely in her direction. It was a message too eloquent to misread. Her heart sank.

"What happened?" she asked, steeling herself for bad news.

"She's disappeared," he said slowly, choosing his words carefully.

Jack always had been tactful, she thought. He was naturally circumspect whenever a sensitive topic was under discussion. Maybe that was why his clients liked him so much. "Do you mean she's gone barhopping?" Lita queried bluntly.

He shook his head and bit his lip. "No. I mean, I don't know. She's not at her apartment, and no one knows where she is . . . She's disappeared."

Lita knew what was coming next.

Jack cleared his throat. "You know how her contract reads, Lita. She opens this weekend at Sydney's. If she's not back by then—or if she's in no condition to sing—you agreed to go on in her place."

Lita leaned back in her chair and closed her eyes. She hated performing. Only for her cousin Melanie would she have ever agreed to do a nightclub act again. Melanie . . . Lita looked at Jack. "Okay, Jack. Did you get me a return reservation, or shall I call for one?"

He looked at her intently. "You haven't heard from her recently?"

Lita shook her head. "No. But I've spent a lot of time down near the water recently. And I disconnected the phone a few evenings just to make absolutely sure Mother didn't wake me up to complain about Daddy's latest date!" Lita smiled ruefully. "If Melanie had tried to call me, she may have missed me." The smile faded when Lita considered Melanie's erratic history. "I certainly hope that didn't happen."

Jack straightened, almost as if a weight had been lifted from his shoulders. He gave Lita a reassuring smile and reached for the phone. "You can't protect her from herself, Lita. And, no, I didn't make a return reservation, but I'll make one now."

"In that case, I'll pack." Lita hurried out of the kitchen and began making a mental list of things to take. "Be ready in half an hour or so," she called back to him as she disappeared into her bedroom. "And go turn off your motor!"

Jack tossed her suitcase into the backseat an hour later, as the sun painted the sky in melting shades of orange, pink, and melon.

The sun had set three hours earlier on the Potomac in Washington, D.C.

Now that night had fallen, Keith Christophe's day was ready to begin. He walked through the side door to his nightclub at eight o'clock sharp, as he did six nights a week. His secretary handed him a sheaf of papers as he passed her desk.

"Good evening, Mr. Christophe. There are just a few things that have to be signed tonight."

He gave her that faint heartbreaking smile that every woman in the club had noticed at one time or another. "Thanks, Felice. Need a cab tonight?"

She picked up her purse and grabbed her coat from the brass coat tree in the corner of her office. "Not tonight, Mr. Christophe." She was smiling happily and stretching out her left hand for him to look at.

He saw the fiery glint of a small diamond engagement ring and nodded his head as if not really surprised. "So Craig finally got the nerve up to ask you," he observed, grinning.

Felice had been in love with Craig Wilson for ten years. He'd been her steady in high school and her long-distance boyfriend in college. All she'd ever wanted was to be his wife.

But when Keith Christophe smiled like that, she felt her heart beat a little harder, and for a moment, she wondered if she were making a mistake. Felice gulped and reminded herself that his smile had the same effect on all women, as far as she could tell. She smiled back, remembering that this was real life.

He held out his hand. "Congratulations, Felice," he said, shaking her hand and lightly kissing her on the cheek. "Let me know when the wedding is."

"Yes, Mr. Christophe," she replied rather breathlessly. "I've got to be going. Craig'll be outside by now."

She hurried toward the door. Her boss, already preoccupied, hardly noticed it close after her.

He rapidly sprawled his signature where it was needed and put the sheaf of papers back on Felice's desk. A frown was shadowing his face as the thought that had been nagging at him all day consumed his attention. He sat on a corner of her desk and pressed the intercom button on her phone.

Marty Kahn was sipping a gin rickey at the bar when the bartender told him Mr. Christophe wanted to see him in his office.

"Thanks," said Marty, slipping off the stool and reluctantly heading for the rendezvous. He'd been dreading this for two days. Now he'd have to tell the boss the bad news.

"Well?" Keith asked bluntly as soon as Marty had closed the office door behind him. He watched Marty shift his slightly pudgy frame from one foot to the other. "Is Melanie King going to perform this weekend or not, Marty?"

Marty shrugged his shoulders and waved both hands angrily in the air. "I wish I knew, Keith! She didn't show up for rehearsal today. No one's seen her since last Friday."

Keith's mouth flattened into a hard line. "She's fallen off the wagon again?" he asked pointedly.

"Damn it, I don't know! I watched her like you told me to . . . I took her home or had one of the boys take her home every night. Hell! We all but tucked her into bed! The only nights we weren't baby-sitting that broad were when you took her home, boss!"

Keith leaned back in his padded leather swivel chair and motioned for his manager to sit down. "Yeah, yeah," Keith said with fatalistic resignation. "Did you get hold of Connery? He owes us a replacement, if I recall the contract we signed with him."

"Not yet, but I've been calling him for two days."

Keith's face hardened into steel. He stood up, straightening his black tie and loosening a button on his tuxedo. "If you don't have any luck by tomorrow at noon, call me at home, Marty. I'll take care of it . . . personally."

Marty felt a faint chill. He was sincerely grateful that

13

he would not be the object of Keith Christophe's personal attention. "Right, boss," he muttered as he trailed after him into the nightclub. Jack Connery had better show up tomorrow with the Winslow dame in tow, or there would be some serious complications in Connery's life, Marty thought nervously. Some very serious complications.

Lita had been trying to sleep on the plane without success. The red-eye flight to Washington had never been a favorite of hers, but the small child kicking the back of her seat for what had seemed like hours on end had made this particular trip almost unbearable. Jack had helped himself repeatedly to the drink cart and had dozed off in an alcoholic stupor, oblivious to her discomfort. Finally the child got tired of kicking and joined the rest of the plane in slumberland, to Lita's relief.

Unfortunately Lita still couldn't relax. The song locked in her head was still bothering her. She closed her eyes and let herself hear it.

> *I'd lived an empty illusion of life.*
> *A dreamer of dreams unmet . . .*
> *Each year they'd faded into regret.*

After a while she drifted into sleep, the melody and words still haunting her. The rest still waiting to be born . . .

Washington National Airport was doing its usual brisk business when Jack and Lita landed a little after dawn the next morning. The long line of taxis, a permanent fixture on the curbing outside, looked exactly as it had the last time she'd landed here.

There was quite a crush at the baggage carousel. Jack struggled to pull Lita's ticket from the inside pocket of his jacket and return it to her, but the jostling was making it difficult. He thrust the envelope into her hands and turned to grab one of their suitcases.

Lita shoved the ticket into her purse without looking at it as she snatched a piece of luggage from the carousel.

They hailed a cab and sped toward Melanie King's town house apartment.

"Are you sure you want to stay here?" Jack asked her as he watched her open the door half an hour later.

Lita stepped inside and looked around. "Melanie?" she called.

Silence.

She turned back to look at the agent. His light brown hair was thinning at the temples. Now, rather unruly from a night sleeping in a plane, it was giving his face a rather desperate look.

Lita told herself to take a firm hold on her imagination and smiled at him gently. "I'm sure, Jack. If it's just nerves or a case of needing to be by herself for a while, she'll be back soon. If it's more serious . . . this is where the first message to that effect will probably arrive." Lita gave his arm a reassuring pat. "Maybe she'll be back this afternoon," she said, forcing some cheerfulness into her voice.

Jack looked lost and helpless. Lita's heart ached in sympathy for him. She'd always suspected that Jack was in love with Melanie. That had been why he'd gone to such lengths to help her get this job at Sydney's. And the job before that. And the one before that.

Now his hard work and Melanie's sensational talent as a nightclub singer were on the verge of being rewarded. This was the big break Melanie had dreamed of for years —ever since she and Lita had been teenagers.

So why had she disappeared? Now, of all times?

Lita pushed a reluctant Jack out the door. "Look, Jack, if I have to stand in for her at rehearsal this afternoon and perform this weekend, I've got to have a little

15

nap and fix myself up. The sea gulls haven't cared what I looked like for the past five years, but as I recall, nightclub audiences want to see someone who looks good as well as sounds good!"

He nodded his head and walked back to the cab, leaning out of the window for one last question. "You'll let me know if you hear anything?" he asked anxiously.

Lita tried to smile but didn't quite make it. "Right away," she promised huskily. She crossed fingers on both hands and held them up for luck. It was an old signal between them. And for Melanie. She had used it before every performance as a good-luck charm.

Jack returned the gesture and leaned back despondently in his seat. The cab sped away in a blur of black and yellow, rapidly disappearing into the Georgetown traffic.

Deep in her heart, Lita could not believe that Melanie would have done anything to jeopardize this opportunity. It was the chance of a lifetime. But what had happened? And where was she?

Where was she?

"Where is she?"

It was the first question Marty Kahn was asked when Keith walked into the club later that morning.

Marty reached for his glass of tomato juice. When the boss came in at eleven in the morning to check on something, it meant someone's head was about to roll. "No one's seen hide nor hair of her. I still got the answering machine when I called her this morning."

Keith nodded, but the diamond-hard look in his eyes made Marty feel very sorry for Melanie King and her agent. They were first in line for execution, as far as Marty could tell.

The bartender handed Keith a glass of tomato juice.

"Thanks," Keith said, downing it and putting it back

on the bar empty. "I'm going to look up Jack Connery. He owes me a singer."

Keith was turning toward the door to execute his plan when an unexpected voice stopped him. "I don't think that will be necessary, Mr. Christophe," Lita began as she walked toward him.

He studied the attractive feminine figure approaching him. There was something familiar about her voice, but it was dark in the club and he couldn't quite see her face. "Why would you think that?" he asked, surprised at her abrupt arrival but too experienced to show it. Then she reached the better lighting near the bar, and he saw her face. "Well, well," he said softly. "Lita Winslow."

She smiled her most gracious professional smile and held out her hand. "In the flesh," she replied.

"Indeed," he murmured.

He took her hand and lifted it to his lips. The warm, brief pressure marked him as an expert. He looked up at her as he raised his head, capturing her with his gaze. She was quite sure kissing the back of a woman's hand was not the only thing at which he was expert.

He ran an appreciative eye over her. Somehow he did it so politely, with such understated admiration, that she found herself taking pleasure in his regard. Unlike most men, he really knew how to do it with style.

He motioned for her to join him at the bar. "If you haven't had breakfast, I'd be happy to order you some," he stated casually.

"Thanks, but I've already eaten."

"I take it that you haven't seen Melanie either?" he asked carefully, treading cautiously until he understood what relationship, if any, there might be between the two singers.

"No."

"Coffee, Ms. Winslow?" offered the bartender, extending her a cup and saucer.

She smiled at the portly man gazing at her with such bashful admiration. "Yes, thanks," she replied gratefully. "And, please, call me Lita."

Keith watched, bemused at his obviously captivated employee. A lot of very good looking women passed through the club, and not many had the effect that Lita was having on Carl. "This is Carl Dietrick," Keith said, helping out his temporarily tongue-tied bartender.

"Nice to meet you, Carl," Lita acknowledged warmly.

Keith turned to his equally dumbstruck manager. "And this is Marty Kahn, Sydney's manager."

Marty licked his lips and bowed his head nervously. "It's—it's an honor to make your acquaintance, Ms. Winslow," he said sincerely, stuttering to get the words out. "Gees, I've been an admirer of yours for a long time!"

"Why, thank you, Marty. And, please . . . it's Lita!"

"Yes, ma'am, er, Lita." Marty stumbled to his feet and glanced at Keith. "I've got to call some wholesalers about deliveries this afternoon, boss," he announced awkwardly. Turning to Lita, he added, "If you'll excuse me? I'm looking forward to hearing you sing again, Ms.— Lita." He ducked his head and hurried off toward the offices in back.

Keith watched him go in amusement. When he turned back to Lita, his eyes were still glimmering with humor. "You have quite an effect on him," he commented, an enigmatic look in his eyes.

Looking at her, he could understand why. Lita Winslow was a very beautiful woman. Her cascade of dark brunet hair framed a face of a classic beauty—high cheekbones, well-molded jawline, delicately arching brows that drew attention to the startling color of her eyes. Her eyes were a deep, rich blue. Clear with a purity of heart, yet hiding something deeper.

Keith found himself wanting to find out what that

deeper something was. It had been a long time since a woman had aroused his curiosity so deeply. And to do it so instantly, so effortlessly . . . It was annoying. He didn't like to be pulled like this. He wasn't used to it. And he didn't care to become used to it.

He drained the coffee the bartender had poured for him and glanced at the corner where the band set up in the evenings. "Are you planning to rehearse with the boys?" Keith inquired coolly.

Lita nodded her head. "Yes, just in case . . ." she replied, her voice trailing off. She refused to let herself think that Melanie might not make it back in time for the performance Saturday. "Am I too early?" she asked hesitantly, seeing no sign of a musician anywhere. Keith smiled faintly and her heart turned over.

"No. They'll be drifting in any minute now," he answered, studying her again in a hooded, unreadable way. "They'll be as star struck as Carl and Marty. Don't be surprised if they spend most of the afternoon shuffling from one foot to the other and staring at you."

Lita laughed in genuine amusement. "I'm not *that* much of an oddity!" she exclaimed. What she really was wondering, though, was whether she had a similar effect on the cool and distant owner of the club. At first she'd thought there had been a hint of masculine interest in the way he'd been regarding her. And then he'd turned away; and if it had ever been there, it was gone.

There was something about him that tantalized her. He was big and rugged and elegant and sophisticated all at the same time. He looked like a man who'd be equally at home in a barroom brawl or a boardroom power struggle. And equally likely to come out on top when the fur finally stopped flying!

"You're certainly not an oddity," he agreed softly, his eyes locked with hers, "but you're a very beautiful woman—and a very famous singer. Ever since you opted for the more solitary life of a songwriter, you've haunted your fans, Ms. Winslow . . . like Garbo."

She couldn't seem to escape his captive gaze, and in a way, she didn't want to. There was something warm and enticing and deliciously dangerous about the intimacy of it. Like falling into the unknown . . . "Lita," she corrected him faintly.

"Lita," he complied in a soft voice that was almost a caress.

"Have I haunted you, too?" she asked while she still had the nerve.

He was silent for a moment. "No," he replied, choosing his words with care. "But then, I'm in this for the business," he pointed out. "As the band keeps telling me, I don't have enough heart to relate to creative types."

The side door opened, and a man wearing a Greek sailor's cap, faded jeans, and a T-shirt bearing the outline of a scantily clad lady sauntered in.

Keith straightened up and got off the bar stool. "Here's the main man in the band," Keith explained, "Gaius Vaughn." As Gaius reached them Keith added, "I don't suppose I need to introduce Lita Winslow, do I?"

"No, sir! You sure don't, Keith," agreed the clearly astonished Gaius as his face lighted up in smiles. He held out his hand to Lita, who took it warmly. "It's a pleasure! It's a pleasure!"

"The pleasure is mine, Gaius," Lita protested. "I've been a fan of yours for a long time. Working with you will be a real honor!"

Gaius snatched his cap from his balding head and swatted it against his knee as he reacted to her praise. "Well, damn! Let's get to it before the rest of the boys get here and start shufflin' and gawkin'!"

Gaius pulled her off the stool and pushed her toward the corner where the band instruments were arranged. Lita cast an apologetic glance over her shoulder at Keith.

He smiled faintly and nodded, his eyebrows lifting as if to say, "I told you so."

"How 'bout warmin' up with a little song or two from that last album you cut?" Gaius suggested, rubbing his palms together in eager anticipation as he sat down at the piano. "How 'bout that one you did—what's it called— 'Love in the Morning'?"

"Anything you like, Gaius," Lita said amiably as she relaxed next to the baby grand.

Lita told herself that the nervous thrill running down her spine had nothing to do with the dark-haired man staring enigmatically at her across a darkened room. A tough-looking man who didn't get involved with "creative types." A man she found intriguing, fascinating, dangerous . . .

"How'd it go?"

"Okay, Jack," Lita replied as she opened the door and let him inside Melanie's town house apartment later that afternoon. "Can I fix you something to drink?"

He frowned anxiously. "You mean you found liquor here?" he pressed, very worried.

"No, no, not that." Lita ran a hand through her hair and sighed. "I meant a soft drink or a cup of coffee."

Jack sat on the couch and let his hands dangle helplessly between his knees. "No, thanks. Sorry. I still haven't been able to locate her. Have you heard anything?"

"No, Jack. I'm really worried. Don't you think we'd better call the police?" Lita asked unhappily. "What if she's hurt and needs help?" His hollow-eyed anguish was painful for her to see.

"Hell, Lita, what can I say? What can I do?" he cried roughly. "Do you want the newspapers to get a hold of this? Start raking up her past? Start smearing it all across the papers? Call her mother? Your mother?" He dropped his face into his hands and his shoulders shook with the sobs he could no longer hold back.

Lita ran to him and knelt at his feet, hugging him instinctively. "You've always loved her, haven't you, Jack?" Lita asked, the tears forming in her own eyes as she tried to comfort him.

"Always," was his choked reply. "Always loved her."

"We've got to get help," Lita said softly, a little while later.

"Yeah," Jack agreed in a ravaged, hard-to-hear voice. He rubbed his face in his hands and took a deep breath. "I guess there's no way to avoid it much longer."

Lita stood up and turned away, giving him a few private moments to pull himself together. She went into the small kitchen and put some water on to boil for tea. "Do you know anyone who could approach the police quietly?" she questioned.

There was a moment of silence.

"I don't," he called back from the other room, "but I know someone who probably does."

"Who's that?" She knew the second before he answered whom he would identify.

"Keith Christophe. He knows just about everybody."

Lita stared blindly out the small window overlooking the canal that ran behind the old town house. So now Keith Christophe would have to know it all. If he didn't already. Her heart sank. No one liked their family problems aired before strangers. And no one liked it less than Lita. She'd spent a lifetime in search of privacy. It seemed that fate was determined to keep it from her, she thought, discouraged. She heard Jack's footsteps as he joined her in the tiny kitchen.

"There's only one problem," he said reluctantly.

"What's that?"

"Keith has a reputation of never doing something for nothing."

Lita remembered the hardness that seemed to lie just beneath the surface—like a man carved of granite, with a heart of steel. "I see," she replied uneasily. "Do we have anything he would want in return?"

She was looking down at the tea she was pouring and didn't see Jack's peculiar expression as he watched her. "Maybe," he started uncertainly. He cleared his throat and began to sound more businesslike. "Why don't you ask him, Lita? Sometimes a woman gets a better reception on personal matters like this than a man does."

She'd been thinking along the same lines herself, but the idea took on a concreteness when Jack said it aloud. "All right, I'll ask him tonight at the club." Her answer was firm.

Jack had no idea that it bore little resemblance to the way she was feeling as she uttered it. He took the cup of tea from her and managed a grateful smile. "Thanks."

"I listened to Melanie's answering machine before I went to the club this morning," Lita mentioned as she took a careful sip from her own cup.

Jack's hand froze, leaving his cup poised halfway to its saucer in his other hand. "And?" he prompted, his eyes riveted on her.

"Nothing that helped. No messages from her. Only routine things, as far as I could tell."

Jack put the cup and saucer down on the countertop and ran his hand nervously through his hair.

"Why don't you get some rest, Jack," Lita suggested, worried about his run-down appearance and obvious agitation. "You can't help her by falling apart yourself."

He ran a hand over his eyes. "Yeah," he muttered, "and I've got to go to New York and Nashville in the next two weeks. Then maybe Los Angeles for a few days. You know how it is in the business . . ."

She pushed him toward the door. "Go back to your

hotel and get some sleep. I'll let you know as soon as I hear anything!"

He nodded his head and awkwardly touched her shoulder. "Yeah, you're probably right."

She tried to give him a reassuring smile. Poor Jack. He'd been there for both Melanie and her during some pretty turbulent years. He'd been a good friend as well as a good agent. She kissed him lightly on the cheek.

"All right," he agreed. "But call me the minute you hear *anything*. Anything at all, okay?"

There was a fierceness in his voice that puzzled her. For a second she worried that if something *had* happened to Melanie, Jack might consider taking revenge on whoever might be involved. Such raw, primal feeling frightened her. She was seeing a side of Jack that she had never seen before. She was staring into Jack's face, but she was seeing the glimmer of a stranger hiding just below the surface.

Lita shook off the feeling of disquiet and smiled at him with great determination. "I promise," she swore emphatically, then she watched him go. Now all I have to do is ask Keith Christophe to help me find Melanie, she told herself, rolling her eyes heavenward at that unwelcome idea. "I wonder what you'll want in return?" she murmured aloud.

She glanced at the clock on the wall. It would only be a matter of hours before she had the answer to that question.

CHAPTER TWO

Lita's cab pulled up in front of the nightclub a little after eight. A chauffeured black limousine with smoked-glass windows and shades half drawn was just pulling away. The small party of people it had discharged were moving into the entrance, their elegant attire drawing interested looks from passersby on the crowded Georgetown street.

Lita followed them into Sydney's and found the evening was getting into full swing. She was startled at how different the club looked, now that it was open for business.

She waited behind the three couples ahead of her at the coat check and curiously observed her surroundings.

The foyer created an ambience of elegant intimacy. Rich dark red carpeting softened the tread of expensively shod feet. The formally attired doorman just inside the entrance made customers feel as though they were being welcomed to a private estate rather than to a nightclub. Everyone in sight was superbly dressed—the men in tuxedos or evening jackets, the women in designer gowns and diamonds.

Lita gave her elegant wool wrap to the attendant and wasn't surprised to see it keeping company with mink stoles and jackets. It was a little late in the spring for fur, she thought in amusement, drifting toward the music. But then, some women would probably wear mink in the summer if they thought they could get away with it!

Her mother was like that, Lita thought with a sympathetic smile. Maybe that was why Lita had never really been too crazy about expensive furs. They reminded her of how desperately her mother wanted to be cared about and admired. Lita had seen how bitterly her mother had been disappointed, and how hard it had been for her to feel good about herself in the face of rejection.

Lita stood at the top of three steps that descended into the main club and surveyed the scene. To her left stretched the long onyx bar, polished until it reflected almost as well as the gold-and-silver-etched mirror that ran the length of the wall behind it.

Men and women were lounging on the tall low-backed stools, swirling drinks and engaging in murmured conversation. Carl looked up and saw her. He nodded a friendly welcome, pouring drinks all the while.

Lita smiled back at him and started hesitantly down the steps.

The main room circled out in front of her and slightly to the right. Tables were clustered here and there and were covered with linen tablecloths of dusky rose and white. A single orchid in a hand-carved lead crystal bud vase adorned each table. Inside the concentric circles of tables lay a small dance floor. Behind it played a jazz combo in the corner.

Music pulsed softly. Sensuous, relaxed melodies massaged tired spirits and made it easy for everyone to forget their cares for the evening. Lita wished she could forget hers. She knew that was impossible, so the next-best thing was to try and solve the main one confronting her at the moment. If she could just locate Keith Christophe, maybe she could make some headway . . .

"Good evening."

Lita started at the voice behind her. She hadn't heard anyone approach, but that wasn't really why she'd felt a sudden twinge of alarm. It was the voice itself that unnerved her. It was Keith Christophe's voice. She'd been hoping that she'd see him first, as if that would somehow help her avoid exactly what had just happened. As she turned to face him she wasn't certain that it would have made the least bit of difference. There was something about Keith Christophe that made her feel like she'd just stepped up to sing and forgotten all her music!

"Good evening," she replied rather coolly.

He stepped down and joined her. "I didn't expect you tonight," he said, giving her a curious look.

He didn't look the least bit surprised in Lita's opinion. However, she had the impression that he didn't let his true feelings show very often. She found herself wondering why.

"I thought I'd get a better feel for the clientele this way," she hedged. That was true enough, but it was far from the whole truth.

"Would you like to meet some of the people who frequent Sydney's?" he inquired.

"Why . . . yes." She hadn't expected that. Somehow she'd imagined him surrounded by admiring women and sitting at the bar, overseeing operations from a cool distance. A personal tour had never really occurred to her. It might make engaging him in conversation a lot easier, however, she thought optimistically.

He touched her back lightly with his hand and nodded toward a table discreetly placed along a back wall where the light was a little dimmer than elsewhere in the club.

"Why don't we start over there?" he suggested neutrally.

Lita recognized a senator and several of his socially prominent companions engaging in animated conversation. Sydney's certainly did attract people who possessed a certain cachet.

The men rose to their feet as Keith smoothly made the introductions. The senator was as charming to her as if she had been a key constituent whose vote was vitally needed for his reelection. His companions were more varied in their reactions. One was obviously impressed at meeting a singer whom he'd admired from an anonymous distance. Another was trying to suppress his irritation at being interrupted from a key point he'd been trying to make. The women were gracious to a fault.

Keith skillfully extracted them a few conversational forays later and casually led her to several other tables whose occupants had been casting admiring glances in her direction.

"If you'll excuse us," Keith interjected at the last one, "I'd like to introduce Lita to our culinary accomplishments."

He smiled and nodded his head in a way that left no room for protests. Murmured farewells lingered as they departed. Keith somehow managed to give off the clear signal that no one was to interrupt them. And no one did, although it obviously required an effort on the part of several single men nursing drinks here and there around the club.

He led her to a small table in a nook behind the bar where they could enjoy the music, watch all the action, and still hear each other talk without any effort. A waiter materialized as if from thin air and took their orders.

There was something about the man that exuded control of everything he surveyed, she thought. The way he held himself, the way he walked, even the way he was sitting there now—relaxed and yet ready to take care of anything that came his way without a moment's notice.

He was still smiling at her, but something flickered in his eyes. "Trying to figure out what it is?" he asked in amusement.

Lita was a little embarrassed. She wasn't in the habit of staring at men. She shook her head and lowered her eyes for a moment, trying to break the peculiar sensation that hovered around her.

"Yes," she admitted. She looked back up at him, drawing on her years of professional performing to put up a good appearance. "People seem to be quite willing to do exactly what you want them to do," she observed, trying for neutral words. "I'd say that's quite an art, Mr. Christophe."

He looked surprised. "Maybe it's because I never make unreasonable demands," he suggested diplomatically. He picked up a small matchbox and fingered it aimlessly. "I hope you aren't intending to keep calling me that," he added. It took a moment for her to understand him. The blank look on her face bloomed into one of comprehension as he explained. "My name is Keith," he said.

He was leaning back in the chair a little. The eyes that had been laughing earlier were serious now. And yet there was a guarded hiddenness about him. She found herself once again wondering what the man underneath was like.

"Keith," she acknowledged.

The waiter arrived with their drinks and food, and they turned to more conventional topics. In between bites of artichokes vinaigrette and sips of champagne, Keith amused her with anecdotes about the people who frequented his establishment. There was the senator's aide who came on Wednesdays with his mistress and on special occasions with his wife. And then there was the well-known Washington hostess who came on the second and fourth Thursdays to gossip with whomever she happened to spy there. And the White House aide who always arrived alone and pretended to run into the attractive and wealthy young woman currently separated from his boss.

"You make Washington sound like Peyton Place!" Lita said, laughing in protest.

Keith raised his eyebrows in mock defense. "Hey! I

29

can't help that! Power and ambition just affect people that way." He gently swirled the golden bubbles remaining in the fluted crystal glass and took a long, cool swallow.

Lita was finding it hard to keep from staring at him in spite of her best efforts to be polite and even a little distant. What did he have that other men didn't? she asked herself in annoyance. Six feet two, muscular and hard as nails under the well-cut tuxedo and blazing white of his shirt. So what? Lots of men took the time to make the most of what nature had given them. And in California, most of them displayed their wealth on the beaches for all to admire! It wasn't as if she'd never seen a man, for heaven's sake!

It wasn't just that, she mused as her cheeks pinkened slightly at the drift of her thoughts. Maybe it was his face. It was rugged and tough, more likely to be found on a longshoreman than a nightclub owner. There was nothing indoorish about it. And the eyes . . . His eyes were almost black, and they seemed to look right through you.

He put down the empty glass and stared back at her. She blinked and looked down at her hands to ensure that he didn't see more than she wanted him to. Eyes could be a window to the soul sometimes and Lita didn't want him seeing into hers.

"Have you heard from Melanie?" he asked cautiously.

That seemed as good a lead as any. Lita took it. "No, I haven't," she admitted unhappily. "As a matter of fact, that was why I wanted to talk to you this evening. I wanted to ask for your help," she explained.

"How can I help?"

It was clear from the way he said it that he wasn't offering any help. He was merely asking exactly how she thought he could do anything to be of assistance.

"Jack says you know everyone in Washington," she began.

"A slight overestimation, perhaps," he pointed out, although he didn't appear too worried about it.

"I'm worried about her." Lita bit her lip and tried not to let herself think about just how worried she really was. "You know, I guess, that Melanie has had a drinking problem?"

He nodded. "That's why I told Connery he'd have to guarantee me a backup—in case she couldn't do it." His eyes flickered over her. "You were . . . you are . . . the insurance policy."

"Yes, but you have to understand . . ." Lita leaned forward, needing very much for him to believe her. "Melanie is recovering. She hasn't touched a drink in six months. She's determined to make something of herself. I just know she's going to do it!"

Keith looked doubtful but politely refrained from voicing his opinion. He opened and closed the matchbox with the fingers of one hand. "What, exactly, do you think I can do to help?"

Lita took a deep breath and looked him straight in the eyes. "I wondered if there were some way to report her missing without drawing a lot of publicity. I desperately want to find her. She may need help. She could be hurt. But she doesn't need to see herself as fodder for the news media or the scandal sheets." Lita's expression saddened considerably. She wasn't sure Melanie was strong enough to bear up under that kind of pressure right now. She had enough stress in her life as it was.

Keith held the matchbox motionless and stared at Lita. "She seems to mean a lot to you," he probed. "Or is it just that you don't want to go on in her stead this weekend?"

Lita didn't know whether to laugh or cry at that remark. "There's nothing I'd like more than to avoid performing in public again," Lita admitted reluctantly. "I quit live singing five years ago, and I've never regretted my decision for a second."

"But you agreed to stand in for your cousin," he reminded her, a hint of challenge in his velvet voice. "Why?"

"Because I love her," Lita replied. She had stiffened defensively, but the intensity in her voice proclaimed the truth of her statement. "She's more like a sister or a best friend than a cousin. I want to help her. Is that so hard to believe?" she asked in surprise at the fleeting look of skepticism that had crossed his face.

The look was gone as soon as it had come. In its place was the tough, polite expression of the nightclub owner. "No," he said, although he didn't exactly sound convinced. He shrugged and looked directly at her. His eyes were as dark and as opaque as the onyx bar. "People have been known to do crazier things than that, out of love."

Lita looked back, unwilling to falter before him like a schoolgirl. And yet there was something unsaid that hung between them—like a warning not quite voiced, she thought. She refused to come right out and ask him what he meant.

Her hazy thoughts were interrupted by a confident masculine voice and the touch of a hand on her shoulder. She turned her head to see a handsome young man leaning over her.

"Lita Winslow?" he asked in admiration and surprise. At her polite smile of acknowledgment, he pulled up a nearby chair and sat down with them. "Good Lord! This is my night! I can't tell you what a pleasure it is to be able to meet you!" he exclaimed. He gave a sidelong glance at Keith, who looked less than thrilled at the younger man's arrival. "Aren't you going to introduce me, Keith?" the newcomer prodded, feigning mild shock at such a display of poor manners.

For a moment Keith hesitated, and Lita wondered if he

were actually thinking of refusing. What in the world was going on? she wondered.

"I'm thinking about it," he stalled, fixing the younger man with a stare that would have quailed most people. Their visitor merely laughed it off.

"I'll do it myself, then," he declared good-naturedly. "I'm Sean Christophe."

Lita, feeling caught in the middle, looked questioningly from one man to the other.

Sean laughed and reached out for her hand. Lita evaded his grasp after a brief squeeze and softened her rejection with a gentle smile.

"Now that my brother's helped you relax, let me entertain you for a while," Sean suggested, appearing totally unphased by the minor setback.

Sean had his older brother's penchant for taking charge, Lita decided. He also had his elder sibling's dark, masculine presence, although Sean was more classically handsome.

Lita looked doubtfully in Keith's direction. He still hadn't indicated whether or not he would be able to help make some discreet inquiries about Melanie. "Well, your brother and I were just discussing something—"

Keith cut her off saying, "Yes, I'll see what I can do about that matter." With that he rose, smiled faintly, and nodded in Sean's direction. "If he turns out to be less entertaining than he thinks he is, let me know. Maybe I can find a replacement."

He turned and left, stopping to say a few words to Marty Kahn at the bar before continuing down the dark corridor that led toward the club offices.

Sean shook his head, muttering something crude under his breath about suitable replacements. "Good-bye, big brother!" he chortled. "Now, let me tell you the story of my life!" he exclaimed cheerfully, turning on all his charm for Lita's benefit.

33

* * *

It was after midnight.

Keith Christophe was sitting in his office, staring at the clock on his broad, uncluttered desk. He felt like he'd been sitting there forever, and he practically had. It had been several hours since he'd left Lita and holed up in his office to attend to a few things.

He knew he was avoiding the club tonight and he knew why. He was avoiding Lita Winslow. And he was deeply annoyed that he felt the need to.

He fingered the gold-filled pen in his hand and stared blindly into the lamplight emanating from the Tiffany shade in a far corner of the soundproof room. Even as he'd signed a few checks and reviewed the bookkeeper's report, he'd seen her. Laughing. Smiling. A graceful young woman of aristocratic carriage and rare charm. A dark-haired beauty with eyes that flashed like midnight velvet.

Midnight velvet!

He was thirty-eight years old, damn it! he reminded himself. He'd been alone for a long time. Why was he letting a twenty-eight-year-old girl hypnotize him?

He saw her face and recalled the gentle sway of her walk and the soft, sultry sound of her voice as she'd sung this afternoon at rehearsal. Well, what man wouldn't want a woman like that? he asked himself angrily.

The phone rang. He picked it up.

"Christophe," he said bluntly.

"Evening, Keith. This is Fallon. Got a message here says to call you," explained the caller in a congenial, unhurried drawl.

Keith swiveled his padded leather chair and stared at the Picasso cutout hanging on his wall. "Yeah. Thanks, Pete. I have a favor to ask of you. It involves a possible missing person. But I'd like you to keep it as quiet as possible, if you can."

"Tell me about it," replied Keith's longtime friend from his desk downtown in the police department.

"There's a singer named Melanie King," Keith began . . .

Somewhere a church bell was ringing one o'clock in the morning.

Lita inserted the key into the town house door and pushed it part way open. She turned a little to face Sean, who'd driven her home in his Maserati and was clearly hoping to be invited in for a nightcap.

"Thanks, Sean. I really appreciate the ride home," she said. She stepped halfway into the darkened doorway and gave him what she hoped was a friendly smile that conveyed her desire to call it a night.

Sean stepped forward and grasped her shoulders lightly. Lita eased herself from his hold and gave him a level look. "Good night, Sean," she said firmly.

Lita recognized the look in his eyes. Sean wanted to come in. Sean wanted as much as he could get away with. But Sean would do what she asked him to do, when all was said and done.

"Sleep tight," he answered suggestively. The humorous light in his eyes softened the insinuating tone of his voice.

Lita sighed. In a few years he'd be as polished as his older brother, no doubt, she thought. Why did that thought bother her, anyway? she wondered as she shut the heavy Georgian-style door behind her and leaned against it. Who cared how Keith Christophe entertained himself?

No sooner had she dropped her clutch on the nearby table than she glanced into the apartment and realized something was amiss. She stumbled back to the door—pausing only long enough to grab her small purse—and rushed down the steps after Sean.

"Wait!" she cried, grabbing his elbow.

He looked at her in astonishment. "What is it?" he asked blankly. He was totally unprepared for the look of fear in her eyes.

"Someone's broken in," Lita said, biting her lower lip as she wondered who that faceless someone could have been. "Could you—could we call someone for help?"

Sean frowned in deep concern and set her inside his car. "Lock the door. Wait here. I'm going to turn on some lights and make some noise and use your phone to call the police."

His dictatorial no-nonsense statements reminded her vividly of his older brother. Lita wished Keith were here instead of Sean. She had the feeling no one would dare to tangle with Keith Christophe, but she wasn't so sure about Sean.

She grasped his wrist before he could leave, and he looked sharply at her. "Whoever it was could still be in there," she reminded him, alarmed at the prospect of his going in alone. "Please, let's find a phone nearby and call. Don't go in there by yourself!"

Sean raised an eyebrow and removed her fingers from his arm. "I may look pretty, honey," he returned silkily, "but don't let the looks deceive you. I can take care of myself."

His eyes narrowed and he turned back toward the town house, taking the steps like a prowling cat. As he cautiously opened the door wide and stepped inside, Lita looked around the street in desperation. Suddenly she found what she was looking for. A telephone booth!

She leaped out of the car and ran to it, fumbling for change and searching her small purse with trembling fingers for the nightclub's number. She heard the phone begin to ring and prayed that Keith didn't turn the phone system off or instruct people not to answer after hours. She looked back anxiously at the town house at the far end of the block.

Please answer, she prayed, biting her lip to keep her growing panic under control.

As the phone rang and rang she kept remembering a similar incident that had occurred five years earlier. God help her if it was going to start all over again, she thought desperately. It couldn't! It just couldn't!

Keith Christophe left his office and strolled out into the club as chairs were being turned up on top of newly bared tables. Piles of soiled linen were being carried out back for pickup by the laundry, and Carl was polishing the mint-clean bar with a soft dry towel.

It was the way the club usually looked shortly after closing. So why was he searching the room? he asked himself sarcastically, as if he didn't know.

"I presume Sean already left?" he asked as Marty joined him.

"Yeah, yeah, boss. A little while ago."

"Did he take Lita Winslow home?"

To anyone else's ear, it would have sounded like a casual, polite question. Marty had known Keith for a long time, however, and he detected a slight difference. There was a trace of real interest in his voice that sounded purely male.

Marty looked at Keith in mild surprise. He'd never known him to be subtle when he was interested in a woman. Of course, the kind of interest Keith had displayed had been of a very basic, functional variety, as far as Marty could tell.

One look at Keith's granite profile told Marty this was not going to be a subject for teasing, so he kept his thoughts to himself. "Yeah," Marty replied, hoping the answer wouldn't be the wrong one. He himself had never been on the receiving end of Keith Christophe's temper, but he hated to even see it, no matter who the poor devil was who'd inflamed it. He shifted awkwardly and waited for a reaction.

Keith merely nodded as if he'd expected as much.

Gaius joined them as the band finished putting their instruments away.

"Say, Keith," he asked, "anybody found Melanie yet?"

"Not that I know of."

Gaius pulled his black cap down tight on his head and nodded thoughtfully. "Well, that's really too bad, man. She's a nice girl. I hope she comes back soon," he said sympathetically. He gave Keith a careful look. "Say, uh . . . Lita really *will* sing if Melanie's not back, right?"

Keith looked at the musician in surprise. "Why wouldn't she? She signed a contract to that effect."

Gaius nodded his head and shrugged his shoulders apologetically. "Yeah, sure. Forget I asked," he said evasively, turning to go.

"Wait a minute, Gaius," Keith ordered. "What makes you think she might not?"

Gaius shifted awkwardly. He hated getting in the middle of things. On the other hand, he didn't want his own band getting tarnished if there were some last-minute complications. "Well . . ." he explained with great reluctance, "it was the way she quit . . ."

"What about it?" Keith prompted him grimly.

"I knew a guy who played at her last gig," Gaius said. "There was something going on. She was scared to death of something. No one was supposed to know about it. They kept it all real quiet. But she's got guts! She stood up and sang in spite of the fact that she was afraid. Leastways, that's what he told me."

All this came as a great shock to Keith Christophe. The information itself was disconcerting, to say the least. Beside that, he was annoyed at his own ignorance of the facts. "Do you know what she was afraid of?" he asked pointedly.

38

Gaius raised his brows and pushed out his lip. "Nope" —he shook his head regretfully—"but the musicians thought she was being threatened." Gaius shrugged helplessly. "Sorry, Keith. I didn't mean to set you to worryin' 'bout this."

Keith gave him a wry grin. "Might as well worry about that as anything," he said. "Good night, Gaius."

As the band leader left, the phone began to ring.

Keith was reaching for his coat when Carl called to him. "It's for you, boss. Lita Winslow. And it sounds like something bad's happened."

Keith covered the distance in a few strides. "Hello," he said quickly.

He heard her sigh with relief, and it gave him the oddest feeling. He didn't have time to consider any of that, however. Lita immediately broke into his thoughts with her news.

"Thank God!" she exclaimed. "Someone's broken into Melanie's town house. Sean's gone inside to take a look around, but he's all alone—" she said urgently.

"Where are you?" he interrupted sharply.

"At a phone booth down the block . . ."

"Stay where you are," he ordered. "I'll be there as fast as I can. We'll call for the police." He hung up the phone and ran toward the back door. "Carl!" he shouted. "Call Pete Fallon and tell him someone's broken into Melanie King's place. Tell him my brother's there and I'm on my way."

Carl was dialing the number as the heavy steel back door slammed shut and Keith slid into the front seat of his car.

Things certainly weren't dull these days, the bartender thought worriedly.

Lita stood rigidly in the booth, staring in apprehension at the front door of the old brick building where Sean had disappeared. She remembered the sharp click as Keith had hung up on her.

It was her only comfort at the moment. It meant he was going to be here soon.

Please, please don't let anything bad happen, she prayed. She couldn't bear it if it all started again and someone else were hurt on her account. The memories began coming back now, and she remembered the cold fear that she'd lived with for so long. For the past four years, she'd managed to put it all behind her.

Now it came back with a vengeance.

Keith arrived first. His powerful low-slung car purred to a halt next to the phone booth, and Lita pushed through the small doorway to be closer to him.

He was out of his car and had a warm hand on her elbow in seconds. "Are you all right?" he asked, a hard, angry look in his eyes.

"Yes—yes," she stammered, "but your brother . . ." She motioned toward the town house.

Keith looked her over and decided everything was exactly as she said. Without another word, he turned and ran toward the town house. He was a big man, but he sprinted as soundlessly as a barefoot youth on the pavement.

Lita wrapped her arms around herself, hugging the woolen shawl closer to ward off the chill and the fear. When the black and white police car appeared a few minutes later, followed by an unmarked car with a detective in it, she hurried toward them.

Keith stepped into Melanie's town house living room and heard his brother's footsteps returning from the back.

"What the devil!" Sean exclaimed, halting as he saw

his older brother at the opposite end of the room. "What are *you* doing here?"

Keith glanced around the mess. Papers had been dropped here and there, a few pieces of furniture overturned and cut up. Whoever had broken in had been looking for something, and they hadn't been too concerned about the damage left behind.

"Anybody still here?" Keith asked sharply, assuming his brother had been checking the premises.

"No. He's gone, whoever it was," Sean replied stiffly. "What are you doing here, big brother?" he asked defensively.

Keith crossed the room and looked into the kitchen, then checked the door to the upstairs apartment. The door was locked and showed no signs of having been tampered with.

"Lita called the club. She was worried about you," Keith said, clipping his words to contain his anger. "What in the hell possessed you to come in here, anyway?" he asked angrily. "If the burglar had still been here, you could have been in big trouble!"

Sean's eyes narrowed in unconcealed ire. "I can take care of myself!" he retorted icily. "You came running in here, too," he pointed out with an air of satisfaction. "If you can, I can."

"Like hell," Keith muttered succinctly.

Before they could escalate their argument, they were interrupted by the arrival of the police and Lita.

Sean shouldered through the small crowd to Lita's side. "I thought I told you to stay in the car!" he exclaimed in annoyance. He glanced resentfully toward his brother, who was engaged in conversation with the authorities, taking things in hand as he always did.

Lita bristled. "I wasn't sure what you might run into. I just wanted to make sure the odds weren't stacked too much against you," she answered.

Sean sighed and pulled her into a corner to sit down in the small loveseat, which had been spared any noticeable attention by the intruder. "I'm sorry," he apologized, loosening his jacket and laying an arm along the back behind her. "I guess it's my problem," he explained with a sheepish grin.

Lita warmed to him and smiled back. Sean was a comforting mixture of man and boy, she thought. He could be infuriatingly persistent, but his charming ability to laugh at himself smoothed over the rough spots. "I'd hardly say it's your problem," she offered. "After all, it wasn't your fault someone broke in and burglarized the place."

Sean lowered his eyes for a moment and glanced in his brother's direction. Keith was looking at him. He didn't look too happy either. Then the detective pulled him into the back, and Sean was spared receiving further nonverbal reprimands for the moment.

"I didn't mean that," Sean explained to her, sliding his hand down over Lita's shoulder. "It's my brother," he went on. "He can be a royal pain in the neck!" He turned cool eyes on Lita as he recalled who had been responsible for Keith's unwanted arrival. "I could have taken care of this for you. You didn't have to call Keith."

Lita saw the expression in Sean's eyes and bit off the first answer that came to mind. Poor Sean, she thought. It must be hard growing up in the shadow of an older brother like Keith Christophe. "I'm sure you could have," she said sympathetically, "but I was scared. I just wanted to make sure no one got hurt on my account."

Sean gave her a charming boyish grin. "Yeah, yeah," he scoffed. "Pay no attention to me, Lita. I know what I sound like."

His eyes were laughing then and Lita began laughing herself. Their gentle camaraderie was interrupted by Keith, staring darkly down at them.

"Have I missed the humor in this situation?" he asked sarcastically, his brows raised in doubt that he had.

Lita was uncomfortably aware of how intimate she and Sean had looked. It wasn't the way Keith seemed to be interpreting it, but it seemed silly to leap to her feet and put some distance between Sean and herself just to prove that. Instead she sat still and tried to compose herself. Looking around the decimated apartment had the opposite effect, and she shivered as anxiety overtook her once again. "No," she replied. "It's not the least bit funny."

Sean drew her closer, as if to comfort her, but Lita saw the triumphant gleam in his eye as he glared at Keith. Lita had no desire to be used by anyone and resented Sean's adolescent attitude surfacing again. He seemed to relapse to age eighteen every time Keith was nearby! Lita stood up and walked toward the police, steeling herself for the unwanted interview.

Keith stopped her with a hand on her shoulder. "The detective is a friend of mine," he explained coolly, looking down at her as if trying to read her state of mind. "His name is Pete Fallon."

"Pete Fallon," she echoed numbly, staring back into his expressionless eyes. His hand was heavy on her shoulder. There was something very comforting about having him near, she realized.

"I told him about Melanie," he added quietly. "Maybe you'd like to speak to him in private about all this." He waved a hand expressively, taking in the wreckage around them.

She nodded her head. "Yes. And Keith . . ." she said hesitantly.

He waited for her to go on, letting his fingers tighten gently over the tense muscles of her neck, almost like a comforting massage . . . or the beginning of a caress.

"Thank you for coming," she said softly.

He gave her that faint smile that made her heart turn over. "Anytime," he replied.

Lita turned and walked toward the waiting Pete Fallon. She didn't see the worried frown that settled on Keith's features—nor did she realize he stood there staring after her retreating figure until she was out of sight.

Lita didn't see, but Sean did. "Well, well," Sean murmured in surprise. "Well, well . . ."

CHAPTER THREE

It was nearing three o'clock in the morning when the police finally left.

Lita stood in the middle of the room, wondering what in the world to do next. Most of the furniture was back where it should be, and the things that had been strewn around the room had been returned to their proper places, for the most part. The silence was almost eerie, and Lita had the chilling sensation that the spirit of the burglar somehow lingered on, threatening to finish what he'd started.

She didn't want to stay here, under the circumstances, but neither did she wish to go to a hotel. Her memories of staying in hotels were vividly unhappy. Besides, if Melanie returned or called, Lita wanted to be there.

If only there were some evidence of forcible entry, she mused unhappily. Unfortunately it appeared that the perpetrator used a key. If that were true, he—or they—could enter the building again tonight. The police had promised to patrol the neighborhood, just in case, but they couldn't sit on the front steps or the back entry until dawn!

She eyed the two tall men talking quietly near the front door. To her surprise they weren't at each other's throats anymore. The brothers Christophe had been impeccably polite to each other ever since she'd talked with the police, as a matter of fact. Lita couldn't help but sigh in

45

relief at that. They were two strong bulwarks, now that they weren't taking snide shots at each other.

Lita was still trying to decide whether to brave staying the rest of the night at Melanie's when she thought of Jack. He ought to know about this. She was in the process of dialing his hotel as the front door closed; when she turned to see who had gone, she was met by a grim-faced Keith Christophe, walking purposefully across the room toward her.

She clutched the phone, still trying to shake the sense of vulnerability that stubbornly clung to her like a second skin. The phone rang. A hotel operator answered.

"May I have Mr. Jack Connery's room, please?" she asked as firmly and as confidently as she could. The operator put her through.

The phone rang and rang, but there was no answer.

Lita slowly hung up the receiver.

"He didn't answer?" Keith asked, although he already had guessed the answer to that question from her actions.

Lita shook her head. "No. He's probably still out drumming up gigs or recording engagements for his clients. They don't roll up the streets in New York at night like they do in Washington," she pointed out, trying to be philosophical about it.

Keith wasn't particularly impressed by that argument, but he nodded agreement and loosened his bow tie anyway.

That small movement caught her attention, and it finally dawned on her that they were alone. He was still in his tuxedo, but he was loosening the top button of his shirt and standing in front of her in a relaxed way that made her want to lean against him for comfort.

She looked up into his eyes and wondered if he could guess her thoughts. She hoped not. But she wished he'd keep looking at her just the way he was now. He was gazing at her like an old friend who was prepared to stand by her, to help her through this . . . until the end, whatever that might be.

She couldn't remember the last time anyone had even given her the impression of being there for her when she needed someone. Jack Connery came as close to that as anyone. Usually it was the other way around. Lita, could you help me with this? Lita, could you fix that? Lita's strong . . . Lita can handle it . . .

The corner of his hard mouth curved, and his grim expression softened into a look of tenderness. "Why are you staring at me, Lita Winslow?" he asked softly, reaching out to tuck a stray dark curl behind her ear, watching it in fascination as it sinuously caressed his finger.

"I . . . was thinking it's been a long time since anyone was there for me to lean on in an emergency," she admitted softly. It was too late and too much had happened this week. All she could manage at the moment was complete candor, no matter how risky that turned out to be in the end.

"Lean all you want," he invited her in a low voice. "I always protect my investments," he added.

And yet there was something in his eyes that said something else altogether. Lita knew she was not just an investment to him, no matter what he said.

"Would you rather stay somewhere else tonight?" he asked hesitantly, his expression turning grim once more. "After all, if someone has a key . . ."

"Yes," she murmured unhappily. "If someone has a key . . ."

She stared at the floor and unconsciously wrapped her arms protectively around herself. The man standing in front of her saw the gesture and felt an unexpected surge of protectiveness. He wanted to step forward and pull her into his arms, fold her dark, silky head close to his chest, and tell her everything would be all right. He'd see to it.

Instead he jammed his fists into his elegant black trou-

47

sers and crossed the room to stare blindly outside into the still darkness. "An old friend of mine is the manager of one of the best hotels in town," he said evenly. "If you'd like to pack a few things, I'd be happy to take you there and see that you're checked in."

A chill of fear ran down Lita's spine.

When she remained silent, he turned to look at her. He saw the expression on her face and wondered what could have put it there. Surely nothing he'd said . . . "What's the matter?" he asked gently, as if coaxing a nervous wild animal to trust him.

Lita tried to laugh but couldn't. "I'm sorry," she apologized helplessly. "I have very painful memories of hotels," she explained vaguely.

Keith was tempted to make some sarcastic remark, but her obvious distress stopped him. Something very painful indeed must have happened, he realized. He recalled Gaius's comments earlier in the evening about the circumstances at Lita's last performance, and he wondered if there were any connection.

"You'd be safe there," he said quietly, trying to soothe her. "Remember, Washington hotels put up celebrities and heads of state all the time. They're very security conscious, Lita."

Her eyes were haunted, and he felt something almost painful stir in his chest as she gazed at him.

"I'm sure they are," she whispered. "I just can't—I'm sorry, I can't stay . . ."

What in the devil could have put such fear in her that she'd start stuttering over a simple refusal to go to a hotel? he wondered in anger and dismay. His fist tightened. If the cause of her distress had been there in the room, he would have been sorely tempted to use it on whatever or whoever it was.

Lita saw his anger but mistook its source. She backed away slightly, a hint of worry in her eyes.

Keith read her reaction instantly and sighed in exasperation, running a hand through his dark hair and shutting his eyes for a moment in order to calm down. "You have nothing to fear from me, Lita Winslow," he assured her with a wry grin. "I just had a sudden urge to choke whoever put that look of fear on your face," he admitted, almost sheepishly.

Their eyes locked and suddenly Lita knew she would never have to worry about Keith Christophe's meaning her any harm. He was on her side. She smiled shyly and felt warmth blossom in her heart as he returned it with a smile of his own.

"If you like, you're welcome to spend the night at my place," he offered gravely. He'd spoken as unsuggestively as he could, wiping every trace of his desire for her as a woman from his mind as he made the invitation. He didn't want her to think he was merely trying to take advantage of the situation.

Lita was frozen with surprise. She saw the sincerity in his face but wasn't sure how he'd take it if she said yes. It was tempting, though, very tempting. She was sure his home would be a safe haven for her. "I . . . don't think that would look too good, Keith," she demurred at length, her voice faintly tinged with apology and regret. "Thank you for offering," she added with obvious sincerity.

The church bell rang four o'clock. Lita knew they couldn't stand in the living room, staring hollow-eyed at the doors until dawn. She had to send him away. He couldn't stand here all night. She'd have to make it through the rest of the night on her own.

Come, Lita, she told herself unsympathetically. You're a big girl. You've lived alone for years. This is nothing new. Nothing else is going to happen tonight. And tomorrow you can get the locks changed and a burglar alarm installed.

"Thanks for everything, Keith," she said, moving toward the door. "You must be tired. I'll be all right. Don't worry about it."

Her hand was almost closing over the doorknob when he realized she was about to usher him out. He covered the distance between them in two long strides, closing his hand over her wrist to stay her.

She looked up at him in surprise. His face, dark and shuttered, was as close as if they were in each other's arms. She could feel the warmth from his body and unconsciously relaxed in response.

"You really want to stay?" he asked bluntly.

"I don't want to," she admitted, her eyes unwavering, though her voice shook a little, "but I'm going to. What if Melanie comes back? Or tries to call?" She hesitated, biting her lip before continuing. "As bad as it is, it's better than a hotel, Keith."

He looked at the rich, deep color of her hair, the creamy, sun-kissed tint of her skin, the melon red of her beautiful lips. He slowly released her wrist, placing both his hands on her shoulders instead and turning her toward the bedroom. "All right," he said calmly. "You go to sleep. If I can't convince you to leave, I'll just have to stick around and play bodyguard."

Keith was pushing her gently but firmly to the bedroom.

"I don't know what to say," she replied softly as she stared at him helplessly.

He grinned at her. "I think the customary thing is 'good night.'"

She laughed softly, feeling for the first time in hours as if she actually could sleep. "Good night," she said. "And Keith . . ."

"Yes?"

"Thank you."

He watched her close the door to the bedroom, wondering why he was finding it so hard to keep his eyes off her. He could hear her rustling around the room, stepping out of her clothes, slipping into a nightgown, brushing her hair. He heard the bed creak softly as she lay down, and he could see her in his mind's eye, her hair spilling around her, her breathing soft and regular now.

He checked the doors and windows, then lay down on the couch and laced his fingers behind his head. "Good night," he said softly.

Keith didn't sleep particularly well for several reasons. Sleeping while trying to be alert to a burglar's return gave him a new understanding of the phrase "Sleeping with one eye open." The fact that his strapping build was a good inch longer than the couch didn't help either, nor the fact that he wasn't sure he wanted to cast himself in the role of Lita's protector.

His mind might have argued against being her guard, but something deeper had compelled him to do it anyway. The beautiful woman seemed to be having an adverse effect on his rational judgment!

Those thoughts jumbled in and out of his restless sleep and occasional wakefulness until the midmorning sun came streaming warmly through the front windows. The sound of the postman pushing mail through the letter shoot in the front door finally put an end to his vigil.

He was sitting on the couch, rubbing his sore neck muscles when he heard Lita's soft tread in the bedroom. He looked up just in time to see her stop hesitantly in the doorway.

"Good morning," she said.

He took in the floor-length blue wool robe, tightly cinched at the waist, and the unruly cloud of dark hair tumbling about her shoulders and grinned at her with instinctive male appreciation. She was beautiful without her makeup, too, he noted in mild surprise. Maybe more

51

than with it; unadorned, she looked younger and less sophisticated—A California girl instead of a famous singer of torch songs in nightclubs.

He ran his hands through his hair roughly, trying to get the circulation going and some energy into his system. "Good morning," he said. "Feel like getting up?"

She lowered her lashes and tried to bury the feeling that had unexpectedly assailed her upon first seeing him. He was so solid and comforting a presence, she'd had the urge to go over, curl up next to him, and put her arms around him for a good-morning hug. This is ridiculous! she admonished herself in alarm. What in the world is wrong with you, anyway?

"Not really," she admitted with a wan smile, "but there are a few things I need to take care of before rehearsal this afternoon, so I guess I'd better. How about some coffee?"

"Yes, thank you." Keith wasn't sure it was a bright idea to keep hanging around, but he needed that java. He had the feeling that the better acquainted with Lita he became, the harder it was going to be to think of her as a glitzy professional woman. He might start thinking that she had a heart as well as a body. He began to frown slightly as bitter memories were resurrected from his past.

Lita had already turned toward the small kitchen, determined to feed the man something. She didn't see the frown or the cynical expression that had come to his eyes.

"Scrambled eggs okay with you?" she called out as she saw that was about all Melanie's refrigerator had to offer.

Keith trailed her to the kitchen and was about to say no thanks. The sight of Lita's shapely form bent over in front of the open refrigerator threw a wrench into his resolve. "Hey, don't bother. Coffee's fine," he protested halfheartedly as he stared in fascination at the graceful curve of her hips and legs molded so intriguingly by the dark blue wool.

Lita looked over her shoulder and misread the look on his face to be that of a man who hadn't slept much and was still rather glazed over from lack of sleep. She smiled at him with genuine warmth, setting her face aglow. "Come on, now. The least I can do is feed the man who pulled guard duty," she teased. She put the ingredients on the counter and began searching the cabinets for bowls, dishes, and a frying pan.

Keith told himself that spending another hour with her couldn't do any damage. Hell! He needed to eat, didn't he? Besides, it was a pleasure to watch her move around the kitchen doing these simple little domestic chores, chatting about the club, and engaging in harmless pleasantries. He set their places at the small table in the breakfast nook and sat down, drinking his coffee and enjoying himself immensely before he knew what was happening.

They ate and conversed amiably, more like old friends than two people who had just met.

"I can arrange to have new locks put on this afternoon, if you like," Keith offered as Lita put the dishes into the dishwasher a little while later. "I'll be glad to talk to the landlord for you, too, if that will help."

Lita smiled gratefully, but there was an amused look in her eye as she replied. "I'll be happy for the help with the locks, but don't give a thought to the landlord. I can vouch for his okay."

"Oh?" he asked, raising a dark brow questioningly.

"Uh-huh. My father owns the town house. He rents out the upper and lower sections as apartments from time to time. Melanie talked him into letting her have it this year, since she was spending a lot of time in the Washington area."

"I see." Keith reminded himself that he had a number of things to take care of besides Lita Winslow, and the

53

mention of her father helped him recall that he wasn't the only person in the world that she could turn to for help. He didn't care to hang around and make a fool of himself over her, so he decided to hit the road and get back to minding his own affairs.

Lita felt the subtle withdrawal, and it came like a splash of cold water. She had been enjoying his company so much she'd forgotten they both had their own lives to lead. She walked him silently to the door, helping him on with his jacket and opening the door for him.

He hesitated on the threshold, turning something over in his mind that he'd been thinking about all morning. "Look, why don't you skip rehearsal, Lita," he suggested, turning serious. "The first performance is in two days. You'd still have time to rehearse tomorrow, if by then it appears you'd have to go on in Melanie's stead."

She gave him a grateful smile but firmly declined with a shake of her head. "Thanks for the offer, but I think I'd better get in the practice. It's been a few years, you know," she reminded him ruefully.

He nodded, acquiescing to her decision. "Yes. For that reason alone, you're going to draw a big crowd, Lita. It seems that it's human nature to want the most what you have to wait for the longest."

"Perhaps," she agreed.

With that he turned and strode down the short cement walk to his car, sliding in like a man whose thoughts were already several blocks away.

She watched the low-slung sports car pull smoothly into the heavy flow of Georgetown traffic and quickly disappear down a side street. If she didn't watch out, she could become very attracted to Keith Christophe, she thought with a ripple of apprehension. He was a complex man. A very complex man. And he was used to playing hard ball in life. That was something Lita had never quite mastered. It was one of the reasons she'd abandoned live performing for the more sheltered life of songwriting and recording.

She unbelted her robe and wandered back into the bedroom. Maybe a shower and some fresh clothes would help her feel like tackling life anew, she thought hopefully.

Lita had barely finished closing the last fastening on a rust and gold paisley dress of soft challis when she heard a knock at the front door.

"Miss Winslow?" asked the cigar butt–chomping red-faced little man who was standing on her front porch and holding a little black bag in his hand.

"Yes," she said, giving him a doubtful look.

"I'm Huey. Keith Christophe said you needed new locks and an alarm system."

He was frowning at her as if she'd been forced upon him unexpectedly and he was hoping to finish here as fast as possible. He also looked more like a pint-size truck driver than a specialist in security devices.

Huey took note of her skeptical expression and shrugged philosophically. It wasn't the first time someone had doubted his line of work. For years he'd been more than happy that that had been the case. But then he'd gone straight, and it had become an annoying liability, as Keith phrased it. Huey preferred to call it a pain in the . . .

"Look, Mr.—uh . . ." Lita searched politely for some words of inquiry.

He shoved the Orioles baseball cap back from his balding forehead and scratched his chin patiently. "Look, Ms. Winslow, Keith wouldn't send no dummy here. If you know him well enough for him to pick up the tab for instant service like this, you ought to know him well enough to know that. Right?"

He stared at her challengingly, shifting from one

pudgy foot to the other and waiting for her to see the light.

"Sorry, Huey," she apologized as she ushered him in.

"Think nothin' of it," he said brusquely, brushing off her concern without a thought. "This happens to me all the time. Believe me, I'm used to it."

Lita couldn't help but smile at the tough little man. She watched him examine the locks with the seasoned eye of a professional. It was immediately clear he knew what he was doing.

"How about a cup of coffee, Huey?" she suggested, wanting to offer some olive branch for her mistake.

Huey looked up at her in complete surprise. He couldn't remember the last time any of his customers had extended the simple, human courtesy that Lita just had.

Seeing his reaction, she headed for the kitchen in triumph. "What do you take in it, Huey?"

"Just sugar," he said, raising his voice enough to be heard in the next room. She was a nice lady, this Ms. Winslow. He could see how his old friend, Keith, could take a special interest in her.

The locks were a snap to change. It took Huey a little longer to suggest the kind of wiring that would be necessary for a burglar alarm. While he was checking around the upstairs apartment, Jack Connery called.

"Oh, Jack, I'm so glad you called," Lita said, twisting the telephone cord around her finger nervously. "There was a little problem here last night," she explained.

"A problem?" he prompted her. "Is Melanie—"

"No," Lita replied, sighing audibly. "I still haven't heard anything from her. But someone broke into the apartment while I was at the club last night."

"Oh, no! Are you okay?"

Lita smiled at the anxiety in his voice. "Yes, I'm fine. Sean Christophe was with me, and Keith and the police showed up. They checked the premises, but we have no idea who it was. They really tore the place up." She hesitated fractionally. "And it looks as if they might have had a key. Jack?"

"Yes?"

"Do you know if Melanie gave anyone a key to this place?"

She could practically see him shut his eyes and hold his breath as he thought. Lita had known Jack for years, since she and Melanie were in college. She knew without asking what was going through his mind right now. If someone had kidnapped Melanie, or waylaid her, they could have stolen the key and found her address in her wallet. It was a very grim thought.

"No," he said at long last. "I don't."

He sounded so distant that Lita frowned in worry. She couldn't prop Jack up right now. She had enough to handle here in Washington. Besides, when the rest of the family found out—Lita didn't even want to think about that!

"Jack," she said firmly, "we'll find her. And I'm sure the break-in was just a coincidence. Please don't worry. It's all over now." She decided to change the subject a little to try and take his mind off the latest hitch in Washington. "I tried calling early in the morning, but you weren't in."

"Yeah. I was drowning my sorrows," he answered slowly. "You'd think I'd be old enough to know better. I've got a hell of a hangover to pay for my stupidity," he added uncomfortably.

"Oh, Jack, I'm sorry!" Lita exclaimed sincerely. "You're one of the nicest guys I know. I wish—" Lita bit her tongue.

"That Melanie could have seen it that way?" he finished for her.

Lita sighed regretfully. "Yes."

Jack laughed bitterly. "Yeah. Me, too."

Lita heard a muffled knock over the phone and Jack's voice shouting "Just a minute."

"Hey, I'm sorry, Lita, but I've got to go."

"Sure, Jack. And Jack . . ."

"Yeah?"

"Take care of yourself, okay?"

"I'll try," he promised.

Lita hung up the phone, but she couldn't shake the feeling of disquiet that had settled over her as she talked to Jack. Something was wrong. He was deeply depressed about Melanie's disappearance, and Lita sensed that emotionally he was hanging on by his fingernails.

She went to check on Huey's progress and reminded herself that she couldn't take care of Jack. If he really began falling apart, she'd suggest he try and get some professional help to get him through this.

At the rate things were going, she might do the same thing herself, she thought with black humor.

Sean Christophe was lounging at Sydney's onyx bar, popping peanuts in his mouth, when Keith left his office in search of Felice later that afternoon.

"I must say, brother, I'm surprised to see you here so early," Sean declared with an exaggerated expression of astonishment on his face.

Keith stopped in front of Carl, who was trying to avoid being caught in the middle of the brothers' ongoing war of words. "Has Felice come back from her break yet, Carl?" Keith asked.

"Nope, but she'll probably be here any minute now."

Keith was turning to go back to his office when Sean caught him by the arm and blocked his way.

"I said—" Sean repeated, his eyes narrowed with repressed anger at being brushed off.

"I heard what you said," Keith said coolly. "And if you were a little older, you might have heard my reply."

Sean glared at his brother in affront. "Meaning your silence was your eloquent way of telling me to mind my own business—that you're not going to discuss Lita Winslow or the incident last night with me?" he challenged.

"Precisely," Keith replied coldly. "Don't you have something to do, Sean? If not, maybe I can find you a job."

Sean laughed humorlessly and lounged against the bar, stretching his hands out flat on it to support him.

"A job, brother? I haven't gone through the trust fund yet! You can do the work in the family, for all I care! There's just one thing I wanted to know," he said, digressing back to his original purpose. "When did you leave?"

Keith clenched a fist. He knew Sean was taunting him purely for the pleasure of getting a rise out of him. Usually he ignored the ripostes and jibes without even getting particularly angry. This was different. He didn't care to have his brother sniping at a suspected tryst between himself and Lita. Especially since it wasn't true. "When it was safe for her to be alone, little brother," he replied softly, emphasizing the words "little brother" to needle Sean back. Keith saw Felice enter the club, giving him a perfect reason to walk away from his brother. "If you'll excuse me," he began, a little sarcastically, "I've got to get my secretary to mail some contracts." Keith turned on his heel and walked away without waiting for Sean's reply.

Carl leaned over the bar and touched Sean on the shoulder. "Hey, go easy, huh?" he pleaded. The two brothers seemed to love each other and hate each other at the same time. Damned if he knew why! But it was always hell around Sydney's whenever Sean started going after Keith.

Sean sighed and grimaced. "Yeah. Sometimes I really

don't know why I dig at him. He's so damned invulnerable! He's always been the big, tough older brother—the man in the family," Sean said bitterly. "When I see a weak spot in his armor, I just want to stick it to him til he cries uncle, you know?"

Carl nodded his head unhappily. Did he ever know!

Sean eased himself away from the bar and stuffed his hands in his pants pockets. "I, uh . . . I think I'll go take a long walk," he told the bartender.

"Hang in there, Sean." Carl watched the young man leave. He gave a sigh of relief. One Christophe was a lot easier to live with than two, he thought as he began racking up the clean crystal and checking his liquor bottles.

Even one could be a hell of a handful!

It was five thirty by the time Felice finally managed to clear her desk and tidy things up in preparation for leaving. She hesitated at her boss's door, ducking her head in shyly and smiling at him apologetically. He'd been holed up in there most of the day, the only one in the club who hadn't come out to listen to Lita rehearse with Gaius and the band. That had surprised her. Felice loved Lita's music and had bought every one of her albums. It was incomprehensible to her that Keith wouldn't at least have taken one small break to relax and enjoy listening to her. Oh, well, she'd told herself in the end, what did she know about a man like Mr. Christophe, anyway?

"Good night," she said.

He looked up and gazed at her blankly. Slowly it dawned on him that the afternoon, which had crawled by at a snail's pace from his point of view, had finally managed to end. "Good night, Felice," he replied. "Going out with Craig tonight?"

That was something else about him, Felice thought admiringly. He always took time to ask about the things that were important to her. Keith Christophe could be tough and demanding, but he'd always treated her as a human being.

She smiled and blushed in spite of herself. She'd been thinking of Craig almost constantly ever since they'd gotten engaged. And a lot of her thoughts were downright lustful! She knew her boss hadn't meant to insinuate that, of course, but she couldn't help being embarrassed at the mention of Craig's name.

Keith saw her confusion and laughed softly. "He's finally getting around to some serious courting, I take it?" he teased her.

Poor Felice didn't know what to say to that and blushed even harder. It was true of course. Until the engagement Craig had been very chaste with her. But recently he seemed almost obsessed with intensifying his hold on her. It was delightful, of course, she told herself. But it was sure getting hard to wrestle out of his grasp on the couch before sending him home every night!

Keith waved her on and shook his head like a man beset. "Tell Craig if he distracts you so much that your typing and filing go to hell, I'll have to arrange a chaperone for you until the wedding!"

"Oh!" she exclaimed in happy outrage.

"Go on!" he ordered her.

She scurried away to her waiting swain just as the phone on Keith's desk began to ring. He picked it up and said a curt hello.

"Afternoon, Keith." It was Pete Fallon. "Just thought I'd check in."

Keith leaned on his elbows and twisted a pencil in his fingers as he stared fixedly into space. "Have you turned up anything?" he asked, a hard edge creeping into his voice.

"Yes and no."

Keith's hand stilled. "Go on," he said.

"Well . . . I don't know where Melanie King is, and I don't know who ransacked her apartment."

A skeptical grimace appeared on Keith's face. "Is that the 'yes' or the 'no' part of your answer, Fallon?"

Fallon chuckled. He was used to Keith's sarcastic rejoinders, and he'd learned to let them roll off his back years ago. "I guess you could say it was the 'no' part, Keith."

"And?"

"And the 'yes' part is that I found a witness who saw Melanie go out Friday night with a man."

"Who was the man?" Keith asked, his interest peaked.

"Don't know yet. We're still working on both ends of this thing. You got anything new to add?"

Keith leaned back in his swivel chair and frowned. "No. There should be a new set of locks and a burglar alarm on the town house by now, though."

"That was smart thinkin'." There was a small silence, and Fallon scented a reason behind it. "You help her with that, Keith?" he asked curiously.

"Yeah."

Fallon sat back in his own chair at police headquarters and considered that for a moment. He knew Keith tried to keep his relationships with people on a purely quid pro quo basis. Was Lita repaying Keith's charity, he wondered.

The steely undertone of Keith's voice suggested that this was different. Fallon couldn't remember Keith's doing something for a woman without receiving something in return. And as beautiful as Lita Winslow was, Pete could think of some delightful ways to be repaid!

"Is there something else I can do for you, Fallon?" Keith inquired pointedly, breaking the rather lengthy silence that had stretched between them ever since he'd admitted fixing Lita's security problems.

"Naw, naw. That's it for now. Keep in touch, though,

okay? If you come up with any interesting new facts . . ."

"Right. You'll be the first to know," Keith promised him. "And Fallon . . ."

"Yeah?"

"Drop in and catch the show." Keith hung up without saying good-bye.

Fallon hung up and grimaced. Keith enjoyed trying to keep a jump ahead of him, damn it! The detective chuckled. Just like when they were kids! Well, it could be construed as good investigative procedure to go to the club and see who was there, what the routine was, ask a few quiet questions about Melanie King . . .

He swung his feet off his desk and leapt to his feet.

Sounded good to him!

CHAPTER FOUR

When Pete Fallon walked into Sydney's that night, he was reminded of the first time he'd seen a classy nightclub: He was immediately on his best behavior, trying hard not to gawk like a fool at the elegant surroundings even as he felt his mouth fall open in awe.

Now, at forty, he didn't care what anyone thought anymore, so he gawked to his heart's content. He was the only one. Everyone else was too busy engaging their companions in high-brow observations to lower themselves to any obvious admiration of their environs. After all, who wanted to appear so gauche! Every so often, however, Fallon intercepted a secretive look that one patron or another gave the club. They were usually feigning looking for a waiter, but he was too shrewd an observer of human nature to fall for that unimaginative camouflage! They were as tickled as he was at being in Keith's sumptuous night spot.

"Would you care for a table, Fallon?" asked Marty Kahn, decked out in evening dress and greeting the clientele as they wandered into the club proper.

Fallon gave the smaller man a pat on the tummy. "Hey, Marty! What's new? Looks like you've been puttin' on a little weight!"

Marty grimaced. "Yeah, well, we can't all run after bad guys to keep in shape, can we?" he retorted a trifle defensively.

Marty was a little touchy about that subject. Even when he and Keith and Pete had played in Washington back alleys after school, he'd resented being teased by the other boys on that score.

Fallon clasped him fondly on the shoulder. "Naw, I guess not," Fallon agreed as he looked over the glittering array of people sitting, standing, and milling around as the band entertained them with some melancholy impromptu jazz.

Fallon noticed Lita Winslow sitting alone at a small table along the far side of the room and cocked his head thoughtfully to one side. "Think anybody'd mind if I went over and joined Lita Winslow?" Fallon asked.

"Of course not."

"Catch you later, Marty."

"Sure thing."

Fallon made his way between the tables as Marty turned to welcome the next group.

Lita recognized the approaching detective and smiled at him in welcome. "Good evening, Lieutenant Fallon. Is this an official visit, or are you off duty?" she asked in a friendly, casual way.

He sat down and wrinkled his brow in mock exhaustion. "In this line of work, sometimes you feel like you're never off duty!"

Lita laughed softly. "I suppose so," she agreed. She wasn't sure whether his reply was intended to evade her question or simply amuse her a little. She swirled the amaretto in the tiny liqueur glass and changed the subject a little. "Do you come here often?"

"Naw," he replied, scanning the room and picking out a familiar face here and there in the crowd. "Keith's place is a little rich for my pocket," he explained with a grin.

"Have you known him long?" Lita asked curiously.

"You could say that," he admitted as he casually surveyed the long bar at the far end of the room and saw the man they were discussing seated on a bar stool between two very attractive young women in low-cut silk dresses that looked like they'd been glued onto their slender bodies. "We grew up in the same neighborhood."

He turned his attention back to the beauty he was lucky enough to be sitting with. Fallon was surprised that Keith wasn't with her. He'd had the impression that Keith was taking a special interest in Lita, but with Keith, it was hard to tell about those things. The man kept his feelings buried pretty deeply.

Fallon ordered a bottle of imported beer from the waiter who'd come to attend them. When the waiter had departed, Fallon thought back on the kids they had been those many years ago in the streets of the nation's capital.

Fallon continued his reminiscing aloud. "Keith was a little younger than I was, but he was such a scrapper that no one dared to mention it to him when we played. He was always in charge, even as a kid. He was the one who chose up sides for the stickball games, the one who settled the petty arguments, the kid who'd take on the bully from the next neighborhood and trounce him into the ground." Fallon reminisced with growing fondness. "I was proud to be his friend," he said. "Too bad you have to grow up, sometimes," he ended wistfully.

Lita looked at him curiously. "You're not friends anymore?" she asked in surprise. That wasn't exactly the impression she'd had last night, although she did admit she wouldn't have guessed that they'd known each other for years.

"Oh, yeah," Fallon replied, giving her a lopsided grin again. "We're still friends, but we've gone our separate ways in life. Keith . . . well, he's got a lot to keep track of. And me . . . well, I can't let myself get too close to a man who insists on keeping friends on both sides of the law." Fallon shook his head regretfully. "It's a damn shame, though. Keith's one of the few men on this earth I would want to be back-to-back with in a dark alley. He's one tough, loyal friend."

Lita had been trying to keep her eyes away from the bar ever since she'd arrived. She knew Keith was there. He'd nodded a welcome to her when she came in. But he'd made no effort to join her, and she'd taken that as a signal that he had other affairs to devote himself to. It hadn't taken her long to realize that the affairs were female: a blond and a redhead.

Fallon's description of Keith's growing up had made her want to see him, in spite of her vow to ignore the man, and she raised her lashes to gaze in his direction.

To her surprise, he was staring at her. Their eyes locked for a moment, and then he turned to respond to something the redhead had said to him.

"It looks like his two friends at the bar want to be friends with him, too," Lita commented lightly.

Fallon turned to see what she was talking about. "Yeah. Women are crazy about him. Always have been," he added wryly. "But my mother wasn't too thrilled at my being pals with the son of a striptease artist and a man who only showed his face once or twice a year." He shrugged philosophically. "No one would be much bothered by it now, I guess. But thirty years ago, even Sydney Keith wasn't good enough for the decent women of this town."

Lita gave Fallon a startled look. "His mother is Sydney Keith?" she asked in astonishment.

"Yeah. Isn't that a kick?" Fallon asked in amusement as he lounged back in his chair. "I sneaked in and saw her act once when I was a kid. She was one elegant, sexy lady. Keith spent most of his growing up punching guys in the nose for making remarks he didn't care for about his mother. I guess that's why he was such a hell of a good fighter." Fallon chuckled. "He had lots of practice!"

"I can imagine," Lita murmured in sympathetic surprise.

Sydney Keith was one of the few burlesque queens to become so famous that even people who never went near a striptease show recognized her name. She'd given a certain respectability to that form of entertainment that had elevated her from the ranks of the common stripper to a pedestal of her own. A Sydney Keith performance was synonymous with sophisticated, tasteful visual seduction. She had established herself as an artiste, and in her field, that was quite an accomplishment.

"I didn't know she had any kids," Lita commented, hoping she didn't appear overly interested in Keith Christophe by mentioning that fact.

If Fallon realized she was obliquely seeking information about his childhood friend, he didn't show it. "People around here knew," he said. "It wasn't exactly a secret, but she didn't want the kids to be caught up in her business. She knew the press and the community moralists could give them a hard time. She was trying to shelter them as much as she could, and she had enough friends in high places to keep the dogs at bay if they came digging for a story about her personal life." Fallon gave his friend a thoughtful look. "I guess, in a way, Keith is sort of like her. They both made friends in all walks of life, as they say—and those friends were always good for a favor. They both know when to call a favor in, too."

That reminded Lita of something Jack had said about Keith Christophe—he doesn't do something for nothing. That was still bothering her. She was doubly indebted to the man now. First, for helping her inquire about Melanie, then for helping her with the break-in. Was there a price for his help that she had yet to hear about? It might be interesting to know what Keith Christophe considered she possessed that would be of comparable value, she thought as a trace of anticipation licked through her veins.

She abruptly told herself not to even *think* about something like that! She searched quickly for another topic. "His father was gone a lot, I take it?" she asked carefully.

Fallon laughed. "That's the understatement of the decade! He was gone more than he was home. And when he was home—well—I felt sorry for Keith and his brother. The whole family was wrapped up in one big love-hate thing. Everyone could see it. But they loved each other too much to throw in the towel and call it quits."

"Ummm," Lita murmured in understanding.

That description had a painfully familiar ring to her. It brought back some vivid pictures of her family life. She was caught in it still, as an adult, but at least now she could escape to her own little castle on the Pacific and hide from the ongoing struggle of wills between her parents for months at a time.

And yet you never really can escape those kind of struggles, no matter how far away you go, she thought sadly. They stick to you like grim death.

"Hey!" Fallon exclaimed humorously. "Don't look so depressed! Keith'll have my hide if his prize songbird isn't happy!"

Lita erased the telltale expression and produced a charming smile in its place.

"Boy, what a dazzler!" Fallon exclaimed with almost boyish candor as he gazed at her in open admiration.

Keith was thinking pretty much the same thing all the way across the room. He'd seen the play of emotions on Lita's face and was trying to figure out what they could be talking about to produce such a panoply. And what in the devil could his old friend Fallon have said to put that utterly captivating smile on her beautiful face, anyway? he wondered in annoyance. Fallon wasn't exactly known

69

for his conquests of the fair sex. Had he been practicing recently?

Keith had never had any problem himself wrapping a member of the fair sex around his finger. Tonight was no exception. It wasn't hard to say the right things at the right times in response to his two lovely companions' efforts at conversation. A suggestive pat on a slender knee, an appreciative smile, an interested look. That was all it took. They were so absorbed in themselves that they didn't really want more. All the blond and the redhead wanted was a politely attentive, suitably enticing male audience.

Keith had filled that bill since he'd learned to tell the difference between boys and girls. He could do it with his eyes shut and half asleep. So it wasn't hard for him to casually return every once in a while to study Lita and Fallon during the course of their conversation while artlessly keeping up with his own.

What was becoming difficult, however, was restraining himself from walking across the club and taking Lita away from Fallon so he could enjoy her company himself! That Keith was determined not to do! He had promised himself to resist that temptation, no matter how hard it turned out to be, damn it!

"Keith! Are you listening?" asked redheaded Gloria with a petulantly scandalized tone.

He gave her a heart-stopping slow grin. " 'Listening'?" he echoed in mild surprise. "Why, Gloria, I think I've memorized every word you've said this evening."

Gloria batted her long black eyelashes at him in confusion. She had the feeling he was poking fun at her, but she wasn't quite sure. She decided that she might look unattractive if she started complaining, so she opted to ignore the double entendre and pretend that he'd meant what he'd said at face value. "Well, then," she murmured in a conciliatory way, "maybe I've talked a little too much tonight. How about a dance?" she asked coyly, flashing him a bright smile.

Blond-headed Mitzi was listening with envy and praying Gloria wasn't passing her by in the Keith Christophe sweepstakes. She held her breath waiting for him to answer.

In all the years Keith had been running Sydney's, no one had ever seen him dance at the club. He had a strict policy of not mixing his business life with his personal life. When he wanted to take a lady dancing, he took her somewhere else. At his own club, he preferred to remain free to mingle with his guests. Mitzi, who was a little more perceptive than Gloria, suspected that there was more to it. Such as not wanting a bunch of jealous females competing for his time and making life miserable for everyone if he danced longer or more often with one of them than with the others.

Keith lifted Gloria's hand to his lips and brushed an apologetic kiss on it. Then he stood up and buttoned his dinner jacket. "You know my rule on that, Gloria. Sorry, honey, I don't break it for anyone"—he gave her an appreciative scan from her casually sophisticated coiffure to her sheerly stockinged feet sandaled in gold heels—"no matter how beautiful."

Mitzi breathed a sigh of relief. Gloria was too self-absorbed to see he was just trying to be nice to her with all that flowery garbage. Mitzi noticed that he gave a last glance toward Lita Winslow before turning away from them to wander toward Marty Kahn for a little chat.

"Carl, give the ladies another round on the house," he ordered as a parting gift.

Gloria sighed and watched him with undisguised admiration. "What a hunk that man is," she said wistfully. "One of these days I'm gonna find his bell and ring it as hard as I can," she vowed fervently.

Mitzi laughed and sipped her new drink. "Don't hold

your breath, Gloria. I have the feeling we may not have what it takes for that."

Gloria shot her friend a crippling glare.

"Sorry," Mitzi murmured, lowering her eyes to her drink to avoid Gloria's nasty expression. "I just have that feeling," she ended lamely.

Sean Christophe had that feeling, too. He began to stroll through the club, having witnessed some of the previous action while leaning against a wall partially hidden in the shadows. Washington was full of pretty young women hungrily searching for a powerful, successful man of their very own. Politicos and their hangers-on certainly attracted their fair share, but over the years, a steady stream had tried out their wiles on Keith. Sean was more than happy to comfort them and regale them with advice, and he didn't mind scoring with them in the least. He was more than happy to oblige them, as a matter of fact. Who cared if his brother was a fool and turned away all this ripe fruit that threw itself repeatedly into his lap!

Sean's gaze wandered around the room, coming to rest on Lita Winslow. Normally he would have moved into Keith's vacant seat at the bar and picked up where his older brother had left off. Tonight though . . .

The younger Christophe smiled at Mitzi and Gloria and threaded his way between the tables, coming to a halt when he reached Lita and Pete Fallon. He smiled boyishly and motioned toward an empty chair between them.

"Good evening, Lita, Pete. Mind if I join you for a while?"

"No. Of course not."

"Not at all."

The band finally played its last song to a small audience at one o'clock. Gaius was exhausted, as were the rest of the guys. The last note wasn't played too soon as far as they were concerned.

Nor as far as Keith Christophe was concerned either. He'd had the galling experience of watching his younger brother dance lazily for the better part of the last hour with Lita. Fallon had left them much earlier, leaving them to each other's exclusive attention.

Keith had been flipping a small matchbox open and shut over and over, his irritation with Sean growing with their every sway and turn on the dance floor. Every time Sean had murmured in her ear, Keith felt his annoyance increase a little. And every time Lita smiled up at him and answered back, leaning against Sean's arms and looking up into his eyes like a long-lost girlfriend . . .

The matchbox snapped shut.

Keith dropped it into his evening jacket and strode toward them. Damn it! Didn't his brother know the music had ended? The musicians were putting their instruments away!

"Lovely, Keith . . . Good night, Christophe . . . Evening, Keith . . . Great band!" murmured the people he passed.

He smiled politely and automatically thanked them, calling most of them by name. When he reached Sean, who was still holding Lita as though waiting for another song to begin, Keith's genial expression began to fade fast. "The party's over, Sean," he said evenly.

Sean was looking over Lita's head at his brother and smiled innocently. "But I still hear music, brother," he replied, giving Lita an extra squeeze.

Lita had enjoyed dancing with Sean. He was a good dancer and an amusing conversationalist. Besides, she'd gotten a little better acquainted with Sydney's and with its tough-minded owner by listening to Sean talk. But she was tired now and more than ready to go home. Furthermore, she didn't have to see Keith's face to detect a hint of irritation in his voice.

She wriggled a little, trying to slip out of Sean's arms. "I think I'd better be going," she said regretfully. Sean gradually loosened his hold and let her go, but he obviously wasn't happy about it, so Lita gave him a warm smile and squeezed his hand in gratitude. "Thanks for keeping me entertained, Sean. It was a lovely evening."

Sean had felt the old surge of rebellion when Keith started exerting his authority, but Lita's kindhearted sincerity somehow eased the pain and he smiled back at her. "Believe me, the pleasure has been all mine, Lita," he murmured sincerely, the steadiness of his gaze lending conviction to his almost hesitantly voiced sentiment.

Keith frowned a little and walked with them to the coat check.

"I'll give you a ride home," Keith announced curtly.

He took the wrap and helped a rather surprised Lita slip it on. It wasn't an offer. It wasn't a question. It was a statement of fact. Lita wasn't used to being ordered about, and there was fire in her eyes when she looked up at him.

"I can call a cab," she protested rather testily.

"Don't be ridiculous," Keith muttered darkly, pushing her toward the back entrance and giving his brother a look that required no words.

Sean couldn't have been more surprised at his brother's behavior. He watched as Keith shepherded a stiff-backed Lita Winslow out of the building. As they disappeared from sight, he couldn't contain himself anymore. He began to chuckle.

"What's so funny?" asked Marty blankly. He'd missed the interesting little scene and had no idea as to what Sean was laughing at.

Sean began to laugh harder. "If I hadn't seen it with

74

my own eyes," he managed to reply between gasps, "I wouldn't have believed it!"

"What in the hell are you talkin' about, Sean?" asked Marty in confusion. It had been a long day. He wasn't in the mood for riddles.

"You'll see," Sean assured him, throwing an arm around Marty's shoulders and walking him outside. "Believe me, Marty, you'll see!"

The street lamps glowed a soft white in the early morning darkness. There were a few cars still cruising the streets of Georgetown, but neither Keith nor Lita were particularly aware of them.

Keith had steered her downstairs to his private garage, his hand like an unyielding clamp on her elbow. He'd handed her into the passenger's side of his car and slid into the driver's seat without speaking, bringing the engine instantly to life and roaring onto the street almost angrily.

Her last view of the club had been of the automatic door to the underground garage slowly closing shut.

He steered the powerful car smoothly down Georgetown's old brick side streets. If he'd been in a better mood, Keith might have pointed out a few of the more famous Georgian houses to Lita. But at the moment, he couldn't have cared less about two-hundred-year-old homes that had sheltered presidents and statesmen down through the ages, so he didn't bother.

Lita crossed her slender legs and silently counted to twenty in French. She had no intention of getting into a temper over Keith's high-handed behavior. That would be sinking to his level, she told herself crossly. No. She'd rise above it all and be impeccably polite, utterly unruffled, and coolly sophisticated!

Keith gave her a sidelong glance and downshifted into neutral as they stopped for a traffic light. "Tired?" he asked coolly. He saw the shapely curve of her leg and knee and was tempted to look higher. Lita turned to reply to his question, and he immediately lifted his eyes to her face, assuming a neutral expression.

"A little," she admitted distantly. "I had a late night," she reminded him.

His eyes seemed to soften a little. "Ah, yes," he said. "Did Huey get all the locks changed?"

"Yes."

"And the burglar alarm system installed?"

"Yes, I—"

"Good," he said brusquely. The light changed and he shifted into gear. The engine purred and the car surged forward like a powerful cat.

To herself Lita counted backwards from five in Spanish. "Thank you for making the arrangements," she said, finally getting to finish her sentence.

He shrugged it off as if it were a matter of great indifference to him. "Don't mention it."

Lita wanted to ask him if she'd be receiving a bill from Huey, since the little man had been very evasive about that. She had the sneaking suspicion that Keith was picking up the tab for the work, and she wanted to avoid that, if at all possible. On the other hand, he was looking so unapproachable at the moment that she doubted she could talk him out of it if he were playing benefactor. She decided to bide her time and tackle that later.

They pulled up in front of Melanie's town house and Keith killed the motor with a flick of his wrist. He held the keys, jangling them softly, as if weighing a decision.

Lita released her seatbelt and moved to get out.

"I assume you still haven't heard from Melanie?" he asked.

Lita let go of the door handle and sank back against the seat. "No. Have you?"

He shook his head. "Pete Fallon had nothing to tell you, then?"

"No, unfortunately, he didn't," she replied.

"You spent a long time talking with him at the club this evening," he pointed out coolly. "I assumed some of that might have had something to do with our missing songbird."

Lita's eyes flashed warningly. "We talked a little bit about her, but since he had nothing to tell me we both felt it would be a more pleasant evening if we found other topics of conversation." She felt her temper rise at the hard cast his dark eyes had assumed. Her emotions were beginning to block her better judgment and she spoke without thinking. "It's a free country, the last I heard. Even in your nightclub, people enjoy the right to free speech."

His eyes glittered angrily, and he reached across her roughly to open the door for her.

Lita swung her legs out and slammed the door shut before he could come around and close it. She was halfway up the walk, retrieving her keys from her small evening bag, by the time he reached her side.

"You shouldn't have bothered to get out," she declared archly, giving him a freezing glare. "I can see myself in."

He took the keys from her and walked toward her door, ignoring her attempt at dismissing him.

Lita found herself in the ridiculous position of standing in the middle of her own walk, fuming because he'd taken her keys and ignored her command, while Keith opened her door and went inside the town house. She certainly couldn't stand outside like this all night! Angrily, she marched into the building after him.

She threw her tiny bag down onto an imitation Queen Anne chair in the corner and dropped her wrap over the back. "What do you think you're doing?" she asked in deep annoyance as she followed Keith from room to room.

He ran a hand along the window sills and doors, paying no attention to her at first.

"Keith!" she exclaimed in exasperation. "What are you doing?"

He wandered back into the living room and dropped her keys onto a cherry highboy against the wall near the kitchen. "Checking to make sure Huey did his usual expert work."

Lita stood, her hands on her hips, her feet slightly parted, the epitome of female frustration and annoyance.

Keith saw the anger, but that wasn't all he saw. He stood and stared at her. Reluctantly, as if he didn't really want to, he let his gaze drift slowly down over her. Her dark hair was slightly tousled, falling softly over her shoulders. The full cut of her dress fell discreetly against the curves of her body. Its aqua tints blended to accentuate the dark violet of her eyes, and its fit hinted shyly at the beauty hidden beneath its elegant folds. Her legs, long and clean limbed, like a thoroughbred's, were well shaped and made to be caressed.

Keith, stunned at the force of his reaction to her, turned a little away and tried to get a grip on himself. He ran a hand through his hair and then jammed his hands in his trouser pockets.

Lita didn't know what to say. That hardly mattered, since her mouth was too dry to utter a word. As he'd looked at her, she'd felt his gaze as if it had been his hands. And, unbelievably, she'd wished it *had* been his hands running over her shoulders and hips and legs. Warm, admiring, wanting hands. She was too shaken to know what to do.

She'd never been one for casual affairs. And she'd never felt the way she had when Keith had looked at her like that. She blushed in embarrassment and wondered what to do. He didn't look like he was ready to leave yet, and a wild, hidden part of her desperately wished he wouldn't go. Mostly, however, she was deeply unnerved by the way he had made her feel. Mechanically she went into the kitchen and opened the refrigerator.

Keith found her a few minutes later pouring herself a glass of milk. "Milk at two o'clock in the morning?" he asked in bafflement.

Lita couldn't look at him, so she stared defensively at her glass of milk. "It's good for you. Want a glass?" she asked, none too encouragingly.

Keith was so surprised that he replied without thinking. "Why not?"

So, a few moments later, they were standing at opposite ends of the kitchen, drinking their milk and staring uncomfortably at one another as if they were on opposite sides of a big negotiation.

Keith put his empty glass down on the counter. He leaned his back against the counter, as far away from Lita as he could get, and looked at her moodily. "If you have to perform on Saturday, are you going to be able to do it?" he asked bluntly.

Lita, holding on to her empty glass as if it were a security blanket, looked at him blankly. Coming out of the blue as it had, it took her a moment to understand his question.

"Well, of course." She straightened up as if that proved it somehow. "Melanie and I are about the same size. I've already tried on the wardrobe she selected for the tour. Everything fits. There shouldn't be any problem."

Keith frowned and shook his head. "That's not what I meant," he said cuttingly. "I've heard there were some threats made against you just before you quit performing. I want to know if that's true and if it's going to interfere with your going on."

Lita paled and walked into the living room to escape

him while she collected her wits. She didn't want to have to talk about that. She was staring vacantly out the front window when Keith reached her.

"Of course I'll go on," she began woodenly. "I signed the contract. You have nothing to worry about. I keep my commitments."

She was only vaguely aware of his taking the glass out of her fingers and setting it down on a table.

"That's not what I'm worried about," he murmured softly. "Is it true, then?" he asked, grabbing her shoulders and turning her to look at him.

She lifted her liquid eyes to his and was helpless to answer. "I"—she struggled with the words—"yes . . . it's true."

His hands felt brutally hard all of a sudden, and she winced in pain. Instantly he released her and stepped back a little.

"I'm sorry," he muttered.

He hadn't realized he was holding her so tightly. All he'd been aware of was how much he wanted to pull her close to him and how intensely he wanted to kiss her. He had unconsciously tightened his grip in an effort to avoid succumbing to his powerful urge, as if he'd been tightening the grip on his suddenly raging emotions instead.

"Look," he said, forcing himself to ignore what he really wanted to be doing with Lita right now, "if someone makes threats, I want to know about it. I don't want to have anything happen to you while you're performing at Sydney's," he argued.

He sounded so cool and rational, so untouched by the horror of it, she thought enviously. She shivered and blinked, wishing she could feel the same way about it herself. She lowered her head and sighed unhappily. "You're right, of course," she mumured with a sense of defeat.

"You don't have to face it alone," he said, a little more softly. "I can help you as long as you're here."

As long as she was here. How long would that be? she wondered. She'd thought when she'd come it would just be for a day or two. She'd fully expected that Melanie would have returned by now. Melanie would have had some fully reasonable reason for bolting like this, and Lita would be catching a plane home.

It didn't look as if things were going to work out that way, she now had to admit. And considering the potent chemistry that was brewing with such volatility between Keith Christophe and herself, her past was not the only danger she was going to have to face for the next few weeks!

"There were a series of things . . ." she said, crossing her arms protectively in front of her. "Things missing from my room, warnings in lipstick on the mirrors in the hotels where I was staying, cut and pasted messages threatening me. My parents hired a private detective. We told the police. No one could ever turn up a thing. In the end, it just wasn't worth it to me anymore. I was tired of traveling; I was sick of the one-night stands, always running to catch a plane, living out of a suitcase. I wanted to enjoy music again."

He listened without commenting. When she stopped he tilted his head slightly to one side. He had the distinct impression she was giving him a very sanitized version of this. He wanted it all. "Exactly what kind of threats were made? Especially the last night?" he asked.

She stared at him in surprise. "The last night?" she repeated, her wide eyes eloquently conveying her memory of the fear she'd experienced then.

"Yes, damn it!" he replied angrily, closing the distance between them and holding her by the shoulders as if he feared she'd run away before he could get an answer from her.

"It was—it was . . . a death threat," she whispered.

He stared down at her fear-darkened eyes and her pale face and wanted nothing more but to fold her into his embrace and vow that he'd protect her.

They hovered just inches apart, all their feelings unspoken.

Lita wished she could just close her eyes and lean against him and totally forget about the past. All she wanted was to feel his strong arms around her, holding her tight, keeping the rest of the world at bay.

That was a fantasy for naive young girls, she told herself bitterly. She knew better. That was never the way it worked out in real life, she reminded herself. All she had to do was recall her own life, and her parents', to know that. No, she'd have to cope with this somehow on her own.

Keith abruptly dropped his hands from her shoulders and paced across the room, staring at the floor before turning to deal with her one last time. "Do you think there could be any connection between what happened to you five years ago and the break-in last night?" he asked evenly. Damn it all, he didn't want to scare her, but he had to ask.

Lita paled again. She hadn't thought of that. "I don't see how," she replied uncertainly. "After all, only a few people know that I'm going to be taking Melanie's place if she doesn't show up in the next two days."

He nodded as if fairly convinced by her argument. "Don't unlock the doors for anyone unless you know them," he advised her.

"No, of course not." She was too upset to be angry at his order. Besides, she was sure he meant it out of concern for her safety. She couldn't really be angry at that. "Thank you for bringing me home, Keith."

He hesitated with his hand on the door, staring at her

enigmatically. "Don't mention it," he said dismissingly. And then he left.

She watched through the window as he got into his car and pulled away from the curb. The last thing she saw was the red glow of the sports car's taillights as they disappeared into the night.

CHAPTER FIVE

Lita spent the next twenty-four hours trying to ignore her attraction to Keith Christophe.

She made her usual appearance for rehearsal in the afternoon and told herself she was relieved that Keith was too busy to listen. She fixed herself a quiet dinner at the town house and amused herself doing some exercises on the living room floor and watching television.

When that became too boring to stand, she searched her suitcase for a paperback book she'd picked up in the San Francisco airport. Unfortunately, the words blurred in front of her eyes. When she read the same page for the third time, she knew it wouldn't work and threw it down on the table in disgust.

She paced around the small apartment, wrapping the soft wool robe a little more tightly around herself, wracking her brains for something that would take Keith Christophe off her mind.

Melanie had rented a piano for her stay in Washington, and Lita sat down on the bench, blindly seeking comfort and escape in the one thing in the world that had always given her that: her music.

She didn't need sheet music to play. She could shut her eyes and it was instinctively there. Lita played the well-remembered ballads and songs of her youth. Songs she'd written, songs she'd loved. The keys felt good under her fingertips. They caressed her, as did the soft and gentle melodies to which she blended her tender voice.

The songs started aimlessly, but soon an unconscious pattern emerged. They were lovesongs, poignant and sad. They were the kind of songs that had made Lita famous, the kind people loved her to sing. And they brought out a hidden part of her that she didn't usually let people see.

She drifted with the moods, letting her fingers begin a song and following it to the end, until she eventually found herself singing the song she'd been working on recently.

She was only vaguely aware that she'd begun singing the unfinished song. The words seemed as natural to her as if the song were already finished.

> *I'd lived an empty illusion of life.*
> *A dreamer of dreams unmet . . .*
> *Each year they'd faded into regret.*
>
> *For years, no one had reached me at all.*
> *Men came and went without knowing how.*
> *There wasn't one for whom I could fall.*
>
> *Til . . .*

Lita's hands froze, poised over the keyboard and she stared blindly at the dark cherry wood of the piano. The rest of the song was there. She could feel it. All she had to do was let it come. Just keep playing and hear the words as they formed on her lips . . .

And suddenly she was afraid. She didn't want to hear the song. She didn't want to know what it said.

She closed the piano and walked unhappily into the kitchen. "Mother always recommended warm tea and milk," she reminded herself aloud. "It can't hurt to try a cup. Maybe it'll still work."

Fortunately, it did and Lita managed to fall asleep, curled in the fetal position, about half an hour later.

"Craig! Please! Stop!" Felice cried, grabbing his hands and trying to pull them away.

At first he ignored her entreaties, pressing his lower body against her in the backseat and reaching insistently into her slacks. He was kissing her roughly, his eyes closed, almost as if he were lost in his own world, oblivious of Felice as a person, concentrating on her as a female body.

She whimpered in unhappy embarrassment as his fingers reached the part of her anatomy that he'd so obviously been seeking for several minutes now.

"Yes," he choked as he pressed his pelvis against her thigh and dug his fingers into her virgin flesh. "Yes . . ."

He began trying to strip off her slacks with one hand, and Felice began to fight him in earnest. "No!" she cried frantically. "Not until we're married! Stop! Please! Please, Craig! Don't . . ." she gasped as she began to struggle for her breath under his crushing embrace.

Dimly her pleas reached him, and he loosened his frantic grip on her. Felice felt his rigid body gradually slacken, and she breathed a sigh of relief as he rolled a little to one side so she no longer had to bear so much of his weight. He buried his face against one arm and his shoulders began to shake. Felice didn't know what it meant, but she sensed that whatever demon had been driving him to attack her was gone for now. She felt so sorry for the forlorn figure, her longtime sweetheart suddenly turned stranger, that she instinctively reached out to touch him lightly on the shoulder.

"What's the matter, Craig?" she asked, whispering in a shaken voice as she anxiously watched him.

"I'm sorry, Felice," he mumbled brokenly against his sleeve. "I don't want to hurt you . . . I swear it . . . I just . . . God! Never mind. Please, try to forget about it."

Felice leaned on her elbow, half sitting in the old car as she straightened her rumpled clothing. It hurt her to see him suffer so, but she really didn't know what to do for him. She'd never seen him act like this, and for the life of her, she couldn't figure out what could have happened to have made him so . . . desperate.

It was the desperate quality of his seduction that had made her recoil, not his unvarnished attempt to consummate their long-term relationship. Felice still lived with her family and had a rather old-fashioned attitude about premarital sex. She'd always dreamed of being a virgin on her wedding day, giving the gift of herself to her husband after they had said their vows.

However, she was physically attracted to Craig, and she was a perfectly normal, healthy young woman. If he had coaxed her and wooed her and courted her patiently, she knew she wouldn't have held out. She would have let him make love to her. After all, they were formally engaged and they'd set the date for their wedding. As far as she was concerned, they were practically married now.

But he hadn't wooed her or courted her. He'd come at her desperately, as if seeking to prove something to himself by stripping her and taking her.

That frightened Felice. Fear had frozen her ardor and had given her the strength to physically resist him.

"What's wrong, Craig?" she repeated, holding her breath as she awaited his answer.

He shook his head and rebuckled his belt. "Nothing," he sighed unhappily. "Come on, let's get back in the front seat. I'll take you home."

Felice was totally unconvinced by his denial, but she couldn't think of a way to get him to explain, so she let it go. Eventually he'd tell her, she told herself hopefully.

He pulled into her parents' driveway half an hour

later. The solid brick homes in the old residential area comforted Felice and gave her the strength to lean over and give Craig a consoling kiss on his cheek. He hung his head as if she'd laid a heavy burden on him by her simple action.

All of a sudden he grasped her hand and held it next to his cheek in a pathetic gesture of appreciation. "I love you, Felice," he whispered, looking at her with haunted eyes. "Please, don't forget that."

"Of course not, silly," she teased him reassuringly, vowing to put aside her own worries and come to his aid. It was probably just prenuptial jitters, she told herself. Everybody got them, she'd been told. She gave him a light kiss on the lips and slipped out of the car. Tomorrow was Saturday and she didn't have to work until Monday. She gave him an optimistic smile. "Want to go for a walk around the tidal basin tomorrow?" she asked expectantly. "We could go for a ride on one of the little bicycle paddle boats . . ."

He smiled wanly and nodded. "Sure, Felice. I can't think of any place I'd rather be tomorrow than with you."

She blushed with pleasure and patted the car for luck as she usually did before leaving him. "Be careful on the way home!" she called out.

He nodded, watching until she was safely inside. Then he backed out of the driveway and drove downtown to buy the early edition of Saturday's *Washington Post.* Surely he'd see a notice somewhere soon, he thought despondently. Then everyone would know. Felice would know . . . He wanted to cry, but he was a grown man and grown men weren't supposed to cry. So he just suffered in silence, hurting like the very dickens. "I'm sorry, Felice," he cried out softly into the darkness as he drove to his apartment. "I'm so sorry . . ."

* * *

Lita sat in the small dressing room Saturday night and stared at herself in the brightly lighted makeup mirror. She'd been sitting there for a good ten minutes, completely dressed and ready to go on. She could hear the sounds of the band members making their way down the hall, joking and laughing, trading stories. They would be warming up in the club in a few minutes. In less than an hour Lita would be standing there with them, singing before a live audience for the first time in years.

All she wanted now was for it to be all over. She prayed for time to speed up so that she didn't have to keep waiting. Waiting had turned out to be the worst thing about this week.

Well, maybe the second worst thing, she amended sadly. She was desperately worried about Melanie now. No one had seen or heard from her in more than a week. With every passing day Lita had visualized worse and worse explanations for her cousin's absence.

"Oh, Melanie," Lita murmured aloud, tormented and frustrated by her inability to do anything concrete to help find her cousin.

Even Pete Fallon had no news.

There was a quiet, authoritative knock at the door. Lita turned a little on the stool and answered. "Come in."

Keith Christophe walked in, closing the door behind him.

Lita hadn't been alone with him since that night he'd driven her home. They'd passed each other in the club a couple of times, but they'd merely said hello before continuing on their separate ways. There was an awkwardness between them that Lita was sure he was aware of, too, yet neither of them seemed to be able to do anything about it.

"Good evening," he said in a low, measured voice. He

perused her slowly, as if giving her appearance a last check before show time. "Do you need anything before you go on?" he asked, raising his dark eyes to hers.

"No. Everything's fine. Thanks."

He nodded absently and walked over to the rack of expensive dresses that lined one wall. He fingered the costly gowns, keeping his back to her. "You look lovely tonight. Are you okay?" he asked distantly.

Lita watched the black jacket rise and fall, stretching over his broad shoulders as he examined the clothes she would be performing in. As usual, he was impeccably dressed.

When she didn't answer immediately, he stopped what he was doing and turned to face her.

Lita tried to smile and shrugged her bare shoulders fatalistically. "No. I guess I can't say that I'm okay," she admitted, "but I'm ready." She lowered her eyes and then raised them again to his. "I'm a professional. I've learned to make myself do what I have to, whether I really want to or not."

Keith had to admire the inner strength of this woman. She was beautiful and radiant; she was talented and accomplished in her field. But the thing that he was coming to find the most appealing about Lita Winslow was her strength of character. She had good reason to try to get out of her commitment. If she'd tried hard enough, he probably would have let her go. Hell! He could have booked another act in a minute. Sydney's was considered a high-class place by performers. It was a jumping-off platform for singers and instrumentalists who aspired to national fame and fortune. It was a club that established entertainers thoroughly enjoyed returning to year after year.

"Has anyone bothered you?" he asked abruptly.

She shook her head. "No."

He stared at her grimly. "We had to change the advertising," he told her, not sounding very happy about it. "Marty called it in yesterday. The announcement that you would be singing tonight ran in today's *Post.*"

Lita knew what he was telling her. Now it was not a secret that she was in town and about to perform in public. If the person who'd terrorized her five years ago happened to be in this area, or somehow heard the news . . .

She stood up and tried to give him a reassuring smile. "Thanks for holding it back until the last minute, Keith. I hope it doesn't cost you in lost revenue," she said sincerely.

He frowned. "I don't give a *damn* about that!" he retorted sharply.

Lita gave him an exasperated look. "I didn't mean it that way!" she exclaimed. Why did he have to take it wrongly?

He paced back and forth across the tiny room. "Look, if you receive as much as a dirty look from someone while you're in town, I want you to tell me. Okay?" he said, beginning to sound angry.

"Sure, Keith. I'll be all right." She couldn't be angry with him. She knew he wasn't angry at her. He was annoyed with himself.

"If I'd known about what happened to you five years ago, I never would have insisted on your being Melanie's backup," he said, looking as if he'd been cursing himself for that recently. "Connery never said anything about it. I want you to know that, Lita."

He'd been getting more and more worried about this whole mess all week. Too many things were going sour. Melanie's disappearance, the break-in at the town house, the past threats against Lita. As far as Keith was concerned, there were too many problems to be merely a matter of coincidence.

Lita saw the worry in his face, and her heart softened

in gratitude. Something melted in her and it showed in her expression. "I believe you," she murmured softly.

He nodded, and the worry disappeared behind the tough facade of the nightclub owner. He touched her shoulder lightly and opened the door to usher her out a little ahead of him. "I'll walk you out," he replied evenly.

It was comforting to sit with him at the bar, listening to the band play and looking over the crowd. The big band sound of "Tuxedo Junction" had attracted a number of couples to the dance floor, where they were slow dancing swing steps of the forties and fifties.

Keith took her hand in his and kissed her palm as the music faded and Gaius stepped up to the microphone to introduce her.

"Good luck," Keith murmured, giving her that hint of a smile that teased her heart so.

She took a deep breath and stood up. "Thanks," she replied. She added to herself, I'll need it.

People turned in their seats to see her as she made her way between the tables. She bowed her head and smiled to acknowledge the applause.

"Thank you," she said, taking the microphone from Gaius, who was grinning enthusiastically. "It's wonderful to be here tonight." She scanned the audience, making each person feel she was speaking just to him or her. "I've been enjoying being in the audience this week, so I know how great the band sounds! I hope you find the singer in the same league."

There were amused chuckles scattered about the room at her modesty. Then the band picked up the strains of Lita's first ballad, and the audience quieted, sitting back to enjoy an entertainment rarity: Lita Winslow, live and onstage.

As soon as she felt the warmth of the spotlight on her face, the hardness of the mike in her hand, the beat of the music from the band behind her, it all came back to her.

The joy of singing, of making other people happy, of sharing the sensuous beauty of a great melody or a poignant lyric. It was what Lita had always loved most about the business. She closed her eyes and sang the opening line, putting her heart into each word.

Sean slid onto the stool next to Keith's at the bar. They watched Lita as she captured the imagination of every person in the club with the familiar tale of unrequited love that had become a standard for just about every serious nightclub singer in the country.

Keith was nursing a bourbon on the rocks, unable to tear his eyes off her.

"Boy, she *is* good," Sean whispered, bending close to his brother's ear.

Keith nodded. "Yeah," he muttered unenthusiastically.

Sean accepted his usual from Carl with a quick grin of thanks and alternated between enjoying Lita's singing and surreptitiously studying his brother's reaction to it. He wasn't sure which was more entertaining.

For once, Keith was too absorbed to notice. All he wanted to do at the moment was look at Lita. Her every gesture, every expression fascinated him. When she held out her slender hand and leaned forward to cry out about the pain her lover had caused her, he wanted to reach out and touch her hand, to soothe her pain. He knew it was just that she was a very affecting performer. He told himself it was just a matter of the phrasing, the way she paced the words, the expressiveness of her delivery. And yet she touched him in a very special way . . .

He followed the cut of her floor-length evening dress, lingering over the swell of her breasts and the curve of her hips under the sequins of midnight blue and glittering silver. Every time she moved, the light caught and reflected her gown, making her shimmer like a goddess of the night. The slit up one side gave elusive glimpses of the shapely leg beneath. She was beautiful to look at.

Most of all, he felt profound admiration. If he hadn't known that she'd been threatened before and had left the business because of that, he'd never have guessed it. Watching her perform, anyone would have thought she loved entertaining—that she hadn't a care in the world other than making sure her audience enjoyed themselves.

The sizzle of the brushes on the cymbals, the deep rhythmic plucking on the bass, the melodic tones of the muted trumpet, and Lita's warm, rich voice filled the club, weaving a sultry, romantic spell.

If it hadn't been for the circumstances that had brought it all about, Keith Christophe might even have enjoyed it.

"Heads or tails?" Sean asked cheerfully. Sean tossed a nickel into the air and caught it in one hand. He waited expectantly for his brother's answer.

Keith was seated next to Sean at the private table in the nook near the bar. Lita had been performing for a week now, and every night he'd found an excuse to spend a little more time in the club, watching her. It was becoming increasingly difficult to come up with new reasons and next to impossible to stay away.

He drained the last of the bourbon and put his glass down with a definite air of finality. He eyed his brother suspiciously. Sean had been uncustomarily easygoing for days. He'd also been hanging around Lita like a groupie, Keith thought sourly. Every time he turned around he seemed to be met with his brother and Lita—taking her for a quick bite to eat after rehearsal, breaking in and dancing with her when a patron started hanging on her, entertaining her when she had some time to kill.

He was generally becoming a damned nuisance as far as Keith was concerned. Of course, he'd seen to it that Sean didn't take her home. Keith had reserved that right for himself.

Keith scowled at his brother as Sean slapped the coin onto the back of his hand, keeping it covered. "Well?" Sean prodded, a definite gleam in his eyes.

"What are we betting on?" Keith asked distrustfully. He'd been the furious recipient of any number of pranks perpetrated by his younger brother over the years. Keith had long ago learned to tell when Sean was trying to set him up. Now was definitely one of those times.

"The winner gets the honor and privilege of escorting Lita home tonight," Sean said, just a little too casually.

Keith leaned back in the chair and gave his brother a quelling look. "I already *know* who gets that honor," Keith replied coolly. "Pick something else," he ordered.

Sean began to grin. "Maybe Lita's tired of your taxi service, brother," he jibed. "Give me a chance to give her a little variety."

Normally Keith would have ignored Sean's teasing, but where Lita Winslow was concerned he seemed to have lost his sense of humor. Maybe it had something to do with watching his brother put his arms around her when they danced, or lean close to her to speak softly in her ear.

Keith's face darkened in anger and he stood up abruptly. "That's the last song. If you want another drink before you go, Sean, you'd better ask Carl for it now. Case closed."

Keith buttoned his white dinner jacket and joined Marty near the door to say good evening to a few old friends who'd dropped by. It required iron determination, but Keith managed to resist the urge to keep looking over his shoulder to see if his brother was following Lita around the club.

Marty looked at Keith in dismay as his boss abruptly concluded a farewell with one of their better-known patrons and headed in the direction of the dressing room.

"Uh, thanks for stopping in tonight," he mumbled,

trying to smooth over the look of surprise on the patron's face. "Glad you enjoyed the entertainment."

Lita recognized the hard rap on her door as the sound of Keith's knuckles. She knew him well enough now to tell that he was annoyed at something from the loud staccato taps he'd delivered. He'd been annoyed at one thing or another all week, it seemed, she fumed silently. Let him wait! There was another sharp rap at the door. Silently Lita counted backward from ten by twos in Italian as she pulled the red sequined evening dress over her head and dropped it over the Oriental screen, which was her only source of privacy within the tiny dressing room.

"Lita? Are you in there?" Keith called, the door muffling his voice but not concealing his tone of command.

"Yes," she called back, much too sweetly to be considered sincere.

"Are you decent?"

"I'm always decent!"

Keith stepped inside and shut the door with more force than necessary. He leaned against the door and glared at her. "You know what I meant," he retorted angrily.

Lita was beside herself. Why, oh, why, was she constantly annoyed with this man? No matter what he said or did, she was irritated with him. They couldn't keep this up for the remaining two weeks of the engagement. They'd both be exhausted, if nothing else.

She looked over the screen at him, having resolved to be polite and calm. All it took was one look at his darkly handsome, thoroughly masculine figure lounging against her door to disintegrate her best-laid plans.

He radiated a dangerous tension, which enveloped her like an invisible net. To her dismay, she realized she was trembling a little, and she took a breath to calm her nerves. Her fingers shook slightly as she finished buttoning her light blue raw silk shirtwaist and fastening its belt.

Keith was silently cursing his stupidity for entering the room. He could only see her neck and head above the discreetly placed screen, but her motions weren't hard to decipher. He felt like he'd suddenly acquired the ability to see through solid matter, because the image of her dressing herself was so vivid it seemed real.

He frowned fiercely, baffled as usual by the intensity of his attraction to her. He whipped up his anger to divert his emotions. He had a clear choice: it was anger or lust. He'd decided anger was by far the best choice for venting his feelings for her. There was no way that lust fitted into the scheme of things. Not this time . . .

He saw her cheeks darken and wondered why she was blushing. She'd removed most of her stage makeup. There was no doubt that the dusky pink that had shadowed her cheekbones was pure Lita. It made her even more attractive, he realized hazily. She was like an alluring rose whose soft, dewy petals had been made to intoxicate a man.

Somewhere, however, there were always hidden thorns to gouge out the pleasure and replace it with pain, he reminded himself bitterly. He had had enough women in his life. And they were all right where he wanted them. Casual friends. Occasional bedmates. They knew the rules of the game. Don't ask for anything. Don't expect anything in return.

Lita watched the increasingly grim expression on Keith's face as she picked up her purse and walked out to join him. It was a chilling experience. He was struggling with some inner devils, of that she was sure. But which ones? And why did they seem to attack him the hardest when she was around?

And why did her heart have to beat harder for this hard, tough man? she asked herself in growing desperation. It was getting worse all the time.

He lifted the car keys from his jacket pocket and rippled them between his fingers. "Are you ready?" he asked stiffly.

"Yes."

She'd abandoned offering to take cabs home after the second night he'd played chauffeur. Keith had made it quite clear that he and no one else would escort her to her door. Secretly she'd finally admitted to herself that she liked it. It was a kind of protective attention she'd never really had before. Not since she was a small child, anyway. She followed him to his car without complaint.

This drive to the town house was even worse than the others had been. The silence between them was strained. The tension seemed to fill the space between them in the close confines of Keith's compactly built car.

He took out his exasperation on the stick shift, changing gears with unusual sharpness. Lita could only sit back, clutching her evening bag, crossing and uncrossing her legs.

Keith pulled sharply into the curb and cut the engine, getting out without saying a word. Lita waited for him to open the door, hoping to make herself play all the right roles, thereby avoiding any prolonged contact with the male who was driving her to distraction at the moment.

As she saw it, the faster she got inside and closed the door behind her, the better off they both would be. It was only too obvious that they couldn't get along. Even as she told herself that, she knew in her heart that it wasn't quite true. She had a sinking feeling she knew exactly why they were having such a hard time getting along. A very sinking feeling indeed. She fumbled with the keys, practically dropping them in her haste to open the door.

Keith swore under his breath, snatched the keys away from her, and opened the door himself. As soon as he handed them back to her, he recognized his mistake. Their hands brushed as he dropped the keys into her palm and they both froze.

Lita stared up into his eyes and saw the desire that he held in check just beneath the surface. A ripple of awareness coursed through her, and she struggled to find something chic and sophisticated to say that would bring the evening to a timely conclusion.

Not a single word came to mind, and she found herself taking a hesitant step backward. She searched for the doorknob blindly with one hand. She fumbled over the smooth hardwood surface and felt a surge of relief as her fingers touched the round metal knob.

But it was too late. Keith had fallen into the mysterious spell of her midnight eyes. He moved forward and reached around her, covering her slender hand with his. He came half a step closer, leaving them just inches apart.

"Go inside," he murmured as his gaze fastened on her slightly parted lips.

He pushed the door open with the palm of his free hand. His body touched hers as he moved forward, pushing her gently but firmly backward into the darkened apartment and pulling the door closed behind them. Silvery light from the street lamps was filtering through the sheer white curtains as Keith pulled Lita into his arms and slowly lowered his head.

Lita closed her eyes without realizing what she was doing and leaned against the warm, solid man who had shadowed her thoughts so disturbingly. She felt his hard, warm lips touch hers and slowly, erotically tease hers with a light, exploring kiss. She relaxed a little and slid her arms around his waist.

A warm, hazy blur of feeling flowered inside her as her lips parted in unconscious welcome and his mouth hardened in response. She felt his arms tighten around her and heard him choke back a groan of pleasure. The heat from his body and the heat from their kiss began to sizzle and blend, raising her temperature from her head to her toes.

He pulled her up until her toes just barely touched the ground and pressed warm, provocative kisses on the corner of her mouth, working his way slowly, exquisitely, across her half-parted lips to the other side.

"Mmm," Lita murmured as her head fell back a little and he continued the tantalizing string of kisses down her tender throat.

He came back to her mouth, running his tongue softly over her sensitive lips. His breath was warm and sweet; the scent of his skin, clean and masculine. He was utterly intoxicating to her. Lita felt herself wanting more of him . . . He lifted her fully into his arms, pulling her to rest on his chest as she lifted her arms, linking them behind his neck.

"Ah," he muttered thickly, brushing a soft kiss against her temple and another against her ear. "I've been wanting to do this ever since the first day you walked into the club."

He moved slowly toward the sofa, savoring the feel of her soft body as it pressed against his. Even through his evening clothes and her dress, he could feel the shape of her breasts flattened against his chest, her stomach against his, her hips just below his arms. Her thighs rubbed lightly against his with every slow stride, making him wonder for the millionth time what they would feel like naked against him.

Keith knew that he was becoming too aroused to let himself continue fantasizing and tried to find something else to concentrate on. He buried his face in her neck and took a deep breath to calm down. Instead he found himself being tantalized by the subtle, fascinating scent of her skin. That hardly helped cool his ardor, but he couldn't help but linger there, savoring the experience in spite of his growing discomfort. A little discomfort was a price he was more than willing to pay for the pleasure of holding her in his arms.

He lowered her onto the sofa and sat down, pulling her onto his lap. He began to caress her back and kiss her throat as he deftly unbuttoned the front of her dress.

His tactic was hardly necessary. Lita wouldn't have thought of protesting. Her whole being had suddenly come alive in his arms. She wanted to sing and to cry at the same time. As long as he kept touching her, kept holding her and kissing her, she didn't care what happened. Being with him was all that mattered . . .

She ran her fingers through his dark hair and kissed him as fully as she could, playing with his mouth with her tongue and thrilling at the tension it produced in him. She smiled as she slanted her mouth against his and opened herself again to his deepening exploration of her mouth as he opened the front of her dress.

She was so eager for his touch that she felt his hand the moment it touched her bare skin. She sighed against his lips as he stopped kissing her and concentrated on unfastening the catch in the front of her lacy bra. For a second her breasts were freed, then his hand closed over first one, then the other, in an infinitely tender caress.

She arched forward as he bent his head to kiss her neck, then proceeded at a provocatively slow pace downward to the gentle swell that ached for his attention. He branded her with each increasingly arousing kiss, leaving a trail of memories burned into her tender flesh. All she wanted was to be his forever. A tiny rational voice cried to her that it was just chemistry, just physical attraction, but another part of her whispered, No, it was more than that, much more . . .

As his mouth closed over one stiff, straining nipple, he felt her tremble and tightened his hold on her in automatic response. She was warm and pliant, eager and responsive, everything he'd ever wanted in a woman. His

101

body was hard with wanting her. He couldn't remember ever wanting a woman more.

"Lita," he groaned as he reluctantly pulled away and leaned back against the sofa, his eyes closing in pain and frustration, "we'd better cut this out."

He pushed her gently back against his arm as his eyes roamed slowly over her face and neck, down to her still-exposed breasts. He ran his hand gently over them one last time before refastening her bra and trying unsuccessfully to rebutton the front of her dress.

She smiled ruefully and did it herself. "I think you're better at unbuttoning than buttoning," she observed teasingly, trying to steady her own nerves a little with humor.

He grinned faintly and raised an eyebrow at her friendly taunt. "You could be right. In your case there's absolutely no good reason for being skilled at buttoning," he pointed out, sounding much calmer than he had the last time he'd spoken.

He gazed at her in silence, enjoying the silvery beauty of her as she finished straightening her clothes. He reluctantly shifted her off his lap and stood up.

Lita got to her feet, amazed that they held her weight, considering how weak they felt at the moment. She was about to offer him a cup of coffee when he spoke, precluding her.

"I never do this, you know," he said seriously.

"Kiss a woman when you take her home?" Lita asked in disbelief. Surely he didn't mean that. The man's kissing was definitely world class!

He grimaced and shook his head. "No. That's not what I meant." His lips were a tight line for a moment. "Get involved with someone who's performing at the club," he explained.

Lita stood looking at him without comment, waiting for him to go on.

He ran his hand roughly through his hair and paced

across the room and back. Then he came to a halt in front of her and placed his hands gently on her shoulders. "I just . . . want you to know that," he added, gazing down enigmatically at her uncomprehending eyes. He kissed her one last, lingering time, then tore himself away and stalked toward the door. "Be sure and lock this after I've gone," he ordered her.

"Yes." His change in mood had caught her by surprise. Yes was all she could think of to say.

She locked the door and turned on the alarm. She knew he had waited to hear the bolt thrown; she'd heard his footsteps fade away afterward. She leaned her forehead against the door and wondered at the tingling sensation she still felt, even though he'd gone.

"Keith Christophe, what are you doing to me?" she murmured aloud. "And what's wrong?"

There was something—she knew that instinctively. He wanted her. Of that she was certain. And yet he was fighting it. The more he wanted her, the harder he seemed to fight against it.

"Why?" she wondered, thinking out loud as she pulled the covers over her shoulders a short while later. "Why?"

CHAPTER SIX

The cold light of day did not help matters as far as Lita was concerned. It only cast a chill over her uncertain memories. Lita awoke to the very disturbing realization that she could fall in love with Keith Christophe if she didn't watch out.

Lita threw the covers over her head and tried to go back to sleep. It was a ridiculous gesture, she knew, but she tried it anyway. She was spared from suffocating herself to no purpose by an unexpected sound.

The phone rang.

"All right, all right," she mumbled, stumbling out of the bed and pulling on her robe as she headed toward the front of the town house. "Hello," she said, trying unsuccessfully not to sound like she was just getting up.

"Lita . . ."

She sat down and blinked in surprise. She hadn't expected to hear from Keith so soon, but she was very happy to hear his voice. "You're up early," she murmured, twisting the telephone cord aimlessly.

There was a barely perceptible pause.

"Yes." He seemed to hesitate, as if reluctant to tell her why he'd called. "There's been some news about Melanie, Lita."

Something in his even, controlled tone of voice gave Lita a sinking feeling in the pit of her stomach. She clutched the phone, steeling herself a little. "What is it?"

she asked, desperately hoping it would be good news but fearing she was about to hear bad news.

"I'd like to come over and tell you in person, Lita," he said. "Could you be ready for a visit in, say, fifteen minutes?"

"Fifteen minutes?" She sensed from the somber tone of his question that he was going to be the bearer of bad tidings. Questions rose up in her throat, but she couldn't bring herself to ask them. She wanted to put off hearing the answer as long as possible, as if it would somehow keep it from being true.

"Fifteen minutes," she repeated. "Yes. I'll be waiting."

There was a moment of hesitation. Then he said, "See you then. I'll be with you as soon as I can."

"Okay," she responded weakly.

She didn't feel the phone leave her hand, nor her barefeet on the carpet as she returned to the bedroom. She was only vaguely aware of pulling on jeans and a sweater. Everything had become very distant and unimportant, all of a sudden.

When Keith's car pulled up in front of the town house, Lita was standing at the window, looking for him. The tiny flicker of hope she'd nursed burned even less brightly as she noted the car that had parked behind him.

Pete Fallon had accompanied Keith. The two men were grim faced as they came up the walk. Lita opened the door for them before they reached the door.

Keith stopped in front of her, searching for the words to break the news to her. Hell! He'd been searching for them ever since Fallon had called him a little after eight this morning. He might as well face it. There wasn't any way to break this kind of news.

"Good morning," he said softly, taking in her worried expression, the brave front she was putting up. He reached out and touched her mouth, soft and appealing in the morning light. "May we come in?"

"Of course."

She stepped back and motioned for them to come in. She saw herself from a distance, as if from outside, following the men into the living room. She didn't want to hear what they were going to say. Instinctively she wanted to avoid it.

Lita hadn't expected it to be like this . . . wanting, yet not wanting, to find out what had happened to Melanie. Now that the news was here, she felt herself going numb, chilled to the bone with fear that it would be very bad news indeed. It was grief's cold denial, nature's original anesthesia, protecting the human mind and heart from a painful, emotional blow.

Anxiously she searched their grim, stolid expressions. There was no room for hope, she realized, seeing their faces. The news was going to be very bad indeed. She blinked hard to keep back a sudden rush of tears. Then the anesthetizing chill turned her blood to ice, and the teardrops froze without falling.

"Please, sit down," she insisted. Lita had the feeling it would be easier for her to take their news standing up.

She looked from one to the other. Fallon was licking his lips nervously, and Keith appeared to be struggling to begin saying whatever had to be said. She couldn't stand waiting another moment and decided to spare them the unpleasant duty they'd set for themselves.

"Have you found her?" she asked, looking steadily at Fallon.

"Yes," he said, sympathy in his eyes.

"Is she . . . alive?" Lita pressed, feeling herself freeze as she waited for the answer. She already knew what it would be, but she had to ask the question as if Melanie still had a chance. She just had to . . .

Fallon's eyes dropped for a second. Then he looked her straight in the eyes, his expression filled with empathy.

He'd had to do this before, but it never seemed to get any easier. "I'm sorry," he answered regretfully. "No."

Lita nodded blindly and sat down next to Keith. "I—I was afraid that was what you were going to say," she said softly. "It's been so long since anyone's seen her, and you both looked so—so grim."

The men were silent, giving her a few minutes to absorb the news. Fallon gave Keith an inquiring look. "Do you want to ask her or shall I?" the detective asked in a low voice, as if hoping Lita wouldn't pay any attention.

"I'll ask," Keith replied evenly. He turned toward Lita. "Does she have any next of kin in this area besides you, Lita?" he asked gently.

Lita pulled herself together. "No. Her father died years ago. Her mother lives in California." Lita looked at him unhappily. "I'm her closest relative in this part of the country. Why?"

Keith's face became even more grim, and he cast a steely glance at his old friend.

Fallon shrugged and shook his head as if in apology. "I'm sorry, Keith. I don't make the rules. Someone has to do it," Fallon pointed out.

Lita looked from one man to the other in confusion. "Someone has to do what?" she asked, a little bewildered by their behavior.

Fallon cleared his throat. "Someone has to identify the body."

Lita paled a little. "Oh . . . I see," she said faintly. "How—how did she die?" she asked, trying hard to brace herself for whatever else was to come.

Fallon shrugged. "We're not sure yet. Her body was discovered this morning by some joggers. At the moment, it appears she was . . . strangled."

Lita was shocked. "Strangled!" She closed her eyes in misery. "Poor Melanie . . . "Oh, God . . ." She felt

Keith's strong, warm hand close over her shoulder in a gesture of comfort.

"If there's someone else who could do it . . ." Fallon suggested hopefully.

Lita shook her head. There was only Melanie's mother and Lita's mother, and she wouldn't wish this on either of them. Lita thought of her father, but he would be too hard to reach. Anyway, it seemed a cowardly way out. In a strange way, she wanted to do it. It was sort of a last favor to perform for her cousin.

Lita drew a deep breath and gazed without wavering at Fallon. "No. There's no one else, Pete. I'll do it." She stood up awkwardly, not knowing exactly what the procedures were when something like this happened. "Do you want me to go now?"

Both men rose to their feet immediately and looked at each other in surprise and relief. She was taking it better than they'd feared.

"If you think you're ready," Fallon said.

Lita nodded. "I wouldn't say that I'm 'ready,' Pete, but I guess I'd feel better if I get it over with."

"Why don't you let me drive you?" Keith suggested as she searched for her purse.

Lita gave him a grateful look. "Thanks, Keith."

He grimly watched her straighten her back and force some determination into herself as they headed toward the car. Lita Winslow had strength of character. He only wished he weren't discovering it under such awful circumstances!

The identification was easier than Lita had feared. Melanie looked like she was asleep. The morgue attendants had mercifully closed her eyes, and the only thing Lita saw was her cousin's face viewed through a small glass window in the casket.

Lita turned away, just barely aware of Keith, who was

following close at her side. "Yes," she said with great sadness, "that's Melanie."

Fallon nodded and led them back to their cars. "I'll need to talk to you, to take a formal statement," he told Lita.

"Of course," she said.

Dry-eyed and silent, Lita sat stone still during the ride to the police station. Keith stayed close at hand in case she needed support. His presence alone seemed to give Lita a little extra strength.

Fallon handled the interview with such kindly professionalism that Lita didn't have a chance to become despondent. In a way, it was helpful to start reflecting on Melanie's life. It was the beginning of saying good-bye. It gradually dawned on Lita that she hadn't had a chance to tell Melanie farewell, and talking about her to others became a means of compensating for that.

"She was just making the big time," Lita told the detective, her eyes gentling with fondness for her cousin. "She'd always dreamed of that. It was all set up. All she had to do was keep her engagements for the next ten months and she'd have been a household name. She was a great singer."

Fallon was an experienced interviewer. He could tell when someone was lying to him or putting him on. He could also sense when a person was lying to themselves. He had no trouble telling that Lita Winslow believed every word she said. Coming from her, he was inclined to accept that assessment of Melanie's life, as well.

"Did she have any enemies? People who would want to see her dead?" Fallon asked crisply.

Lita's first impulse was to give him a shocked no for an answer. She bit her tongue and counted to five. He deserved, and Melanie deserved, a thoughtful answer. "I haven't spent every day of the past ten years with her," Lita explained slowly. "Melanie and I grew up together, of course. We lived next door to each other and spent a great deal of time together." Especially when our parents were having problems, which seemed to be continuous, she omitted to say. That wasn't pertinent. It was . . . private. "We came here to college, mainly to escape our parents," she told them, smiling wistfully at the long-ago memory.

"Here?" Fallon asked in surprise. Lita mentioned the name of a well-known women's college for upper-class girls, and the detective made a note of it.

"We desperately wanted to get away from home—to try our wings a little, you know," she went on. "But we knew it would be safer in a place like this—where there were so many famous people and children of famous people, that we would just be like one of the crowd."

Fallon nodded. She didn't have to explain what she meant. Everyone knew Lita's mother was a well-known film actress and her father a wealthy financier. Melanie's mother had been a successful model and was always written up in society pages, especially when she was seen dating a particularly eligible bachelor of hefty means.

It had been natural for Lita and Melanie to gravitate toward the entertainment field. They'd grown up in it. Doors opened for them more easily than for most.

Keith had leaned his chair back and studied Lita from beneath half-closed eyes, toying with a paper clip as he listened to her talk. He, of course, was also aware of her family background, but hearing it from her own lips gave it a special reality that it had lacked before. Like Fallon, Keith was an expert at reading between the lines. As she related the facts Lita had no idea how much she revealed to the faintly startled Keith Christophe.

"I think that was the happiest time of life for both of us," she said softly, remembering. A fond expression lighted her face. "We were free for the first time, really. It was wonderful! We could get up and plan for the day

110

without checking with our mothers." She laughed softly and gave Keith and Fallon inquiring looks. "Do you have any idea what that was like for us?" she asked doubtfully. "Going from sunny California under the daily eye of the press, our parents' agents, our housekeepers, and our parents, who were going overboard with limits on our social lives because they felt so guilty about being gone more than they were home?" Lita sighed wistfully. "Sorry. I guess I'm not exactly answering the question am I, Pete," she apologized.

He shrugged. "Take your time. I'm listening."

Lita tried to focus her thoughts. She had wanted to begin at the beginning, and somehow the year they'd first come to Washington to go to college seemed as good a beginning point as any. "Well, we dated, we studied, and we learned about life outside the California fishbowl. We grew up a little. I guess it was during those years that I admitted to myself that singing and writing music were two things I was fairly good at. I started performing a little during vacations, and Melanie, well, she wanted to get into the business, but she always seemed to get side-tracked . . ."

"Sidetracked?" Fallon asked encouragingly when Lita's voice trailed off a little.

Lita blushed a little remembering in vivid detail a couple of incidents that she had no intention of revealing to anyone, ever. Melanie had gone overboard in one unfortunate aspect of her newly found freedom. "Melanie kept falling in love," Lita explained lamely. "There was always a guy after her. And it would always be the same. She'd let him pick her up, she'd fall into his lap like the trusting little romantic she was, and then he'd leave." She gave the two silent men condemning looks without being entirely aware of what she was doing. "She'd be broken-hearted and cry, go out to every party she could get to, and then it would start all over again."

Fallon and Keith had both been startled at her censuring look, but they were both seasoned enough to take it in stride. They merely looked at each other briefly, wondering whether that pattern had continued into the present —and if so, who some of the men had been.

Lita chewed her lip thoughtfully, then decided to say what she was thinking. "I think that was the beginning of her drinking problem," she said at last. "She was terribly insecure, and . . . well, whenever an affair ended she'd start partying and drinking, seven nights a week. If only she could have seen herself as I saw her—her family—Jack . . ."

"Jack?" Keith asked, his interest picking up at the mention of the name.

Lita nodded. "Jack Connery. He was always in there pitching for Melanie. We met Jack here in Washington the last year we were in college, as a matter of fact. He was always encouraging her to go into the business, and he did everything he could to try to keep her on the straight and narrow. He was determined to prove to her what a dynamite person she really was."

Lita was surprised to feel tears gather in her eyes from out of nowhere. She swallowed and tried to control the threatening sorrow. "Now she'll never know," Lita murmured huskily. She wiped the tiny trail of moisture angrily from her cheek. "In answer to your question, Pete, I don't know of anyone who would have tried to hurt her. Melanie was afraid of life, terribly insecure, and desperate for affection. She'd give a stranger her last dime in return for a heartfelt thank you. But no, I never heard of her ever having an enemy."

Fallon tapped his pencil on his notepad a couple of times. "Uh, could you give me the names and addresses of any old friends who might still be in the area, recent boyfriends, family?"

"Certainly," Lita agreed, holding herself together with

112

sheer determination. She had too much to take care of to give in to the terrible grief she felt. Maybe later . . .

As they were leaving the police station later Keith turned to Lita. He'd been listening as she talked and had begun to realize there were a large number of people who needed to be notified of Melanie's death—quickly—if it were to be done before the news broke in the papers. He held her shoulders lightly in his hands, wondering how in the world a woman could look so strong and so vulnerable at the same time. "Would you like me to call anyone for you?" he asked quietly.

She leaned her forehead against his chest, curling her arms up against him as if to soak up his force a little. His arms closed around her comfortingly as she shook her head.

"No," she mumbled, "but could you take me back to the town house?"

He kept one arm around her shoulders and led her back to the car.

The rest of the morning and early afternoon were swallowed up in long, teary telephone conversations. Lita personally broke the news to her father, who was in Ottawa on business, and to her mother, who was in Hollywood at work on a new film. Much to her surprise, her mother, after breaking down for a few minutes of weeping, summoned her strength and insisted on being the one to break the news to Melanie's mother.

"She's my sister," the actress reminded her daughter. "I'd never forgive myself if I let her hear it from anyone else . . . or over the phone." Lita heard her mother sob once and then struggle to find her voice. "I'll call you tonight, darling. We can make the funeral arrangements here . . ."

"Yes, mother. Thank you," Lita murmured.

Keith watched her replace the phone and stand in the

middle of the room, staring unhappily at the instrument. "How did she take it?" he asked cautiously.

She blinked and looked at him like a person who didn't quite recognize her surroundings for a moment. "Much better than I'd expected," she admitted in surprise. "I was preparing to have to do everything—call people, begin making funeral arrangements, coordinate things . . ." She waved a hand as if trying to underline the duties that had been whisked away. "But after she got over the first shock of the news, she insisted on telling Melanie's mother in person and taking charge of the funeral plans."

Keith frowned slightly, trying to make sense of why that should be such a major accomplishment for Lita's mother. "She doesn't usually help out like that?" he asked as tactfully as he could.

Lita shook her head and smiled sadly. "Not that I can recall. Baking cookies was too much for her to manage without help when I was a child. I was always the person who handled things when there wasn't a servant in sight or another adult for her to appeal to for help." Lita moved toward the antique writing table and picked up the photograph of Melanie's mother and Lita's mother playing volleyball on the beach. "Mother and Aunt Joelle had grown up learning how to be beautiful, amusing, entertaining women. Helplessness was encouraged," she added, none too pleased at that last observation. Lita realized she was rambling and attempted an apologetic smile. "I'm really sorry," she told him. "You've been wonderful to stay with me through this. Since it looks as if Mother will be handling some of the things now, I only have to call Jack and sit here to find out what they need done next."

Keith saw the shadow in her eyes when she mentioned Jack Connery's name. He shoved his hands in his pants pockets and stood even more rock still than he had been.

He had no intention of leaving her just yet. "You're worried about how Connery will take the news?" he guessed.

She nodded her head and sank down on the Queen Anne chair. "Yes, I am," she answered, sighing audibly.

Keith thought back to his conversations with the agent, recalling the tough arguments Connery had given him in trying to land the engagement for Melanie. There had been a special intensity underneath it. At the time, he'd assumed that Connery needed the business as an agent, and that that was why he'd been so aggressive. Now he wasn't so sure.

He remembered how frequently Connery had dropped by the club to check on arrangements or talk to people. It seemed above and beyond the call of duty, no matter what kind of a financial position he or Melanie had been in. He was checking up on Melanie, and considering the drinking problem Melanie had, Keith assumed at the time that Connery was just trying to protect his investment.

There was another possibility, of course. The usual one when it involved a man and a woman. "Was Connery in love with Melanie?" he asked carefully.

Lita looked up at him in surprise. "How did you know?"

So *that* was it, he thought, slowly turning the information over in his mind to see whether that changed things. Maybe. "Lucky guess," he replied vaguely. He paced to the window and turned a little to face her. "Would you like me to call him?" he asked, his dark eyes fastened on her in an expression of controlled sympathy.

She shook her head. "No. I think it would be easier for him to hear it from me," she said, having resigned herself to the unpleasant task.

"Why don't you try and reach him now, Lita?" he suggested. "Then I'll take you out for a cup of coffee. If anyone calls, they can leave a message on the machine," he pointed out, anticipating any possible resistance on that score.

He made sense, she had to admit. She certainly was not relishing the prospect of sitting in the lonely town house, waiting. "All right," she agreed, lifting the phone and searching for the number Jack had left. "He's in Nashville now, talking to some producers and publishers. I doubt if he's seeing anyone on Sunday, though, unless it's at a restaurant. Maybe I can catch him before he steps out."

Jack answered on the seventh ring.

"Jack?" Lita asked dubiously. She'd hardly recognized his slurred voice.

"Lita . . ." he said slowly, as if trying to focus his thoughts. "Is that you, Lita?"

"Yes. Are you all right? You sound . . ." Her voice trailed off. He sounded like he was at death's door.

"I sound hung over," he declared disgustedly, a little more like the old Jack. "You always were a soft touch when it came to telling it like it is, you know, Lita—"

Lita interrupted, not wanting to prolong the agony of telling him. "I have bad news, Jack."

"Melanie?" he asked tensely.

She heard a ragged intake of breath, and her heart ached for the man's pain. She certainly knew how he felt. "Jack, I'm terribly sorry to have to tell you like this, but —but Melanie's dead."

"No!" His cry of pain and denial ripped through the distance between them. "No . . ." he moaned, beginning to sob.

"Jack!" she cried. "Oh, Jack . . ."

Lita was feeling completely wrung out by the time she got off the phone with Jack.

Keith checked his wristwatch. "Look, it's the middle of the afternoon, and neither of us has had anything to eat yet," he pointed out reasonably. "Let's go get a bite. Now's probably the best time to leave. Everyone will be busy with other matters for a while."

Lita nodded mutely and accepted her purse as he handed it to her.

Keith took her to a little Greek restaurant in the downtown area. On Sunday afternoon, downtown Washington looked like a ghost town. The broad streets and towering stone buildings that bustled with activity all week were deserted now.

The light Mediterranean meal tasted good, much to Lita's surprise. The olives, feta cheese, tomatoes, and herbs brought her gently back into the present. Keith had not pushed her to eat, but he hadn't slighted himself either. He'd ordered in Greek, saying a few personal words to the waiter as well. As he dug into his *paidakia tis Scaras* with relish she couldn't help asking him about that.

"Where did you learn to speak Greek?" she asked curiously, between spoonfuls of the tasty avgolemono.

He tilted a dark eyebrow and grinned a little. "At my father's knee," he replied, none too helpfully.

Lita finished her serving of the Greek-style chicken soup and gave him a humorously chastising look. "Your 'father's knee'? You wouldn't care to tell me what that's supposed to mean, would you?" she prodded him.

He grinned a little more broadly. "My father's Greek."

"Oh." That explained his dark good looks, she thought. "Does he live in Greece?" she inquired, trying to sound merely interested, not prying.

"Some of the time. He spends a month or so there during the course of a year. Mostly he tries to be on a ship as much as he can . . . coming or going. Staying in one place never held much interest for him, I'm afraid."

There was a trace of anger underlying the last part of that statement, Lita thought. The precision with which

117

he cut the last piece of his lamb confirmed that she was right.

Lita leaned back in her chair a little as the waiter removed their plates and brought them cups of strong Greek coffee. The aromas of their meal lingered pleasantly in the tiny restaurant—roast lamb, lemon, olive, a hint of garlic, a whisp of oregano . . .

Keith drank his coffee and looked thoughtfully at Lita. As soon as Fallon had awakened him with the bad news this morning, he'd begun turning over the implications of Melanie's death in his mind. His worries kept plaguing him, refusing to fade away with the passage of time. What if Melanie's death had something to do with the break-in at the town house? What if they both were somehow connected with the threats against Lita in the past? Did that mean that Lita was in danger? Or was Melanie's death unrelated? A tragic coincidence?

Lita watched his expression darken and wondered what grim thoughts were running through his mind. She didn't have long to wait to find out. Before she could ask, he spoke.

"Considering what's happened," he said slowly, "I think it would be a good idea for us to dissolve the contract, Lita."

She hadn't given a thought to the contract in days, and his broaching the subject came as a total surprise. She looked at him in pure astonishment. "Well . . . I'd be grateful for a day or two to attend the funeral, of course," she reluctantly agreed, "but I'm prepared to finish the engagement."

His expression went from dark to darker. "Look," he said grimly, "I don't know what's going on, but I sure as hell don't like it! I think you'd be safer back home in California until Fallon figures out what's been happening —and who's responsible."

Lita finished her coffee and carefully put the thick cup

down on its heavy saucer before raising her eyes to gaze steadily into his. "We just had new locks and a burglar alarm installed," she reminded him. "Besides, I feel I owe it to Melanie—"

He leaned his elbows on the table and snorted dismissingly. "That's ridiculous!" he exclaimed, beginning to lose his temper in spite of his best intentions.

Lita's back stiffened and she glared at him. "It may be to you, but it isn't to me!" she snapped back angrily. "I'm going to do it, whether you like it or not!"

For a moment, she was sure he would erupt in real anger. A muscle tightened in his jaw, and his eyes glittered a hard, dangerous black. Then he grabbed his napkin and slapped it down on the table, waving an authoritarian hand in the air for his check. The waiter flew to Keith's side.

"You're a damned fool," he muttered as he pulled cash out of his wallet and tossed it on top of the bill.

They both rose stiffly to their feet, and Lita lifted her chin defiantly. "I'm a pro," she corrected him coolly.

He muttered something under his breath that Lita wisely chose not to ask him to repeat. They stalked to his sports car in an awkward silence and endured a chilly ride back to the town house, which was now fully drenched in the warm spring sun.

"Call me if you need any help or change your mind about terminating the contract," he said tightly.

He jotted down a phone number on a scrap of paper that he'd retrieved from the glove compartment and handed it to Lita, who accepted it without great enthusiasm. He walked her to her door and waited impatiently for her to step inside.

"I'm sorry," he said, looking very irritated as he stood there, staring at her at eye level even though she was standing on higher ground, inside the house. "I liked Melanie," he admitted rather hesitantly, as if he wasn't used to revealing that kind of information. "If there's anything I can do to help you, call."

Lita's annoyance had been gradually melting away during the drive home. Now that she was faced with Keith's leaving her, she realized he'd devoted almost his entire day to helping her. She was tempted to lean forward and put her arms around him and lean on him. She could get used to having this man around. But that was dangerous. Keith Christophe had all the earmarks of an experienced, if not confirmed, bachelor. He obviously had women friends; he clearly was not lacking for companionship if he wanted it.

Lita felt herself growing warm and melting inside a little as she gazed into his mysterious dark eyes. I can't afford to let myself get involved with Keith Christophe, she told herself. Unfortunately, her heart kept fluttering like a schoolgirl's, making a mockery of her best intentions.

Keith stepped forward, pulling her head toward him in a motion so swift she was only aware of it when it was too late to do anything about it. He kissed her with all the anger and frustration that was still pent up inside, bruising her mouth. And then the sweetness of it melted his anger, and his arms were wrapped around her and they were lost in each other's tenderness.

He tore himself away and stepped back, keeping her at arm's length as if he didn't trust her to stay away from him—or him from her. "Remember," he ordered her, "call me if you need me."

"Yes," she murmured, still feeling dazed by the need that had been so quickly aroused between them.

He stood on the step, as if struggling with himself over something. After a few strained moments he dropped his hands from her and strode back to his car.

Lita was haunted by his parting comment for the rest

of the night. She needed him, all right. But she was deter-mined not to call.

Keith spent what was left of the afternoon and evening telling himself that Lita Winslow was just another good-looking woman and he didn't really care if she left for California tomorrow and he never saw her again. But he didn't believe it.

He went to the fitness club located on the ground level of the Crystal City high rise where he lived and worked out until he was ready to drop. The weight-training equipment exhausted his physical energies, but it only dulled his fundamental problem.

He wanted Lita Winslow. He wanted her with an ache that grew sharper with each passing night. He longed for her smiles and whispering kisses. He hungered for the feel of her close to his heart. He wanted her more than he could ever remember wanting a woman, and in ways that were sometimes unfamiliar to him. In quiet ways, in inti-mate ways, in profoundly primitive ways.

He grabbed a towel and stalked into the showers, let-ting the sharp, needlelike spray punish him.

He couldn't let her get to him like this, he swore, clos-ing his eyes and turning the water to a softer, more sooth-ing level. He'd seen what had happened to his parents. He had no intention of getting that involved with a woman, especially one who was a performing artist. Ab-solutely not.

The warm water ran over his hard body, and he found himself fantasizing that Lita was standing there with him, and it was her hands caressing him instead . . .

"No!" he muttered angrily, turning off the water with a sharp jerk and toweling himself dry with a vengeance. "You're not going to do it!"

CHAPTER SEVEN

It was all over the newspapers by the following morning.

Lita looked away every time she neared a news stand, not wanting to see even a single word of it in black and white. She could have stayed in the town house and avoided the exposure entirely, but Lita wasn't used to being confined and found remaining inside for long periods a suffocating experience.

"I wish I were home," she admitted softly as she walked along the early morning streets, clogged with Monday morning commuter traffic. Home. A comfortable, modern bungalow sprawled on a hill overlooking the sea. Home. Where I found comfort, peace, and escape from life's pain. Home. Where my heart is at ease . . .

The image of Keith Christophe in rolled-up jeans and a loose cotton shirt, standing on a craggy ledge and holding out his hand to her, leapt unbidden into her thoughts.

Home and Keith Christophe. Why would she put them together? she wondered uncomfortably. He was hardly the image of a stay-at-home man. And as far as she knew, he had no particular connections with the West Coast. Except for her, of course. She was a West Coast girl, all right, but he was an East Coast businessman. Just like her father. And Lita well knew the chasm between East and West. The temperaments were too different—one free and easy, the other formal and controlling.

A horn blared as Lita stepped onto the street, nearly

being run over. She quickly stepped back and glanced at the light across the river of traffic. DON'T WALK was clearly displayed in bright red.

"Maybe I should stick to walking around the backyard," she muttered under her breath in embarrassment. "We don't need two funerals in one week!"

Unlike the streets the sidewalks weren't crowded yet, so Lita strolled at a leisurely pace, admiring the determination of the flowering trees and shrubs that grew hardily amid the stone and clapboard of two hundred years of unbroken human occupation.

In another week or so the fruit trees would be brilliant —blindingly white or pink or red. Their delicate petals would paint the town in southern pastel shades in vivid celebration of life. It had been Melanie's favorite time of year. Spring. Lita remembered fondly how they'd loved it. Spring breaks had been eagerly awaited and enthusiastically enjoyed during their stay in Washington. Dear Melanie.

Lita blinked back the tears that threatened suddenly. "I'm going to miss you, Mel," she whispered. Lita stopped to lean on an antique iron fence surrounding a tiny public park nestled in an out-of-the-way side street. "I'm going to miss you . . ."

It was hard to accept the fact that Melanie was gone. It was harder still to conceive of anyone's murdering her. Lita felt an unfamiliar surge of fury at her own helplessness.

Melanie had loved life with an exuberance that had sometimes been breathtaking. She had had her demons to struggle against over the years, but she had been determined to make something of her life. It was despicably unfair that someone had robbed her of her chance.

"They won't get away with it, Mel," Lita swore softly.

A warm breeze gently rustled the delicate green leaves

of a young dogwood, making it bob and weave a little, as if in agreement.

Lita turned to go back, determined that Melanie's murderer would be made to pay for his deed—even if it took her every waking moment and her last dime to accomplish it!

Inside, her heart was breaking.

There would be no more midnight phone calls filled with girlish laughter, no more soulful letters in which she and Melanie let down their hair and shared confidences. No more joy in each other's accomplishments or sorrow for one another's pains.

Lita brushed a tear away.

"Oh Melanie," she murmured, fighting an upsurge of despair.

The phone was ringing off the hook when she got back. The funeral arrangements had been made, and to Lita's astonishment, Melanie's funeral was to be held in Washington.

"In Washington?" Keith repeated her announcement in surprise later that afternoon when she wandered into the club. "Why?" he asked bluntly, not bothering to try to camouflage his surprise at all.

Lita sat down across the desk from him and shrugged. She wasn't certain that she'd been given the real reasons, and if she had she definitely didn't agree with them!

"Well, my aunt said she thought that Melanie had been very happy here, Mother thought it would be a lovely final resting place, and Father insisted that the funeral could be arranged with less press coverage and scandal mongering here." Lita threw up her hands in a gesture of irritated futility. "I really don't understand why they're doing it this way! Personally, I think they're crazy if they think they can control the press coverage more easily out here! Washington has as many journalists per square inch as L.A., from what I've seen." She sighed, running out of steam. "It's certainly one of the few times in my life that I can remember all three of them agreeing on anything!"

It was obvious that their agreement was the only bright light to the funeral plans as far as Lita was concerned. She shook her head a little to chase away the dismal thoughts that had been poised to overwhelm her. "That wasn't really what I came to see you about, though," she told him briskly.

"Oh?" he replied, raising a dark brow questioningly.

"No." She drew a breath as if preparing for a difficult role. "I wanted to talk to you about Melanie," she explained, her voice betraying her still-bruised emotions when she said her late cousin's name.

Keith held his gold pen with both hands, fingering the ends absentmindedly as he waited for her to continue. "All right," he agreed, although the slight frown that had creased his brow was not exactly encouraging.

He had made it perfectly clear that he thought it unwise for her to remain in town and foolish to continue performing. Even so, Lita thought that his subtle resistance to talking about Melanie was a little strange. She brushed her feelings aside and concentrated on her reason for coming to see Keith.

"I wanted to find out how she'd spent her time here in Washington. She was here for almost a month." Lita looked at him expectantly. To her surprise, he didn't answer right away. It was almost as if he were trying to decide what to say and what not to say. That bothered her.

"I'll tell you what I know," he agreed. "But that isn't very much."

Lita waved her hand slightly, brushing off his warning. Anything would be better than nothing.

He pursed his lips pensively and gathered his thoughts. Fallon had asked him the same thing, of course, but talking to Fallon and talking to Lita were two different things. Besides, talking to Pete had raised some questions in his own mind about exactly how Melanie King had been spending her time, and Keith wanted to find out the answers to those questions himself before he aroused any suspicions. Melanie King's death had occurred much too close to home, as far as he was concerned.

"I first met her when Jack Connery introduced her to me here at the club about six weeks ago. She appeared to be very happy and very excited about performing at Sydney's. She made a big hit with everybody here at the club. She was charming and ebullient, like a young girl out on her own for the first time, in a way . . ."

Lita listened attentively, but she was struck by the aptness of Keith's description. "Like a young girl on her own for the first time" was the way Lita had thought of her for the past couple of months. It had been as if a great weight had finally been lifted from Melanie's shoulders and she'd seen her way into the future. "That's very perceptive," Lita murmured.

Keith looked at her strangely. "You think so?" He shrugged indifferently. "Just normal business acumen, in my opinion . . ."

Perhaps, Lita mused. And yet it wasn't the kind of insight she'd have expected from a completely casual observer who didn't know Melanie very well. Lita would have expected Keith to have described Melanie as excited or enthusiastic, charming or beautiful, talented or hardworking, even struggling to prove that her past wasn't her future.

But to so accurately describe the inner Melanie. Lita felt a stab of jealousy as she wondered if his relationship with Melanie had been closer than just that of owner and performer. After all, Lita reminded herself, he hadn't been strictly businesslike in his relationship with her.

"We knew about her problem with the bottle," he was

126

saying, "so I had someone see her home every night after rehearsal. Of course, there were a couple of weeks between her arrival in town and her beginning to rehearse when nobody did that. And most of the time, she wasn't here at the club."

Lita tried to disregard the suspicions that had begun eating at her and concentrated on getting as many facts as she could from Keith. "How much time did she spend here?"

"More than I would have expected," he admitted. "She dropped by almost every evening for a little while. She said she wanted to get to know the clientele. That made sense to me at the time. It would give her a feel for the kind of entertainment that would be popular and the kind that wouldn't."

Lita, already sensitized by her earlier suspicions, was struck again at the oddity of Keith's words. He'd said that it made sense at the time, as if now, in retrospect, he had some doubts. She felt a sinking in the pit of her stomach.

Over the years, Lita had learned the hard way to trust her feelings. Much as she didn't want to trust these, she was afraid she'd have to. There was something Keith wasn't telling her. "Did she leave with anyone in particular? Make any friends?" Lita asked, hoping to encourage a fuller reply as well as get the answer to those two specific questions.

"She spent some time in the club with a number of people. Some of them were patrons, others were apparently people she knew and had invited to meet her here."

He hesitated only a fraction of a second, but Lita immediately felt the missed beat in his speech.

"All of us spent some time with her, of course," he said smoothly.

Why had he hesitated in saying that? she wondered as a chill of concern feathered her spine.

Before Lita could say anything else, the door was shoved open and Sean burst into the office. "Damn it! I just spent the past hour talking to Pete Fallon about Melanie King—"

By the time Sean had reached the middle of the room, it dawned on him that Keith was not alone in his office. The younger Christophe stopped dead and whipped around to see Lita staring at him in complete surprise. His angry expression changed to one of discomfort, and he cleared his throat awkwardly. "Sorry," he mumbled apologetically. "I thought you were alone . . ."

Keith nodded curtly and fixed his brother with a hard look. Sean immediately fell silent and looked uncomfortably from his brother to Lita.

"We'll be finished in a little while," Keith told him in that no-nonsense way he used when issuing orders. "Stick around. I'll buzz Carl when we can talk."

Sean, to Lita's great surprise, turned to leave without an argument. Lita reached out and touched Sean's arm, holding him lightly. "You were talking to Fallon?" she echoed. "About Melanie?"

Sean looked down into her soft, vulnerable eyes and opened his mouth before he thought about it. "Yes. I'm sorry, Lita," he offered sincerely. Then a darkness settled in his dark brown eyes, and he looked away as if he were ashamed to let her see into them.

"Did you get to know her?" Lita asked impulsively, tightening her hold on him as he began to move away.

Sean blinked and looked at Keith for a second. Then the younger brother's face became strangely expressionless and he pulled loose. "Sure," he admitted a little too lightly. "We all did. She was a fun-loving girl," he added, almost defensively. "People around here know how to have fun. She was a natural here."

Lita stared at him in dismay. Why was Sean acting so strangely?

128

Sean couldn't look Keith in the eyes as he left. The younger man lowered his head as he shut the door, gazing blindly at the dusky rose plush carpeting instead.

Lita noticed that Keith and Sean were both behaving oddly. Something was wrong, and Lita was very worried that the "something" did indeed involve Melanie.

Keith looked at her and realized that she'd picked up the unspoken currents of communication and immediately set himself the task of deflecting her curiosity. "I didn't want to get into a discussion with Sean about your cousin's death," he explained calmly. "Sean liked her, and he's pretty upset that she was murdered. He'd taken her home that night and feels somehow responsible."

Lita was surprised to hear that small detail. That could mean that Sean had been the last person to see Melanie alive—except for the murderer . . .

Keith saw the speculative shadow on Lita's face and frowned slightly. "We tried to keep a protective eye on Melanie," he said evenly. There was a hardness in his eyes that belied the calmness of his words. "In a way, Melanie's death is a personal insult. We want to find out what happened as much as you do."

"Thanks for caring," Lita said honestly. And yet that didn't quite explain why Keith had avoided having a discussion with Sean in front of her, she thought. Perhaps he thought it would be too upsetting, she mused. Surely he realized she was already upset, though. There wasn't much else that could top what she'd already been told!

The phone rang, and Felice told Keith he had an important call. He covered the mouthpiece and explained to Lita, who rose to her feet to leave. She hesitated with her hand on the doorknob, the door open just enough to let in the soft, slow sounds of Gaius playing "Someone to Watch over Me" on the piano.

"Keith—if you know anything, or hear anything, please tell me," she said slowly. She raised her eyes to his, and for a moment, the magic flowed between them so strongly that she ached to hold out her arms to him. She saw the simmering heat in his eyes, the tightening of his hand on the phone, and guessed he felt the same. "She's dead," Lita reminded him, her heart twisting in pain. "There's nothing worse that I could learn. Remember, I knew Melanie better than anyone else."

A shadow of pain crossed his eyes, then was gone as he ruthlessly erased all expression from his face and nodded curtly.

Lita lifted her chin angrily at his obvious dismissal. She slammed the door on her way out and walked out of the club without responding to the friendly hellos that followed in her wake.

She was certain now that there was something he wasn't telling her. Lita was furious. It was her cousin! She had a right to know! He had no business deciding what to tell her and what not to tell her!

Lita walked briskly through the streets until she'd worn off some of the edge of her anger. When it dropped to a low, intense simmer, she was able to stop fuming and begin thinking.

Keith wasn't the only source of information at the club. If he wouldn't tell her what she wanted to know, she'd find someone who would.

Lita gave a sizzling performance that night. Every eye in the house was riveted to her. She immersed herself in the music in an attempt to stem the constant flow of pain she was feeling from the loss of her cousin. Privately, she dedicated a song to Melanie and she brought the house down.

Keith sat at the bar and nursed a drink, trying to ignore the fire ignited inside him every time he looked at Lita.

But Lita wouldn't even look at Keith. When she wasn't

singing, she laughed and conversed with the customers. She even accepted invitations to dance with half a dozen especially eager swains who had come alone. She was determined to conduct her own investigation into Melanie's death, and for that reason, she had to mingle with the customers, even though she was sad and confused. But she was a big girl, and she had to hide her feelings and do her interviewing in the most effective way possible for a woman. Flattery always seemed to loosen the tongues of males. Soothe their egos with a little batting of the eyelashes and they babbled like babies.

And babble they certainly did. Lita got quite an earful from the regulars in one long evening of skillful listening. Unfortunately, it only made her worry more about why Keith had become as silent as a stone on the subject of her cousin Melanie. It appeared that Melanie had been seen in the company of a number of men during her stay in Washington. But the names most frequently mentioned were Keith and Sean Christophe.

"Mind if I cut in?" asked Sean of the dashing Senate staffer who'd been holding Lita in a tight clinch for the duration of a slow fox trot. Her partner grimaced but gradually loosened his arm and turned her over to Sean.

"Thanks," he said, hoping he'd get another chance to dance with her later.

Lita smiled pleasantly, but there was no encouraging light in her eyes, and the man was sophisticated enough to recognize her subtle rejection. He shrugged his shoulders philosophically and eyed Sean enviously.

Sean chuckled and pulled her close as the music swelled. "I see you've broken another heart!" he whispered devilishly into her ear.

Lita tossed back her head and pushed his shoulder a little away, her eyes glittering with annoyance. "Don't be ridiculous! I have yet to dance with a man whose heart was the least bit involved," she retorted, keeping her voice low so that the other dancers wouldn't hear.

Sean chuckled more and pulled her head close to his cheek as he led her through a slow, intimate rendition of the tango. Lita couldn't struggle without making a scene on the floor, so she ceased her efforts to wriggle away from him and glued herself to him to keep from falling as he pulled her backward in a low dip.

"Why, Sean, I didn't know boys your age knew the tango!" she purred, wide-eyed as she mercilessly stepped on his instep.

She had to hand it to him—he never missed a beat and kept right on smiling as if they were having a wonderfully private little conversation along with the indecently close dance.

"Boy!" he protested in an outraged whisper between smiling teeth. "I'm no more a boy than you're a girl!"

Lita leaned so far back in the next dip that he almost toppled over.

"If you need proof that I'm a girl, I'll be happy to mail you a copy of my birth certificate!" she said sweetly, taking a deep breath as he finally loosened his grip a little in defeat.

Sean laughed and looked down at her with a devilish twinkle in his eyes. "That wasn't what I meant and you know it!" he teased her. He looked over her head and grinned down at her. "If looks could kill, I'd be dead and you'd be next in line," Sean told her, sounding very amused.

Lita gave him an uncomprehending look, not appreciating his choice of words. "What are you talking about?" she asked.

He held her a little closer but danced with more decorum than he had at first. "Keith . . ." he replied.

The music ended, and Lita was again swamped with admirers seeking a dance or conversation, and Sean let himself be pushed out of sight before she could ask him to explain what he meant. When she turned to look toward the bar, Keith was watching him intently, but he didn't seem murderous to Lita. And he had Gloria chattering at his side to divert him, she noted with a pang of displeasure.

Who cares who he likes to spend the evening with? she asked herself angrily. He's not my type. I don't want to get involved with him. He's not interested in me. Well, she wasn't so sure all of that was true, but she didn't want to lower her defenses anymore where he was concerned.

So she gave a brilliant smile to the three nearest gentlemen and asked them all to join her for a drink at her table. They couldn't believe their good fortune and fell all over each other in very proper fashion trying to take her arm, hold her chair, and motion for the waiter.

Lita gave Keith a cool smile and turned all her charm on the three strangers who were next on her list to "interview."

It was closing time when she finally managed to disengage herself from Sydney's exceedingly sociable clientele. She was still trying to say good-bye as she backed into the hall on her way to her dressing room, with an especially persistent beltway bandit still clutching her hand.

"That's really interesting," she exclaimed enthusiastically, interrupting the man's nonstop description of his firm's sterling track record. "I'm sure I'll be reading your name in the newspapers one of these days," she added, trying for just the right blend of admiration and a tone of permanent farewell.

The man looked crestfallen and a little annoyed at her comment and came to a halt, still hanging on to her hand. "Well, I've already been written up a lot," he told her immodestly. His condescending smile clearly told her that he'd now decided she was beautiful but probably

133

dumb—a Californian in showbiz who never read anything but *Variety* and suntan lotion labels.

Lita's smile froze over and she jerked her hand away. "Sorry, I guess I don't read the comics enough," she declared, and hopped into her dressing room before he could figure out the insult.

She was leaning against the door in relief and slipping out of her shoes when she heard a soft laugh on the other side and a short, familiar rap.

"He's gone," Keith said as she opened the door.

He was leaning indolently against the wall, his arms crossed in front of his chest, staring at her enigmatically. "You certainly put your heart into entertaining my customers this evening," he commented casually.

Lita turned her back on him and moved behind the screen. "I'm going to change," she said pointedly, ignoring the undertone of sarcasm she had sensed in his statement. She waited, giving the door a significant glance. When Keith merely shut the door and sat down in the chair in the corner, she frowned for the first time in hours. "I said, I'm going to change," she repeated, annoyed. "Would you mind leaving? I'll be out in a few minutes if you need to talk to me about something."

The corners of his mouth curved slightly upward. Lita wouldn't have called it a smile under any circumstances. The hard look in his face made his half grin even more chilling.

"I can wait," he replied evenly, stretching out his long legs and crossing them at the ankles as if taking possession of the area indefinitely.

Lita flashed him an angry look. "I want you to go!" she repeated emphatically, gripping the top of the screen in her ire.

His dark, unyielding eyes bored into her. "I'm staying," he announced bluntly.

Lita wanted to stamp her feet and shake her fists in

frustration. She refused to give him the satisfaction, however, and confined herself to shaking in rage. Damn him! She stripped off her evening gown and tossed it over the screen, grabbed the soft cotton slacks and loosely cut crocheted top she'd brought to wear home, and jerked them on in record time. She grabbed her purse and marched stiffly toward the door, turning angrily toward Keith. "What do you want?" she asked challengingly, still furious with him.

He hadn't expected the question, having been lost in fantasizing about her dressing again, and looked at her blankly. The first answers that came to his mind had to be discarded as too revealing to admit, he realized, and his cheeks darkened as he scrambled to come up with a believable answer to her question.

He'd spent one of the worst evenings in his recent memory watching every man in the club try to seduce Lita. The more he'd watched, the harder it had been to just sit there without interfering. He'd forced himself to stand on the sidelines just to prove to himself that he could do it. He was determined not to let her get so far under his skin that he couldn't control himself. No matter how hard it might prove to be.

He couldn't remember ever being so relieved that an evening had come to an end. All the men would go home now and Lita would go sleep in her own bed, safe and sound, away from the lusty and admiring stares. And then he'd stumbled on the last lothario and had felt the urge to pick the man up by his coattails and toss him into the back alley! If it hadn't been for Lita's clear rejection and put-down of the man, Keith would have been hard put to remember that he was the club's owner and wasn't supposed to treat his patrons to that kind of brutality!

As it was, her deft deflection had humored him a little, and he'd been enjoying being closeted with her while she changed. It made him feel like her guard—or her lover . . .

Why had he come in here anyway? he asked himself in disgust. He'd sworn all evening that he was going to meet her in the hall and drive her home! But it had been as natural as breathing to follow her into the dressing room and wait for her to change.

He snapped to his feet and reached for his keys. "Ready to go?" he asked brusquely, jerking the door open for her.

"What do you want?" she asked again, still angry.

He directed her out into the public area of the hall. He needed to get out there before he did something foolish, like slam the door shut, lock it, kiss her into a frenzy, and make love to her until they were both exhausted.

"To see you safely home," he answered as a frown gathered on his dark, tough features. "I parked in the garage. Let's go."

With that curt order, he strode down the hall, arm in arm with Lita, who was trying to decide whether anyone in the club would have the nerve to take her home if she refused Keith's offer. Probably not, she decided. And at this hour, she didn't really want to take a cab. She still occasionally had nightmares about the threats that had been made against her. She wasn't stupid enough to put herself into a potentially dangerous situation just because she was furious with Keith Christophe!

Not a single word passed between them on the ride home. By the time they arrived at the town house, the strain between them was almost palpable.

Keith opened the car door and Lita swung her legs out, accepting his hand reluctantly. She hadn't wanted him to touch her, not even in that small way. His grasp was warm and firm and sent electrical energy sizzling through her.

She stood in the doorway and turned to bid him good

night. It only took one look for her to realize how hopeless it was becoming to fight her feelings. The moment her eyes met his, she began to melt inside. Her heart seemed to beat a little faster, even though it was already pounding. And that dark, brooding look in his eyes. She wanted him to take her in his arms and possess her in every way a man could possess a woman—body, mind, and soul.

"Are you planning a repeat performance of tonight?" he asked bluntly, his eyes narrowing as he recalled in vivid detail how she'd spent the evening.

At first she didn't understand what he was asking. "Well, of course," she said rather crossly. "I told you I was going to finish the contract—"

He shook his head, cutting her off. "Not that," he said shortly. "I mean personally entertaining all the stray men who frequent Sydney's."

His eyes were hard and angry, to Lita's surprise. Surely he didn't intend to prohibit her from talking to people! Then an awful suspicion assailed her. What if he knew she would eventually unearth enough facts to discover whatever it was he was hiding? "I don't think there's anything to be afraid of," she argued. Her expression became guarded.

"I'd hate to see you get into something you couldn't handle." That wasn't exactly his concern, but he decided it was close enough. And if she knew him a little better, she'd know exactly what it was she should be afraid of, he thought grimly.

"Look," she declared heatedly, "I've been taking care of myself and everybody else in my life since I was big enough to walk. I've lived alone for years without any problems. I've traveled and lived to tell about it. The men at Sydney's tonight were all perfect gentlemen. So don't worry about it!"

A drunk staggering by a nearby street lamp waved to

them and started up the walk to join their heated debate. Keith turned his frustration and fury on the ragged fellow and glared at him with such potency that even through his alcoholic stupor the man got the message and wandered unsteadily off in the opposite direction.

Keith pushed her inside, stopping himself in the doorway. There was no way he was stepping all the way into the town house himself! He wasn't stupid enough to do that! Not the way he was feeling!

"You may be an expert in taking care of yourself," he said through gritted teeth, "but as long as you're working in my club, you'll avoid encouraging men to hang all over you. I don't relish the prospect of punching out a patron or friend just because they can't keep their hands off you!"

Lita had been angry before, but his irrational attack brought her to flames. "Of all the stupid, idiotic, asinine—" she cried indignantly.

Before she could completely enumerate the adjectives that she felt suitably described his comment, his control slipped and he hauled her fully into his arms and cut off her speech with a burning kiss. Lita squirmed in his arms, furious at his actions and terrified that she'd forget she was furious any minute now. He held her head still with one hand and clamped her body to his with the other. As the warmth and wanting flowered in the kiss the anger melted away and another kind of fire took its place.

Lita felt his embrace change subtly as he stopped restraining her and began holding her instead. His arms were strong and hard, making Lita feel soft and meltingly female. The more she relaxed into him, the more his arms tightened. Their kiss became a coaxing, pleasuring, tantalizing caress of two mouths hungry for each other. The hungering flooded the rest of them, and soon they were both gasping for breath and tottering on the brink of a

138

passion that would not be assuaged with deep kisses and tightening embraces. Keith reluctantly loosened his arms and rested his head against Lita's.

"Why are we standing in my doorway?" Lita asked unsteadily, beginning to feel like an adolescent girl.

Keith ran a hand slowly down her back, following her soft, tempting curves. He sighed and placed a warm, lingering kiss on her neck. "Because if we go inside, I'm going to take you to bed," he told her bluntly.

Lita knew their relationship was too tenuous to begin an affair. Assuming, of course, he was suggesting that. A one-night stand could be what he had in mind, she told herself. Lita was afraid of that. She didn't want to be anybody's one-night stand, but she especially didn't want to be that to Keith. "I see," she murmured unsteadily, still shaking a little from their kissing. "Well, maybe you'd better go home, then."

He kissed her softly along her jawline and hugged her one more time. "Yes," he muttered, not sounding too enthusiastic about it, "maybe I'd better." He let go of her slowly and stepped back outside. "Lock the door," he said, gazing at her expressionlessly now.

"Of course," she retorted, stung by his ability to recover so easily when she was still shaking like a leaf and wanting him with every inch of her body. "Good night," she muttered angrily at the closed door.

She marched straight into the bathroom to shower and change into pajamas. She refused to watch him drive away.

She kept telling herself she didn't care on and off all night as she tossed and turned. But something had happened to her bed. It was suddenly too uncomfortable for words. No matter how hard she tried, there wasn't a comfortable position to be found in it.

As a last resort, she tried counting wolfhounds in Russian. That helped. It had been a long time since she'd studied any Russian.

But the last image in her mind as she drifted off to sleep wasn't a wolfhound. It was a dark-haired man with a longshoreman's face and a magnetic appeal that was turning her blood into rivers of fire.

CHAPTER EIGHT

Melanie's funeral was held late the following morning.

The small group of mourners dressed in black clustered together in a soft spring rain as the priest intoned the prayers of the burial service.

They prayed together, their voices low and suffering in spite of the message of thanksgiving and hope that had been woven into the rite over the centuries. Melanie's mother, wearing a veil of heavy mourning, clung to her sister's arm, her shoulders visibly shaking with sobs as the priest concluded the service. Lita's father was standing behind them like a sentinel, there to shore them both up whenever their courage began to fail.

The celebrant's voice, calm and strong, offered the final prayer for all of them. ". . . Father of all mercies and giver of comfort: Deal graciously, we pray, with all who mourn; that, casting all their care on you, they may know the consolation of your love . . ."

They collectively murmured amen and stood silently next to Melanie's grave in farewell before slowly turning away and making their way back to the line of black limousines awaiting them.

Keith stood off to one side, watching as the small group, still stunned at Melanie's unexpected death, embraced one another and tried to give and receive some comfort before returning to their separate lives.

The family had wanted a very small, very private service, but out of appreciation for the efforts Keith had made for Melanie, they had asked Lita to invite him to attend.

"Oh, Lita," Melanie's mother murmured brokenly, "I still can't believe she's gone."

Lita put her arms around her aunt and held her tightly. Tears glittered on her eyelashes, but she forced herself to hold them back. She had to be strong for them, she reminded herself. "Me either, Aunt Joelle," Lita sadly agreed.

Joelle King slowly disengaged herself from her niece's tender embrace and pulled the heavy black veil down over her tear-ravaged face. Silently, Lita's father, Tate Winslow, handed Joelle into the waiting limousine. He turned to give his daughter a kiss on the cheek before leaving himself. "You're sure you want to finish the engagement?" he asked under his breath, his brows narrowing in a frown. "If you want to get out of the contract, I'll have my lawyers take care of it for you."

Lita patted his cheek fondly. That rather summed up the story of her relationship with her father, she thought. He'd have someone take care of it. He had always been coming or going, but he'd never stayed around long. When she was small, she'd tried desperately to be the perfect little girl, thinking that if she achieved perfection, he'd stay and play with her. Gradually she'd realized that that had nothing to do with it. Her father was obsessed with his work. His drive to compete, to vanquish his rivals in business, was the all-consuming motivation of everything he did.

He'd spent a lifetime trying to show his affection to his daughter by offering her access to the many services and powers his success had acquired. By now Lita had reconciled herself to the fact that that was as close to emotional support and caring as her father could get. It still hurt and disappointed her, but it was easier to endure at twenty-eight than it had been at eight or eighteen.

"Thanks, Daddy"—she smiled up at him—"but I want to stay here awhile," she explained. "And, Daddy," Lita added, recalling how chivalrously her father had attended her mother and aunt in their hour of need, "thanks for helping. Mother and Aunt Joelle never could have managed without you. And I . . . I wouldn't have known where to begin," she said honestly.

He shrugged and nodded as his eyes sought the slender figure of his wife. Lita watched the shadow of unhappiness cross his face and her heart wrenched. Her parents loved each other passionately, but they could not live together. When they'd lived together, they'd made each other miserable. When they separated, they missed each other deeply. But they'd finally settled on a legal separation, and they tried to keep in touch, getting together for holidays or special occasions. Their problems had never been solved, naturally enough, by avoiding them like that, but neither could completely sever the ties that bound them.

"I think Barbara held up like a real trooper," her father observed, a hint of surprise and genuine admiration in his dark gray eyes as he continued to watch his wife. "She's done much better than I expected," he admitted.

Lita nodded her agreement. "Yes. It always seemed to me she dug down deep and found the courage when she needed it, Daddy," Lita said softly, holding his elbow fondly and leaning her cheek against his arm.

Maybe that was why she had never sought a divorce, Lita thought. Her mother was dependent in many ways, but she had a kind of determined grit in a few areas of her life. Her career had been one. Her husband and daughter had been another.

For a dreadful moment Lita felt like she had when she was ten and her father had told her he was moving permanently to the East Coast and would only be visiting her on holidays. Her mother and he simply couldn't get along, he'd said grimly. Lita's heart had broken. She'd stared at him, pleading silently with her eyes for him to stay, to try harder, to be a family.

It hadn't worked, and she'd spent years trying to recover from that shattering blow. And yet today she felt the same stubborn flicker of hope in her breast. Maybe they could get back together someday . . .

Just then, Lita's mother finished embracing a longtime friend good-bye and walked carefully through the damp spring grass to join them. She held out her hand to her husband and looked at him with a confidence and strength that Lita rarely had seen in her mother. "Thank you, Tate," Barbara told him sincerely. "I know you're busy. You always have such a crushing work schedule," she said sympathetically. "We should get you back to the hotel and to the airport."

Her father seemed surprised and took Barbara's black-gloved hand in his and tucked it under his arm protectively. "I think I can spare enough time to take you and Joelle to get something to eat and talk a little longer. There isn't any hurry. My plane will leave whenever I tell the pilot I'm ready to go."

Lita blinked in surprise. Her father was dragging his feet. That had to be an all-time first! And her mother was graciously urging him to go. Instead of crying for him to stay.

Barbara lifted her veil and kissed Lita fondly on the cheek. The years had been very kind to her beautiful mother. Even with tears staining her cheeks, there was a fresh, healthy glow to her skin. She was still a box office draw of considerable strength, and it was obvious that the makeup department wasn't particularly responsible for that fact.

"Darling," her mother murmured affectionately, "I do

144

hope you'll come down to L.A. when you fly back. Joelle and I will be there for the next month at least and would adore having you with us."

"I'll try, Mother," Lita agreed, giving her mother a supportive hug.

Barbara glanced at the tall dark man standing near the curb and playing absentmindedly with a matchbox in one hand. She gave Lita a speculative look. "I enjoyed meeting Mr. Christophe," she said, a soft gleam in her eyes. "He's quite impressive, isn't he?"

To Lita's surprise, her father scowled and began pulling her mother toward the limousine.

"Yes," Lita reluctantly agreed. "I suppose he is."

"Good-bye, darling," her mother called out as she slipped into the limousine beside her sister.

"Good-bye, Mother," Lita called back as her father closed their door and got into his own limo.

Keith, who had insisted upon driving her, joined her as they drove away. "About ready to go?" he asked quietly.

"Yes."

They walked at an unhurried pace to the black Mercedes that Keith had driven, side by side but not touching.

"I saw Jack Connery," Keith said as if making simple conversation to fill the silence that had fallen awkwardly between them.

"Yes. He's really taking it very hard," Lita replied sadly.

Jack had arrived by cab a few minutes before the interment and stood at the back of the crowd, his head bowed. He'd barely spoken to anyone, just a hoarse phrase or two to the immediate family and a poignant embrace for Lita.

"He said he'd just flown in from Nashville to be here for the funeral. He left immediately afterward to catch a plane to L.A." Lita explained as they stopped and Keith unlocked the Mercedes.

Keith held the door for her and closed it after she'd swung her black-stockinged legs neatly inside, walking around to the other side to slide in beside her. The engine came quietly to life and Keith swung the expensive car smoothly into the nearly empty street.

"He must have loved her a great deal," he observed quietly. "He looks like he's been drinking himself into oblivion."

Lita frowned. "Yes," she agreed, worried. "I've never seen him drink like this before. He looks just awful."

Jack seemed to have aged twenty years in the short span of a few weeks. Lines of anguish and suffering lined his face. He'd lost weight, giving him a gaunt appearance. The dark circles under his rather bloodshot eyes, his unsteady speech, and his defeated walk all gave him the stamp of one who had been delivered a blow that was too great for him to endure.

"How long has he loved her?" Keith asked curiously, turning the corner and easing into heavier traffic.

"For years," Lita replied. "I'm sure that Melanie didn't realize it. She loved him like a brother, but she would have confided in me, I think, if she thought he felt any differently about her. Melanie was a little wild and rather blind about a lot of things, but she had a tender heart when it was all said and done. She'd have worried about him, I think. Maybe even tried to get another agent . . ."

Keith nodded his head thoughtfully. "Yes, that's the way she struck me," he agreed slowly.

Lita turned to look at him, careful to appear as neutral as she could, under the circumstances. He'd just given her an opening to a subject that had been bothering her a great deal, and she had every intention of pursuing it as tactfully as possible. "Did you spend a lot of time with her, Keith?" she asked with polite, cautious interest.

He gave her a sideways glance and then concentrated

146

on the traffic. "I wouldn't say a lot," he replied, shrugging it off a little. "But I spent more time with her than I usually do with performers. By a long shot."

"I'm sure that meant a great deal to her," Lita said, trying to ease the conversation into a productive channel.

Keith raised a dark brow. "Maybe. She seemed to enjoy the company of most of the people here in Washington that I saw her with."

"But you're special," Lita told him.

He grinned faintly but kept his eyes straight ahead. "Is that so?"

Lita blushed slightly, more out of annoyance with herself than anything else. "Well," she added a little stiffly, "you have a reputation of being a lone wolf. She'd have been flattered for the attention, I think."

He pulled up in front of the town house and killed the engine. Then he turned in the seat, resting an elbow on the steering wheel to look at her. "So I have a reputation as a lone wolf, do I?" he asked, gazing at her with great interest. "Would you care to tell me how you came by that impression?"

Lita could hardly tell him that's how he made her feel. That right now she felt like Little Red Riding Hood staring into the hungry jaws of the Big Bad Wolf! "Some of Sydney's patrons love to talk about you," she replied. "And I, being a polite entertainer, listen to them."

He seemed to be trying to decide whether or not to swallow that when all of a sudden a light went on in his eyes and he leaned a shoulder back against the seat. "Is that what you were doing flirting with all those guys the other night!" he exclaimed as if the thought were dumbfounding.

Lita stiffened and her eyes flashed angrily. "I wasn't flirting!" He grinned at her, looking almost relieved, she thought.

"If there's anything you want to know, just ask," he told her. "I'll tell you."

But how would I know if it were the truth? she wondered, aching to be able to believe him.

He stretched his arm along the back of the seat and touched her dark hair with his fingertips, staring at it in fascination. "Are you taking tonight off?" he asked quietly.

Lita shook her head. "No. I think it would be harder sitting here at the town house. Performing gives me something to do."

He nodded sympathetically. "Do you want to come to the club with me? I can wait for you to change and drop you off."

She smiled gratefully. "Thanks. That would help."

"No problem," he said as he opened her car door and offered his hand to help her out. "Just consider it part of the service."

Why did he have to make it sound like part of the business? she wondered with a surge of unexpected unhappiness. When he'd made the offer, her heart had leapt with gratitude. But the crack about its being part of the service made her blood freeze over. "I'll only be a minute," she said coolly as she walked quickly toward the apartment.

She changed in record time, not wanting to give any impression of wanting to linger in friendly conversation with Keith. She'd had very bitter experiences with a businessman once before in her life. She wasn't about to voluntarily invite a repeat performance of that kind of bitter pain. Absolutely not!

Keith was sitting in the Queen Anne chair, his eyes closed, his hands clasped behind his head when she returned. She felt her stomach tighten and her pulse speed up a little as she soaked up the look of him. His dark suit was stretched a little over his shoulders and thighs, out-

148

lining his well-muscled contours and emphasizing his rugged, masculine appeal.

She realized she was staring at him and lifted her gaze to his face. His eyes snapped open, and they stared at each other for a long, tense moment.

Lita broke the strain that had arisen so quickly between them by looking away and moving toward the door. "I'm ready if you are," she announced with much more conviction than she really felt at the moment.

He followed her, straightening his stylish tie with his left hand and watching her back and hips in her gold lamé gown in begrudging fascination.

"I'm afraid I am, too," he muttered.

Lita gave him a perplexed look as they walked back to the car. "What?" she asked, thinking she couldn't have heard him right.

"Me, too," he said more clearly and definitely with more finality. "Let's go."

Keith was ready, all right. But he was damned if he was willing! He wouldn't act on his urge to pursue Lita Winslow, no matter how much he wanted to.

His position was hard to take, since every night he sat at Sydney's bar, nursing his drink and watching Lita seduce the club with her songs. The two weeks of Lita's engagement seemed to drag on like grim death. At the end, he was beginning to wonder if she'd ever leave. He began having visions of being hung on the rack of unfulfilled desire for the rest of his days.

"Just tonight," Keith muttered to himself as he swirled the bourbon slowly over the ice cubes in his glass. "Then she's out of my life, and everything will be back to normal around here again!"

Carl was hanging a glass on the overhead rack and watching the dark look on his boss's face, wondering how much longer Keith would hold out. He'd known Keith

Christophe for years, and he'd never seen the man like this. It was as if he'd become obsessed with the woman. Obsessed with a burning need for a woman that had him losing sleep and drinking more than usual. An obsession that made other women look pale and uninteresting in comparison.

"What are you staring at?" Keith snapped at the bartender.

Carl's shaggy brows lifted innocently, and he busied himself wiping the bar with a white towel. "I was just thinking that you look tired," Carl said quickly.

Sean joined them and grinned as he slapped his brother on the shoulder. "Yeah! Don't snap at Carl," Sean admonished his annoyed elder brother. "It's not his fault you can't get a decent night's sleep anymore," he argued with a sly look in Lita's direction.

Keith's jaw tightened and he gave his brother a cold stare. "I don't recall inviting you to sit down," Keith replied curtly. He wasn't in the mood to put up with his brother's taunts tonight.

Sean lazed against the bar and gave Lita a very admiring look. "Well, I can't say as I blame you, brother," Sean went on recklessly. "I'd lose sleep over her, too."

Keith's expression grew harder, and anyone but his brother would have dropped the subject. Sean, however, had never had his brother in this vulnerable a position and wasn't about to miss the opportunity to take advantage of it. He leaned closer so that only Keith could hear his words. "She feels so good in a man's arms," Sean said under his breath. "It's no wonder that the guys want to dance with her."

Keith knew what his brother was doing, and for that reason, he forced himself not to rise to the bait. Only his iron will kept him seated, however. The image that Sean's words had evoked was adding unneeded fuel to the growing jealousy that had plagued Keith daily since her arrival.

"No, it's no wonder," Keith agreed, lifting his tumbler for another drink.

Sean heard the heat buried beneath the controlled reply, and it was all he could do to keep from laughing out loud. Why in the hell didn't his brother just let himself go after Lita, anyway? He certainly had no scruples where a number of other ladies had been concerned over the years. It must be that Lita was somehow different from the others and his brother instinctively realized it, Sean thought.

"Hey, Carl," Sean said, turning away from his brother for a moment, "since this is Lita's last performance, why don't we have a little party after hours for her? As a kind of send-off . . ."

Keith dropped the tumbler roughly onto the bar and stood up. The last two weeks had been pure hell as far as he was concerned. All he needed was to have a private little party with Lita and the boys! Like rubbing salt in open wounds! At least with the club in operation, he found it easier to keep away from her. There were too many people around to do anything. Like seduce her, for instance, he thought as heat grew in his loins at the thought.

He'd only had to drive her home and not go into her town house. That he'd been able to do. They'd even managed to have some interesting conversations about a lot of things during the drives. They'd gotten to know a little about each other's likes and dislikes, he recalled.

He'd come to like her as a person, respect her as a professional, admire her as a performer.

And want her with a burning need that was beginning to consume him alive.

Keith slipped off the bar stool and gave Sean and Carl curt nods. "I've got some work to do," he announced unemotionally. "See you later." He stalked into his office and closed the door, shutting out the sounds of laughter intermingled with the soft, sensuous music of bass and piano and Lita's melodious voice . . .

When the last song was sung and the applause ended, Lita replaced the microphone on the stand and stepped down off the raised stage where the band was arranged. She smiled and shook hands, graciously acknowledging compliments and taking the time to chat politely with several people. It took her twenty minutes to make her way through the sophisticated crowd, and by the time she'd reached the dressing room, she felt like she'd run a gauntlet.

The knock at the door a few minutes later didn't sound like Keith's.

"Yes?" she called out as she began freshening up a little.

"Lita? It's Sean . . . The boys and I would like to throw you a little going-away party," he explained, his voice muffled by the closed door. "Could you stay a little while tonight?"

Stay a little while longer. There was nothing she'd less like to do, she thought with a sinking feeling. She'd been as nervous as a cat for days, counting the hours until her obligation was met and she could leave Keith's club. "Well—" she began.

Sean heard her negative tone and interrupted before she could turn him down. "Great! We'll be waiting for you by the bar."

"No! Sean! Wait."

Lita's heart froze. He'd left, misunderstanding her comment for a yes, no doubt, she thought in dismay. She pulled the zipper up on the dress she'd been taking off and dashed for the door. She had to make it clear before the party got under way, she thought frantically. She couldn't take an intimate little gathering with Keith Christophe in attendance! She knew she was dying for the man, and being with him in such close quarters would be fatal! At all costs, she had to get out of here as fast as possible!

She hurried into the club and was opening her mouth to insist that she had to leave right away. But before she'd uttered a word, she was drowned out by a boisterous rendition of "For She's a Jolly Good Lady" by a raucous all-male a cappella choir. She stood there helplessly staring at them in confusion as Sean, Marty, Carl, Gaius, and the guys in the band sang lustily, laughing at themselves as they crooned.

"Thanks, fellas," she said, moved by their enthusiasm and kindness. "You've been wonderful to work with . . ."

Before she could shift into an apology to the effect that she couldn't be staying for more farewells, Sean swooped to her side and pulled her to the bar, pushing a glass of champagne into her hand and urging the group to turn on the recordings that had been made of the evening's performance for a little background mood music.

"Hey! We didn't sound half bad tonight, did we?" Gaius shouted, slapping his thigh and taking a long swallow of his beer.

The rest of the band agreed with him, and their enthusiastic replies drowned out Lita's efforts to excuse herself.

Lita took a drink and felt the cool liquid slide down her throat like golden bubbles of light. She glanced nervously around the room and quickly realized that Keith wasn't there. That came as such a relief that she relaxed and took another drink in minor celebration of the fact. If he wasn't here, maybe it wouldn't hurt to stick around a little bit and say good-bye. After all, she'd grown fond of the guys during her stay in Washington. They'd been kind and thoughtful to her and great to work with.

When the boys in the band began talking about up-coming gigs and tours they'd be taking, she listened with interest and took another cool drink. "How many weeks do you usually spend at Sydney's?" she asked curiously.

Gaius replied for them all. "Oh, about twenty six, I'd say. Then we spend about two weeks recording—and maybe six weeks traveling as a band to seven or eight gigs . . . New York, New Orleans, Miami, Philadelphia, Los Angeles, San Francisco."

The other band members mumbled "Uh-huh" between swallows of their drinks and added a few other cities they'd been to in the past few years.

"Then we all split up and go our own way some, too," Gaius explained. "That way, we can each be the 'guest artist,' you know?"

Lita's eyes were warm as she put her hand gently on Gaius's arm. "I'm glad to hear it!" she commented with genuine warmth. The musicians in Gaius Vaughn's band were each brilliant—technically and musically—as far as she was concerned. For a man who claimed to have no sensitivity to creative types, Keith Christophe had impeccable taste in the musicians he'd employed, she thought.

Keith Christophe. She couldn't seem to keep from thinking about him, she thought ruefully.

Lita finished her champagne and tried to concentrate on the stories the band members were regaling them with about performances that had been harrowing in one way or another.

"Now for the pièce de résistance!" Sean exclaimed enthusiastically as Carl returned from the kitchen with a cake and some plates.

Lita Winslow, in icing, decorated the top of the sheet cake, and there was a suitable round of applause for the pastry chef before the laughing group began tasting his handiwork.

"I wonder where Keith is?" Sean asked innocently, provoking a chorus of echoing voices.

"Yeah!" Gaius exclaimed, polishing off his piece of cake and heading toward Keith's office. "Say, the boss shouldn't miss this!"

Lita almost choked on her cake and wished Sean could have waited a few minutes before asking about his brother's whereabouts. She'd look pretty peculiar running through the hall to the dressing room with her mouth full of cake! All she could do was sit uncomfortably on the bar stool and hope that Keith hated farewell parties—especially hers!

Gaius knocked on Keith's door and barreled in as soon as Keith barked permission to enter. "Hey! You're missin' all the fun, man!" Gaius exclaimed, grabbing Keith's arm and hustling him out of his chair before he fully realized what the band leader was about.

"I don't want any fun!" Keith objected emphatically.

"Hey! Sure you do! You work too hard! Besides, this is Lita's last night with us! We got a cake an' everything!"

Gaius was wiry and an expert manipulator, a veteran of many years of having to get himself and his band jobs. Between his physical determination to dislodge Keith from the office and Keith's underlying ambivalence, Gaius prevailed.

Sean clapped his brother on the back with suspicious good humor, Lita thought.

"Good work, Gaius!" Sean exclaimed. "Keith never learned to relax and play. He was always the responsible one in the family," he explained with just a touch of sharpness. "He never learned to let himself go."

Keith was staring at Sean with barely visible irritation. "It's a dirty job," Keith muttered sarcastically, "but someone in the family has to do it."

Sean maneuvered Keith a few steps to his left until he was next to Lita, who was licking icing off her fingers and

155

searching for a napkin so she could make an escape at the earliest opportunity. Sean's eyes narrowed as he noted the skittish look in her eyes and the fact that his brother was pointedly avoiding looking at her.

"Say, Gaius?" Sean asked genially.

"Yeah?" the bandleader replied cheerfully.

"Can you find the song you guys did with Lita toward the end of the evening—'Night and Day'?"

Gaius stopped the tape recorder and reeled in at high speed until he found the section he wanted. "This ought to be it," Gaius said, pushing the play button down.

Sean pushed his brother into Lita's arms before either of them could do anything to stop it. "Everyone else has danced with her, brother. This looks like it's your last chance to have that pleasure," Sean said, a soft taunt barely underlying the comment. "Otherwise, you may go through life wondering what it would have been like . . . wondering what you'd missed."

The bassist was plucking the lead-in as Keith stared down into Lita's startled eyes. Sean pushed them so close that Keith's chest was brushing her bare arm and the tantalizing scent of her perfume was teasing him. It had been tough trying to keep away from her. At this close range, he could feel his will dissolving second by second. The need to hold her was relentlessly swallowing his determination to keep his distance. "May I have this dance?" he murmured, placing a proprietary hand lightly on her waist.

Lita had been telling herself to leave for several minutes, but every time she looked at Keith her strength failed her. She stared up at the dark-haired stranger who'd come to be so dear to her for reasons she could not fathom. The rest of the room receded and there was only Keith. "Yes," she whispered shakily as she preceded him to the darkened dance floor. She was only vaguely aware that the others began filtering out of the room.

He put his arm around her back and pulled her gently into his body, holding her cold hand in his.

"He was right," Keith murmured as he leaned his jaw against her dark hair.

Lita let him pull her into him, thigh to thigh, flattening her gently but firmly against his hard body until she was no longer certain where she ended and he began.

"It would have been hell going through life wondering what I had missed," he muttered, as if the admission freed him from some inner battle.

Lita wanted to sigh with pleasure. Being in his arms was heaven; listening to his voice, hearing his sweet words, gave meaning to the word *wonderful*. She indeed felt, for the first time in her life, as if she were full of wonder . . .

Lita's voice joined the instrumental lead and she had the strange experience of feeling as if she were talking to the man in her arms with her singing and her body at the same time. From the way Keith's arms tightened slightly, she wondered if he felt the same way and was pleased by it. " 'Night and day, you are the one . . .' "

Lita closed her eyes and leaned her cheek along his hard jaw, relaxing trustingly into his strong arms as he moved them slowly through the music. The song was being played in the slow, evocative tempo of a ballad, and they moved so slowly that it was more like embracing than dancing. Lita felt her entire body begin to come alive. She felt like she was glowing, and every sensitive nerve ending was attuned to Keith Christophe. His clean, masculine scent, his strong, muscular arms, the steely length of his thigh wedged against hers, the erotic pressure of his knee guiding her slowly into the next step . . .

If she could have died, it would have been then and there, in the exquisite pleasure of being lost in his arms.

The song continued and Keith pulled her hand in close

to his body and placed a soft, long kiss on her temple. "Cole Porter wasn't the only one," he murmured, a faint smile touching his lips.

Lita barely heard him through the haze of warmth that was enveloping her. "Hmm?" she asked through the dreamy pleasure that was surrounding her.

His lips caressed her cheek and came to rest over her ear. " '. . . this longing for you follows wherever I go . . .' " he quoted.

The words, whispered against her ear, sent a cascade of goosebumps down her neck and shoulders and over her spine. I know what you mean, she echoed silently.

Lita was drowning in sensation. Keith's hand slid down into the small of her back, pressing her snugly against his hard midsection and slowly, sensuously, massaging her lower back. His mouth traveled down a little below her ear, and his tongue traced a path of liquid lightning whose miniature bolts struck every nerve cell in her upper body. Lita moaned softly and pressed against him, tightening her arms without conscious thought.

She didn't need to think. She needed to be close to Keith. As close as humanly possible.

Keith suddenly stopped moving and pulled her completely into his arms, pulling her upward as he lowered his mouth savagely to hers. He kissed her with a hot, burning need that ignited her own fires of longing. The deep, soul-wrenching kiss brought tears of frustration and desire to her tightly closed eyes, and she put her arms around his neck to hold him as hard as she could.

Roughly he pulled a little way, letting their lips part by just a fraction of an inch as he pressed her tightly into him. "Let me make love to you," he muttered as he began to place open-mouthed kisses provocatively on her throat and slid one hand slowly down her back in a gesture of masculine desire.

Lita told herself she should say no. She would be leaving for the coast soon. She couldn't handle a sexual encounter with a man as devastating as Keith Christophe. She would pay for it for the rest of her life . . .

"Tonight," he whispered unsteadily, cupping her face in his hands and placing a soft, teasing kiss against her lips.

She opened her eyes and tried to find the will to deny them both what they so clearly wanted. Instead she fell into the hypnotic spell of his passion-blackened eyes and found herself thirsting for his loving.

He trailed soft kisses across her jaw and ran his fingers into her hair, creating waves of pleasure in their wake.

"Oh, Keith," she managed to moan, "we can't. I'm leaving soon."

He kissed her fiercely then, as if branding her with his mouth. "Then give us both a memory to treasure," he urged her huskily. "Damn it. I haven't slept for weeks. I feel like a dying man, Lita. All I can think about is wanting you, touching you, kissing you, making love to you . . ." He ran his hands over her hips and slid them up to caress her breasts and sides.

Me, too, she wanted to admit. Instead she slid her arms around his neck and kissed him back. "All right," she said softly, "your place or mine?"

CHAPTER NINE

The view from Keith's apartment was spectacular.

His Crystal City high rise overlooked the Potomac. The huge picture window and balcony looked out onto the dark, glistening river and the jeweled buildings dotting its banks. At night the floodlit national monuments were a clear, ghostly white against the darkened backdrop. The Kennedy Center, the Washington Monument, the Jefferson Memorial—the giant alabaster buildings suddenly seemed close kin to the temples of ancient Greece.

Lita stood admiring the breathtaking beauty of it while Keith slipped out of his tuxedo jacket and loosened his black bow tie, admiring a more private view of his own.

She was silhouetted against the elegant vista of nighttime Washington, the sequins of her ruby red dress glinting in the soft, low lighting of the apartment. Her bare shoulders gleamed enticingly, and Keith found himself urgently wanting to run his hands over them. And over the rest of her.

He silently crossed the room, his firm tread barely audible.

Lita felt a soft tremor of alarm whisper down her exposed neck and back. Where Keith was concerned, her hearing, her awareness in general, was exquisitely sensitive. She had seen his every movement as clearly as if she'd been looking at him—the desultory way he'd shrugged out of his jacket, the casual flick of his wrist as he'd tossed the bow tie on top of it a moment later, his confident strides as he closed the distance between them.

The feel of his hands, warm and hard, against her shoulders came as no surprise. And yet she leapt as if she were startled. As his hands slid down over her cool skin, acquainting himself with the feel of her back and arms, the startled feeling did not lessen. It grew more intense.

Keith put his arms around her and pulled her back against his hard body, burying his face in the soft cloud of her dark hair, pressing an erotic kiss against the exquisitely sensitive nape of her neck. Lita closed her eyes and gasped a little, laying her arms on top of his to hold him fast. Keith's brief muffled laugh made her smile.

"I'm not about to escape your clutches," he teased reassuringly, in reference to her tightened grip on his embracing arms.

She held him a little harder and leaned her head back against his broad, comforting shoulder. "I hope not," she murmured back fervently, humor in her voice.

He kissed her neck and ignited a flurry of startled feelings everywhere his lips touched. The feelings were so absorbing that she unconsciously loosened her hold on his arms, and he took the opportunity to run his hands over her stomach and breasts in leisurely exploration. Even through the fabric of her gown, goosebumps followed wherever his fingers roamed, and Lita began feeling oddly short of breath.

"You're the most beautiful woman I've ever seen," he murmured huskily as he turned her to face him.

He sank his hands into the dark cascade of her hair and gently pulled her head back. His eyes traced her features in an intimate gaze, their dark recesses revealing how much she affected him. "Beautiful," he breathed as he lowered his head and covered her mouth with his.

Lita slipped her arms around his neck and closed her

161

eyes as a rush of desire poured through her. His lips were warm and hard, teasing and commanding. As he moved his mouth slowly back and forth her mouth parted for a deeper kiss, and Lita felt her knees begin to grow weak as her heart started to pound.

She moaned softly and tightened her arms, pressing her willing body firmly against his. Her gesture of desire and surrender stripped away the last of his defenses, and he suddenly jerked her hips against him in a move of pure masculine possession.

Their kiss deepened and Lita felt a fiery shower of desire from her mouth to her toes. Never had a kiss been so earth-shattering in its intensity. It was as if they were stripped naked and their souls were reaching out to each other.

She felt his hand halfway down her back and vaguely realized that he was unzipping her dress. When he'd completely lowered the closure, he gave the front a gentle pull and the expensive gown slithered to the plush carpeting in a soft swish.

"No regrets?" he asked softly, looking down at her.

She knew he was giving her a last chance to change her mind. She reached up and pressed her lips to his hard cheek and rested her head against his. "No regrets," she assured him in a soft, sure voice. She had never been so sure of anything in all her life, she realized. She wanted to belong to Keith Christophe. Even if it were just for tonight. She would pretend that it was the beginning of forever. Just pretend . . .

"Tonight you are mine," he murmured, nuzzling her neck. Then he lifted her into his arms and carried her through the darkened room down the hall to his bedroom.

It lay hidden in shadows accentuated by the night colors of the decor: a dark walnut dresser, an ebony chair upholstered in a maroon print, the rich mahogany of the ornately carved headboard on the double bed. The heavy curtains were drawn, but as her eyes grew accustomed to the darkness, she realized that their colors matched the russet and cinnamon shades of the bed's heavy coverlet. Keith's tread was muffled by the Oriental rugs that covered the floor and lent the room the atmosphere of an Eastern potentate's quarters.

He hesitated, holding her for a moment longer. Then he bent his head and kissed her mouth with exquisite thoroughness.

In the arms of the sheik, Lita thought hazily as she felt him lower her slowly to the softness of the waiting bed.

Her body was still vibrating from the aftereffects of his kiss as he straightened. She watched him in fascination as he undid the studs of his tuxedo shirt, one at a time. He tugged the shirttails loose, and the corners of his mouth curved upward in pleasure at the look of rapt appreciation on her face. He unfastened his expensive gold cuff links and dropped them with the studs onto the antique night table next to his bed, hesitating in his disrobing long enough to give her another soul-wrenching kiss.

"Shall I help you?" she asked, her voice shaking. All of her was beginning to shake, she realized vaguely. If the man didn't hurry up, she was going to be writhing in agony.

Keith clamped his jaw shut and jerked the cummerbund loose. He stepped out of his formal black trousers and deftly shed the rest of his clothing, forgetting that he'd intended to take his time.

Looking into her face had put that plan completely out of his mind. All he was aware of was how desperately he wanted to strip the rest of the clothes off that delectable body of hers—how urgently he needed her.

"Yeah," he muttered thickly as he pulled the satin slip and underwear quickly off her trembling body. "Help me," he encouraged her, lowering his mouth to her naked breasts. "I'll show you how . . ."

His tongue teased her stiff nipples and she arched her throat in a spasm of delight, moaning her pleasure and urging him on as she slid her hands over his shoulders and back.

He groaned and buried his face against the softness of her breasts, trying to control the surging passion that was threatening to overwhelm him. He wanted to bring her to ecstasy. It wasn't enough just to satisfy himself. But as her hands slid over his back and began caressing his buttocks and thighs, he knew he'd never last. "I'm sorry," he groaned, gritting his teeth. "I can't wait . . . I've got to have you . . . now."

Lita had felt the hard, pulsing evidence of his wanting pressed between her thighs. His urgent need made the dull ache in her own belly nearly unbearable. At his words, she wriggled lower in the bed, pressing herself enticingly against him. "I can't either," she gasped, wanting desperately to be part of him.

Her words, and the tortured way she said them, more than convinced him. He pulled her into his arms and thrust forward. In one firm stroke, they were joined and they each gasped in relief and pleasure.

He was still for a moment, savoring the warm, silky feel of her. Then slowly he began to move rhythmically. Her legs tightened around his thighs, and she eagerly met him halfway, inflaming him even more with her responsive movements.

As he felt the beginning of the end take hold of him, she pressed up hard and clenched her fists. He buried his face in her neck with great relief and reached his own intense release in the waves of her own pleasure. They lay together, enjoying the pleasantly draining sensation of love's aftermath and savoring its feelings of deep fulfillment.

He inhaled the soothing scent of her neck and smiled against her shoulder. "You sure know how to help," he murmured, rousing himself enough to run one hand over her waist and hip in leisurely possession.

"Ummm," Lita managed to reply as a smile curved her own lips. "I didn't notice that you needed any," she teased him, leaving her eyes closed so she could concentrate on the wonderful feel of his body lying fully against hers.

He chuckled softly and sighed with pleasure. He should have done this days ago, he thought ruefully. That made him grin. Of course, if he had he'd have had to cancel her last few shows because he'd never have let her out of his bed!

Lita sensed his good humor and half opened her eyes. "What's so funny?" she asked, smiling at him.

His grin broadened. "I was just thinking that if I hadn't been so damned determined not to let you under my skin, we could have done this days ago."

Lita ran a hand tenderly over his rock-hard ribs and ruffled his hair playfully. "You're a confident one, aren't you?" she asked with mock indignation. "Do you think I'd have fallen into your bed just because you finally were ready to?"

He raised himself onto his elbows and grinned down into her beautiful face, her cheeks still showing the telltale blush from their passionate embrace. "I think you and I have been simmering at the same temperature ever since we met." He lowered his mouth to her throat and traced a tantalizing pattern on her tender flesh with his tongue. "I think we've been hot for each other for days," he added in a disgustingly satisfied voice. "And I think if we hadn't found an excuse to go to bed with each other, we'd have spent the rest of our lives wondering what would have happened if we'd given in to the urge—to say nothing of weeks or months of suffering the painful congestion of the frustrated lover . . ."

Lita grabbed a pillow from beside her head and hit him over the head with it, laughing at his outrageous candor. "You!" she gasped as he fought back by tickling her bare abdomen and waist. "You, sir, are *no* gentleman!"

He captured her thrashing legs between his and began running his hands over her breasts and the soft flesh of her stomach. "Dead right," he agreed in a strange, intense voice.

The playful fighting and tickling quickly changed into something else as he ran his hands up the insides of her satiny thighs and began massaging her velvety womanly flesh in slow, knowing strokes. His mouth closed over one breast and his pleasingly rough tongue circled its hardening nipple with relentless precision.

Lita moaned and ran her hands down his hard, hot physique, seeking to torture him in a similar way. She felt his whole body go rigid as her fingers closed over his pulsing need. Seeing how quickly, how strongly, he responded to her lovemaking only served to intensify her ministrations.

With a fierce moan, he pulled her hands away and shoved his knee between her parting thighs, once more joining them with a sense of renewed passion and urgency.

"Oh, yes, yes," Lita sobbed as he plunged against her again and again.

She heard his muffled voice and felt his body shuddering hard against hers as waves of satisfaction hit them. It sounded like he was saying something in Greek, but she didn't need to understand the words to catch his meaning. It was the expression of joy at being one with one's beloved. In any language it was the same.

I love you, she replied in silent echo, tightening her

166

arms around him to convey the same message with her body. I love you.

The sun had been up for hours by the time Keith first opened his eyes. The room, shrouded by the heavy curtains and receiving only indirect light from the hallway, was still in semidarkness.

His leg was stretched possessively across a shapely thigh, and one arm had the pleasure of resting along a soft, feminine ribcage. His head was pillowed next to a fragrant cloud of silky black hair. His nostrils were filled with the sweet scent of the woman who had warmed his bed all night.

He turned carefully and looked at her, feeling a deep, quiet pleasure in her innocent, sleeping features—the rhythmic rise and fall of her breasts under the thin sheet; the way her hand lay, half curled, palm up, on the pillow next to her head.

He'd never felt anything quite like it. It was as if she belonged to him. After last night, he thought, perhaps that was the best way to describe it. A wry grin tugged at his mouth. That wasn't the usual thought that came to mind under circumstances like this. He usually couldn't wait to get his clothes on and leave.

The wry grin changed slowly into a more serious, thoughtful expression. He couldn't very well grab his pants and go this time. It was his apartment they were in. Not hers. Not some hotel.

He picked up a strand of the soft black hair spread across his pillow and rubbed it softly between the thumb and forefinger of one hand. Lita Winslow was in a category by herself. In every way. How had the woman gotten to him like this? he wondered in frank admiration and astonishment.

The object of his admiring reverie stirred and gradually became aware of the heavy male leg and arm half pinning her to the bed. She stretched and rolled her head over to see if he was awake and was greeted with two warm hands grasping her head and a firm, tender kiss being placed on her mouth.

She slipped her arms around his neck and gave him a hug, smiling contentedly as he drew back to look down at her. "My, you do know how to wake a girl up," she teased him.

He was tempted to wrestle playfully but decided that might lead to a prolonged stay in bed, and he wanted to spend some time with her in other ways before she had to go. So he threw the covers off her and got out of bed amid her shriek of protest that she was cold.

"Time to get out of bed, my dear." He scooped her up and carried her into his bathroom for a shower.

Lita laughed and turned on the taps as he held her in his arms. "I'll wash your back if you'll wash mine," Lita offered with a generous smile as she reached for the scented soap on a rope hanging nearby. It was a spicey scent that reminded her of Keith, she realized as she lathered his broad shoulders and well-muscled back. Good Lord, now I'm going to smell like him, too!

"What's so funny?" Keith asked, raising a dark brow in curiosity.

"No one will be able to tell us apart in the dark," she hinted, holding the soap up under his nose as a clue.

He pushed the soap away and ran his hands over her breasts and hips, giving her a devilish grin. "I seriously doubt that," he replied.

And then he forgot his intention to stick to a less intimate form of human interaction and used his turn at soaping her to pick up where he'd left off the night before.

"What magic hands you have," Lita said, sighing as he toweled them dry and tugged her after him into the bedroom to finish what they'd started in the shower.

When their breathing finally returned to normal, Lita opened her eyes and gave him an impish look. "I wouldn't have minded being wet," Lita assured him, kissing him soundly as he held her in a warm embrace.

"I didn't want you to drown," he argued.

But I *am* drowning, she thought. I feel lost and adrift. I only feel whole and safe when I'm with you, Keith Christophe. And what in the world can I do about that?

He stared into her wide, vulnerable eyes and felt his heart twist painfully. If he weren't careful, he would really be in bad shape, he realized. He could fall very deeply in love with Lita Winslow. Of that, he was now dead certain. And to his disgust, he realized that that scared the hell out of him. "Midnight velvet," he muttered, looking into her beautiful blue eyes. He pulled her head close to him, tucking her under his chin. Just think about today, he told himself. Tomorrow will just have to take care of itself, damn it!

Lita burrowed against him affectionately and they pulled the covers back over them again. Neither wanted to spoil the peaceful, contented feeling. It was a rarity in their lives, and each wanted to savor it fully before the dream had to come to an end. They relaxed, and before long, they both drifted off into a restful sleep.

Lita awoke to the sensation of something tickling her nose. She brushed it away, but her hand found nothing but air. Reluctantly she opened her eyes a little and tried to focus on the elusive object that had roused her from a delectably deep sleep. The object in question turned out, much to her surprise, to be a long, scarlet feather.

"I was beginning to think you weren't going to wake up until this evening," teased her dark-haired lover as he grinned down at her and ran the feather over her cheek in a delicate caress.

Lita glanced at the small brass clock next to Keith's bed and sat bolt upright. Keith, who was propped on one elbow, twirled the feather absently and watched in fascination as the covers slipped down, exposing the enticing feminine curves of Lita's upper body.

"It's two o'clock!" she exclaimed in shock, turning on him in consternation. "I can't believe we slept this late!"

He laughed and lay back, lacing his fingers behind his head. "You shouldn't keep such late hours if you want to be an early riser," he teased her with a completely straight face.

Lita put her hands on her hips and gave him a friendly glare. "You're not in a position to talk," she pointed out, climbing out of bed and searching the room for her clothes.

Keith watched her nude form with admiration as she gradually collected her satin underwear and put it on. "I like my position just fine," he retorted as his eyes hungrily took one last look at her shapely bottom before Lita's slip slithered over it. He could really get used to watching her dress, he thought. He couldn't let himself think along those lines.

He tossed the covers off and got out of bed. When Lita looked up, he was disappearing into a walk-in closet. A moment later he reappeared in a pair of gray wool slacks. "Help yourself to the bathroom," he suggested casually as he opened a dresser drawer and pulled out a navy turtleneck sweater and walked toward the hall. "I'll see if there's anything to eat. Help yourself to the toothbrushes."

She stared at the empty doorway. "Help myself to the toothbrushes?" she muttered under her breath.

When she opened the medicine cabinet a few moments later, she saw a small supply of disposable toilet articles. She took what she needed and proceeded to freshen up. She told herself she should be grateful for his being so well stocked. But why did he have all these little things, anyway? she thought miserably. Women must stay here often. That was the obvious conclusion.

She lowered her head and shut her eyes. "You have no right to be upset by that, Lita Winslow," she told herself softly. "He's a free man."

But that wasn't really it. All of a sudden she felt like one of a herd. Just another woman he'd taken to bed. And it hurt.

She tried to shake the feeling and wandered through the elegant apartment in search of its owner. Obviously there was no going back, so she might as well go forward.

She found Keith slicing a melon and warming some gourmet muffins for their long-overdue breakfast. The automatic coffee brewer had just about filled its glass pot with delicious-smelling hot coffee.

Lita joined him in the small breakfast nook in one corner of the well-equipped kitchen.

He noticed the change in her as soon as he looked at her. It wasn't anything he could pinpoint exactly. She didn't look sad or withdrawn, but he knew she was beginning to have second thoughts about having spent the night with him. Normally that wouldn't have bothered him. He rarely got involved with women who worried about that. But Lita's regret was a stiff blow that rendered him speechless. He couldn't think of any glib words to use.

He joined her at the table and lifted her hand to his lips. "I've never brought another woman to my apartment," he said, raising his head slightly to look up at her, his eyes dark and intense.

Lita looked at him in surprise. She hadn't expected that. Nor the way he was looking at her. As though it were very important to him that she believe what he'd said. "Never?" she asked lightly, a skeptical laugh punctuating her challenge. Her forced smile receded as his unwavering, serious eyes locked with hers.

"Never." His fingers tightened around hers and he pulled her into his arms. He lifted the soft hair off her neck and placed a soft kiss on her sensitive skin.

"You don't have to say that, you know," she murmured. "I'm a big girl. All grown up. It's all right."

His hands were suddenly on her forearms, holding her a little away so that he could see her face. "I know I don't have to," he responded. "And for your information, I haven't done anything I didn't want to since I was ten years old. That, I'm sure you know, was quite a long while ago." His hands relaxed a little, and he gradually released her altogether. "I told you because it was the truth"—he hesitated—"and because I wanted you to know that." He frowned and reached for a warm muffin and some butter, clearly not interested in explaining further.

Something about his actions warmed Lita's heart. For the life of her, she didn't know why that should be. But she felt as if a heavy weight had been removed, and she was smiling as she got up to bring the coffee to the table. So maybe he had friends stay overnight unexpectedly, she thought. If Huey was any example, some of them probably needed a toothbrush! The idea brought a smile to her lips as she poured Keith a cup.

"That's better," he approved softly, his dark eyes gleaming at her over the hot cup of coffee he was lifting to his lips.

Lita's smile warmed and the sparkle was back in her life again. A glorious, wonderful, heartwarming sparkle. With a solid and fascinating male at its source.

He put down his cup and watched her thoughtfully. "Are you planning on staying in Washington for a while?"

Nothing in the way he had asked gave her a clue about his feelings on that subject. He was totally neutral, as far as Lita could tell. That didn't really surprise her, though.

172

Men were often like that—hiding their feelings. Of course, she couldn't help but hope Keith wasn't as neutral as he wished to appear.

She sipped her own coffee, holding it in her hands for a moment, trying to decide what the answer to his question was. "I'd like to," she admitted, "but I've got to fly back to California tomorrow. There's some business I have to take care of immediately. I can't do it long distance." She glanced up at him, and he nodded almost imperceptibly and leaned back in his chair.

There was a moment of silence as cold reality dashed away their private world and thrust them back into the present.

"And after that?" Keith inquired casually. He picked up a matchbox with Sydney's monogram from the center of the table and began idly flipping it open and shut.

"I . . ." Lita hesitated. Afterward, what? She'd been determined to stay in Washington until the police had found Melanie's murderer. But now, after having become so involved with Keith, she felt awkward about it. She forced herself to control the feelings of unease that suddenly plagued her. She couldn't afford it, under the circumstances. She looked steadily into Keith's enigmatic dark eyes. "Then I'm coming back. I want to get to the bottom of Melanie's death."

His hand closed over the matchbox, and he nodded his head in understanding. Naturally she'd want to be close to the investigation, he told himself. She wasn't the type to forget someone who had been close to her for so many years. There were few people he knew who would be willing to do the same for him, he thought cynically. Most were strictly the fair-weather variety of friend. "I'd like to help," he told her. And his unflinching gaze told her he meant it.

"Thanks, Keith," she replied gratefully.

He seemed to be trying to decide what to say for a

moment. When he finally spoke again, however, Lita was startled by his change of subject.

"You're different from most of the beautiful girls in this business," he commented thoughtfully. "I don't think I've ever seen or heard a single word of gossip about Lita Winslow. Not in the trade journals, not in the scandal rags, not even the usual talk that you hear from the other artists who've performed at Sydney's."

" 'Gossip'?" Lita repeated in surprise.

"About your life, your travels, the men in your life," he clarified. "*Is* there one?" he asked bluntly.

Well . . . if I counted you, perhaps, she thought in uncomfortable amusement. She decided against saying that out loud, however. "There've been one or two over the years," she admitted cautiously.

"And now?" he asked pointedly, locking her gaze with his.

"Now," she answered softly, "there isn't anyone."

His eyes flickered subtly. "No one at all?" he pressed her, as if finding that hard to believe. His eyes traveled over her appreciatively, underlining the reason for his doubt.

Lita smiled at him teasingly. "I didn't say there *never* had been anyone," she pointed out. "I said there wasn't anyone now."

He supposed he deserved that. Naturally there had been one or two heartthrobs in her life. He didn't particularly want to know about them. And yet he found himself uncharacteristically curious about Lita Winslow. He wanted to know how she spent every day. Who her close friends were. Who else she would kiss and caress with the same abandon she'd kissed and caressed him. That thought was too galling to contemplate, so he ruthlessly quashed it and turned his thoughts to the future.

He didn't want to let her walk out of his life. Not just yet. And he didn't want to pursue her in the ways he'd pursued the few women who had interested him in the past.

No expensive flowers, elegant dinners, costly trinkets. That wasn't what he wanted for Lita Winslow. With her they'd seem like the hollow gestures they had been. Payoffs for services rendered. The manipulations of a carefully calculated game of conquest and surrender.

He wanted Lita. Yet, oddly enough, he didn't just want her surrender. He wanted *her*. He wanted her trust and her affection, her laughter and her sadness, her joys and her sorrows.

Those jewels were not acquired through some manipulative courting ritual. They came with time spent together in many different ways. Quiet ways. Intimate ways.

"A penny for your thoughts?"

Lita's soft question pulled him back from his private musings. He smiled faintly and stood up. "I was wondering how to convince you to spend some time with me," he admitted, offering his hand to her.

She took it and he raised her hand to his lips as she came to her feet. His lips, firm and warm on the back of her hand, sent a now-familiar current sizzling through her. He looked up at her as he slowly raised his head, and the touch of his gaze had a disturbingly similar effect.

Lita didn't smile. It was too serious a moment for that. There was something there between them that was too strong for nervous laughter or coy flirting. She slid her arms around his neck as he pulled her slowly into his arms. She rested her head against his and closed her eyes, floating into the sensation of being in his protective embrace. "I wouldn't mind being convinced," she murmured against his neck.

His arms tightened. "Tomorrow I'll take you to the airport," he said huskily.

"Okay," she replied, beginning to feel a little like a dreamer.

"I'll pick you up when you fly back," he offered as he let his hand slide slowly down her back.

"That would be nice," she admitted softly, letting herself fall into the hazy joy of being in his arms again. The brief time they'd been physically separate had suddenly seemed like an eternity.

He began moving slowly out into the living room, dancing in a slow, sensuous way. Lita felt him lean down a little near the smoked-glass stereo cabinet. There was a soft click. Keith straightened again and tightened his arms around her. And then there was soft music to go with their swaying dance steps.

"And then we could have dinner together," he suggested, lifting her hair away from her ear.

"That sounds lovely . . . ah . . ." she moaned softly as his breath warmed her ear and his tongue sent soft flashes of lightning down her body. "Do you hear music?" she asked huskily, beginning to feel a little disoriented.

He laughed softly and nuzzled her throat. "When you're around, I always hear music, sweetheart," he murmured, moving his lips provocatively against hers in reply.

Then there was nothing but the feel of his mouth moving against hers in a warm, teasing kiss that lasted forever. Even so, it was not long enough.

It was not long enough at all.

CHAPTER TEN

The Pacific Ocean hadn't changed in the brief time Lita had been away. It was as strong and powerful as ever.

Lita wished she could say the same for herself.

It was late afternoon. She'd returned home the previous morning and spent the day trying to catch up on her sleep and the four large bags of mail that had been waiting for her at the post office.

Having only managed to plow through half of it, she was beginning to regret her decision not to have a secretary to handle some of her routine correspondence. It was flattering that people wrote her letters, of course, but it was extremely time-consuming to try to respond personally to each and every one of them. Especially now. Time was a very precious commodity for her at the moment.

Lita took a glass of iced tea out onto the rustic patio and pulled her dark glasses down to shield her eyes from the setting sun. Maybe she could get through most of it by tonight, she told herself optimistically.

A gull swooped down, perching on the low stone wall that edged the patio, his unblinking, sharp-eyed gaze searching for possible morsels from the remains of Lita's lunch.

"All right, all right," she grumbled good-naturedly as she pitched him the crusty heel of her French bread. "But that's it! You don't want to become too dependent!"

The gull brazenly plucked at the tasty offering and flapped his wings slightly, as if dismissing her comment as unworthy of notice.

Lita laughed and shook her head. Sometimes you realize your dependency too late, she thought. That made her think of Jack Connery for some reason. And thinking of Jack made her smile fade.

"Poor Jack," she murmured sadly. "Maybe if you'd kept your distance from Melanie, things would be easier for you now." She shook her head and ran a hand through her windblown dark hair. "Last time I was talking to a sea gull. Now I'm talking to myself! What's next?"

She grabbed the letter opener and reached for another letter. As soon as she saw the handwriting on the front of the envelope, her blood chilled and her hand froze in midair. It was Melanie's handwriting. And it had been postmarked the afternoon she'd disappeared. The last Friday of her life.

Lita wasn't even aware of how much her hands shook. As she opened the letter from the dead girl, the surroundings began to recede. There was only the numb realization that this was the last time she would ever hear from Melanie. Poor, talented, beautiful Melanie. A warm and shimmering young woman with so much to offer. Poignant, sad Melanie. A lonely, vulnerable girl who hadn't had time to soar, free and whole, into her shining tomorrows.

A teardrop fell on the delicate coral notepaper as Lita unfolded it with trembling fingers and silently read the last words she would ever have from her cousin.

Dear Lita,

I can't tell you how excited I am! Rehearsals are going great. The band is wonderful. The club is out

178

of this world. And so is the club owner and his brother!

I know you're going to scold me, but I've met the nicest men since I've come back to Washington. Even though Keith keeps a close eye on me, I've managed to have a good time. Just like when we were in school. Remember?

There are three of them that would make even your heart do flip-flops! I'm trying to decide which one I'm the craziest about.

And it's especially fun since it makes them all a little jealous to think that I might belong to someone else. Tonight, after rehearsal, I'm going to meet one of my Washington "beaus" and we're going to stroll along the busy avenues, as they used to say! (No bars for me! Don't worry!)

I know you don't understand, but I can't help it, Lita. It's just a thrill like nothing else in this world to make a man jealous. They want you so much more, then. And do they ever show it!

I can't wait until my Greek finds out. You know what they say about Greek men and their tempers!

Speaking of men with tempers, Jack's been dropping in when he's in town. Long-suffering, ever-patient, devoted Jack. I bet nothing ever gets him in a temper!

Now there's a man who makes a perfect brother, but I wonder who'd want such a sweet, patient man as a lover? If I hurry, I can slip away tonight right after he leaves and just before Sean picks me up. Jack made me swear I'd stay away from the guys, so he might be a little annoyed if he catches me out on the town. But I figure, he's always forgiven me my weaknesses before—and besides, a girl has to have some fun in life. All work and no play makes Melanie a dull, dull girl!

If you were here, I'd hug you to pieces! If you hadn't agreed to be my backup, I know Keith wouldn't have hired me. And I'd probably be crawling into a bottle instead of trying on designer dresses for a class act at Washington's best nightclub! I can't tell you how much it means to me!

If you could stop in while I'm here, you'd see exactly what I mean. It's just like we always dreamed, Lita. Only it's better. Because this time, it's real.

As ever, Love from Mel

Yes. This time it was real.

Lita put the letter down on the table and stared blindly at it. A part of her wished that she'd never read it. Irrationally she felt guilty for not having been there to keep her cousin out of harm's way. Melanie had been an adult, yet she had never learned to see the dangers of life until it was too late.

"I should have been with you!" Lita cried brokenly. "You were still such a baby, Melanie!" Angrily Lita got up and headed for the rocky cliffs. A climb along the stone-studded beach might help. It often had in the past.

The past, however, was gone.

"What did you mean when you said you had three Washington beaus, Melanie?" Lita asked softly.

She stood on the edge of the ragged cliffside, the wind snatching her words as they fell from her lips. A wave crashed into the rocky piles that stubbornly jutted up from the thin strip of beach below. The pounding of wind and water worked relentlessly against Lita's pain until it was numbed and nearly forgotten.

Only Melanie's words remained. They were sharp and clear in Lita's memory. "Three men," Lita reasoned aloud, jamming her hands into the back pockets of her faded jeans. "Sean's obviously one of them . . . Is Keith another?"

That thought produced an unwanted sliver of jealousy. Had he been more interested in her cousin than he'd let her know? she wondered in unhappy dismay. There wasn't any way to find out at the moment, so she just had to shove that unpleasant thought to the back of her jumbled mind until she could sort things out.

"The third man . . . Who was he?" she asked out loud, as if addressing the wind. The wind whipped her hair, and she wrapped her arms over her head to keep it from blinding her.

Lita didn't recall anyone at Sydney's mentioning a special man in Melanie's life. And she'd "interviewed" quite a remarkable coterie on precisely that subject while she'd been performing there. They'd all been drinking and had been eager to please her, so there was no reason to think that there was some conspiracy of silence afoot, she reasoned.

So . . . the third man must have been meeting Melanie secretly. That would make sense. Melanie had been quite clear in her letter about her reasons for doing things that way. But why would the man have gone along with it? Most men couldn't have helped but brag a little about getting Melanie's attention—even if it were just over a drink at the bar, confiding in an old buddy . . . Unless he had had something to hide.

"Oh, God. Who did you get mixed up with, Mel?" Lita cried out in fury and frustration. "What kind of man would do something like that?" She brushed away an angry tear with the back of her hand and vowed she'd find the answer to that question. "I'm going to get some exercise, finish the blasted mail, and go back to Washington!" she swore with every ounce of determination she possessed.

Lita climbed slowly down the ragged stone path, using

her sandaled toe to push aside a tangle of seaweed and driftwood. It had been awhile since she'd been able to walk in the fresh salt air and listen to the soothing rhythm of the ocean. That's what she needed now. It would nurture her. Renew her. And then . . .

"Then I'll go back," she told herself, "and find out."

The cold she felt had nothing to do with the slanting rays of the setting sun as day turned relentlessly to evening. She was afraid of what she might discover. What if Sean were somehow involved in Melanie's death? Or Keith?

"No!" Her slender foot, numbed by the cooling temperature, slipped on a rock and she stumbled slightly, catching herself on a large boulder with both hands. She hung her head and closed her eyes as tightly as she could, as if that would chase away the unwanted thoughts that began to gnaw at her.

"I know them," she said, forcing herself not to shout at the waves breaking just below her. "They couldn't know anything about her disappearance. I would have known."

But *would* she have known? a small voice asked. They were charming men. And Lita was not exactly an objective observer of their behavior. Especially of Keith's. She had felt that Keith wasn't always laying all his cards on the table with her. There were times when she'd wondered if he were holding something back . . .

She plunged her hands through her hair and covered her ears as if desperately trying to shut out a voice carrying unwanted tidings. "I couldn't be that wrong about Keith Christophe," she swore. "I just *couldn't* be that wrong about him."

Lita looked upward, searching the heavens for answers. There was only the evening star materializing like a brilliant diamond in the darkening sky as the yellows and oranges of sundown melted into the pastel blues and purples of nightfall. She wrapped her arms around her chilled skin, hugging herself for warmth.

If only it were Keith's arms keeping her warm. His words soothing her fears. His strong, hard lips and firm body comforting her in the way a man comforts his woman.

She pressed her hands against her temples and closed her eyes, took a deep breath, and reopened them. She'd better be getting home before the light faded altogether and she broke her neck going back up the unlit trail. With steps made brisker by the damp, cool breeze, she scrambled back up to her house. Every inch of the way, she clung to the memory of the enigmatic man who had become so dear to her heart.

As memories of Keith Christophe mercilessly teased her the third verse of the song she'd been struggling with for more than a month began haunting her ascent. She could hear the poignant lyrics and melody as clearly as if she were singing.

> *Til you . . . You touched the soul of my heart.*
> *You warmed the fires of love.*
> *You taught me all, only to depart.*

Somehow Keith had done just that. Touched her heart. Her lonely, longing heart. The part of her she'd guarded so well for all those years, telling herself she was too lighthearted to get really involved with a man. Keith had broken through her defenses as if they weren't there, with those dark and penetrating eyes and that tough and distant manner of his.

She broke into a run as she reached the crest of the hill, as much to escape her disturbing thoughts as to elude the chill night air. Running got her inside and warmed up fast enough. However, as she showered and changed for bed a little while later she realized that nothing else had changed. Everything in her life seemed to be hanging in a state of suspension, waiting for something to happen. No matter how fast she ran, those things remained.

She couldn't concentrate on her work anymore. The new song wasn't quite finished yet. Her relationship with Keith was definitely in midair. She wasn't even sure that what they had together could be called a relationship. And the truth about her cousin's death had yet to be unearthed.

For the first time in years Lita felt deeply alone as she snuggled down into her bed. Deeply alone and terribly lonely. Not since her father had left her mother had she felt quite so much in need of someone. And it wasn't just anyone she needed. It was a tough, dark-haired Greek with a faint, heart-stopping smile and a past that seemed shadowed by the seamier side of life. He was the man she longed for.

Lita pulled the light blanket more snugly around her and curled into a tight, protective ball.

Tomorrow was another day. Things would look better then, she told herself hazily as sleep crept into her exhausted form. Everything would work out.

And yet the last conscious image in her mind's eye was the dark and dangerous glitter in Keith Christophe's . . .

The glitter in Keith Christophe's dark eyes would have done justice to Lita's image of him right about then. As she fell asleep, he was closing up and preparing to leave Sydney's for the night. On the way out he'd run into Sean staggering out of one of the offices.

"I thought you'd left already," Keith said shortly, eyeing his brother with measured coolness.

Sean grinned coldly and bowed like a cavalier. "Still keeping an eye on me for Momma, are you Keith?" he asked challengingly. "Haven't you noticed, brother? I grew up. You don't have to do that anymore."

Keith's mouth tightened into a straight, hard line as he looked his well-liquored brother over from head to toe. "No. I hadn't noticed," he replied, his disapproval evident.

Sean's eyes hardened with antagonism and he leaned forward menacingly. "No. You wouldn't," he sneered, his words slurring from the half fifth of Keith's best Scotch he'd polished off while lazing in the office. "You never have," he added in a more jovial tone, waving one arm in the air as if in explanation.

"You're crocked," Keith said curtly. "Get into the car. I'll drive you home."

Keith reached for his brother's arm, but Sean recoiled, snatching his elbow back before Keith could touch him. "Oh, no," Sean muttered as he sagged against the wall and put out a hand in a gesture of refusal. "I'll get home under my own steam, brother. Just like always. Just like you. You never get drunk," he said loudly, letting his eyes close to shut out the hall, which seemed to be slowly spinning.

Keith watched in silence as Sean began to slide very slowly down the wall. The kid just couldn't seem to shake his damned inferiority complex. What was he supposed to do about it?

Before Keith could finish his thought, Sean slid the remaining way to the floor, his head falling forward onto his bent knees as he passed out cold. Keith knelt and hoisted his brother over his shoulder in a fireman's carry and headed toward the exit. One of the janitors passed them. Keith stopped dead and stared for a second.

"Night," Keith said curtly, staring through the man with cold eyes.

The janitor tipped his fingers to his head in farewell as he held the door for the tight-lipped, tuxedo-clad club

185

owner carrying his unconscious, equally well dressed brother over his shoulder like a man leaving a combat zone. "Night, Mr. Christophe," he replied nervously. "I didn't see nothin', Mr. Christophe," he whispered as loudly as he could after the big man's retreating back.

"Right," muttered the thoroughly frustrated club owner. "Thanks, Grady."

Sydney Keith's residence on elegant, old-money Foxhall Road was grand in every sense of the word. The long, curving drive cut a perfect semicircle through the precisely manicured lawn, which was edged with flowers, shrubbery, and stately trees. The house was a nineteenth century robber baron's contribution to Washington architecture. Its twenty-five rooms and four-car garage came complete with a carriage house and a ten-feet high wrought-iron fence to discourage casual visitors.

Keith pulled up in front and turned off the ignition.

Even at two thirty in the morning, the twin lights on the front entrance burned brightly. The sun never set on Sydney's palace.

Muttering a colorful string of unprintable Greek phrases aimed at his drunken brother, Keith hoisted Sean onto his shoulder for the second time and staggered up the semicircular steps of fine brick. He was in no mood for polite conversation. He hoisted the giant brass doorknocker and rapped the metal lion's hard nose sharply against the black oak door.

Sean's weight was giving him a tremendous pain in the neck, literally and figuratively, and Keith shifted his brother's weight to ease the pressure. "Damn it, Sydney! Open the damn door!" he bellowed as the seconds dragged painfully by.

The door flew open and a stately beauty stood irately in the center of the entryway, glaring icily at her elder son and his disreputable-looking baggage.

"How dare you use that tone on my front steps!" she exclaimed furiously. She stepped back and waved him inside. "Get inside before you wake the entire neighborhood!"

"The neighborhood is sound asleep, quivering behind their burglar alarms and dreaming of tomorrow's power plays," Keith snorted derisively as he strode into the drawing room and dumped his brother on the settee.

He wondered if anyone could imagine what life with the famous Sydney Keith had really been like all those years. She'd been an ambitious young woman who'd worked for years to finally make it big, and when she had, she'd truly struck it rich. And she'd wanted the world to know it. It was curious to him that such determination hadn't aged her at all. Even now she was more attractive than most women twenty years her junior. And she was as domineering a beauty as there was. That was an annoying trait he could have done without tonight.

Sydney flowed after him, her diaphanous rose-colored nightgown and robe fluttering around her like a soft cloud. She frowned worriedly and bent down over her unconscious younger son. "What happened?" she asked, raising her delicate features inquiringly to look in Keith's direction.

Keith straightened his jacket and loosened his tie. "What always happens," he said sharply. "Sean's been drowning his sorrows in a bottle. This time alone. I guess the girls couldn't keep up with him tonight."

Sydney touched a manicured hand to Sean's brow, smoothing away the dark strands of hair that had fallen over it in disarray. He was still her baby. Sadly, she had long ago realized that was part of Sean's problem. She had stubbornly resisted letting him grow up and take the knocks life routinely handed out to the young. She sighed and straightened, looking thoughtfully at the morose and tired-looking Keith. "What are we going to do, Keith?"

she asked, a note of desperation creeping into her silken voice. "We've got to help him."

Keith shrugged noncommittally. "I think he's had too much help, Sydney. It's time he helped himself."

It was bluntly stated, but he'd said as much to her many times over the past ten years, and she never seemed to hear. He was sick and tired of picking up the disasters in his brother's reckless wake. And he was becoming dangerously annoyed with Sean's unrelenting barrage of personal snipes and potshots. What to do about it, however, was not such an easy thing to know.

Keith strolled over to the huge oil painting of his mother that dominated one end of the room. She was standing alone in a satin sheath with above-the-elbow gloves and three-inch heels. The ensemble was a study in gleaming white, down to the knee-length boa draped casually around her neck and flowing over her shoulder. It was the most famous image of Sydney Keith there was.

The dark red rose, just beginning to bud, had been her trademark. She held it in her hand, drawing it along one cheek seductively, her eyes daring the one gazing at her to come hither. She was still a seductive, elegant beauty, he thought, turning to admire her. She had class. She always had.

But her children and her husband had been her weaknesses. She couldn't deny them anything. Her husband, a grown man, had taken everything with great pleasure and arrogant satisfaction. Her eldest son had been so busy defending her and his family from the taunts of the world that he'd grown tough in spite of her softheartedness.

Sean had been a different story. Sean had it easy. Protected. An adoring mother. A fiercely protective older brother. A father who doted on him like a visiting uncle when he came to town.

Sydney could read the thoughts as they chased through Keith's mind. She was alone in that regard. To most of the world Keith was an enigma but not to her. It was partly because his guard was always a little down with her. But it was also because she was finely in tune with the moods and feelings of the men in her family.

She smiled impishly. Of men in general, she had to admit. You couldn't strip for men for twenty-five years without learning to read their faces accurately.

Before Keith and Sydney could come to grips with the problem, Sean began to come around. "You're a beauty . . . Come back, pretty girl . . ."

"Is there a girl involved in this?" Sydney asked in surprise. Sean had always been a casual lover of women as far as she knew. Like Keith, he made sure no one got near his heart.

Keith shook his head. "No."

Sean slowly began sitting up, sliding shaking hands up to either side of his head as if to keep it from spinning. "So, you brought me home anyway," he mumbled indistinctly, his eyes still closed. "I'd have thought you'd be home dreaming of pretty Lita."

Sydney saw Keith's face darken in anger. That was interesting, she thought. "Lita?" she asked, her musical voice as neutral as she could make it.

"Lita Winslow," Keith supplied before his brother could elaborate. "She sang at the club recently."

Sean seemed to be coming back to the real world. His eyes opened, and he leaned against the upholstered back of the settee.

"And the most beautiful songbird we've ever had," Sean added, a knowing smile curving his lips.

Keith's mouth was a hard, straight line. Any other man would have gotten the message and dropped it. Not Sean. Drunk or sober, he wouldn't miss the chance to rile his older brother.

Sydney stepped between them to keep their squabbling

under control. *"The* Lita Winslow?" she inquired curiously.

Sean grinned sloppily and nodded. "The one and only. She swept big brother here right off his feet."

Keith gave Sean a disgusted look and turned toward the door. "Stay off the sauce, Sean."

Sean staggered to his feet and bowed erratically.

"Yes, sir," he slurred, a hateful look in his eyes. "You're just lucky I didn't try to get around you with Lita the way I did with Melanie," he boasted angrily. "Women don't always prefer the big-time club owner to his wastrel brother, you know."

Sydney looked from Keith to Sean in alarm. There was something more to this than met the eye. The rift was deeper, the problem worse than before.

"Shut up, Sean," Keith ordered him coldly. "We'll talk when you're sober."

Sean laughed bitterly. "Yeah. Get your lawyers out of mothballs, Keith. Little brother's gonna need someone besides you to bail him out of this one."

Sydney's skin paled and she gave Keith a stricken look. Suddenly she looked her age. She rushed to Keith, who had stopped halfway to the door at Sean's outburst. "What is he talking about, Keith?" she asked urgently, her slender fingers clinging to the fine black material covering his shoulders. "What does he need a lawyer for? What's this all about?"

Keith gently took her hands in his and kissed them, then led her to the staircase in the foyer. "Nothing for you to worry about, Sydney. I'll take care of him. And any trouble he's in."

"But, Keith . . ."

He pushed her gently up the first marble stairstep and shook his head. "He's drunk. He's unhappy. You know Sean." Keith hesitated for a moment, considering. Grimly he plunged on. "I think you should give him the boot. He needs to move out of here, get his own place and get a job. You know it. I know it. And he knows it. If you want him to take over the club, that's fine with me. I can hire him. Or I can sell it to him. Either way, Sean needs to see himself as a man on his own, able to fend for himself. In my shadow, he just can't believe he's got what it takes."

Sydney looked down at her dark-haired son with stricken eyes. She'd always known what he was saying was true, of course. But it hurt terribly to hear it said so frankly . . . especially with Sean sitting in the other room in the condition he was in.

Sydney ran a hand affectionately through Keith's hair. He'd taken the blame on himself, as usual. "It isn't just your shadow that's caging him, Keith," she said with a regretful, guilty sigh. "It's mine. And the net I've thrown around him since he was a baby. Your father was always free as a bird. I never could cage him. And you were always so tough, even as a small child. I was so proud of you. I encouraged your independence. And then, I was working all the time and you were out of my clutches more than Sean was." A shadow crossed her delicate features. "Sean was my baby. I had more time for him. I'm afraid I clung to him too hard, for too long."

A tear threatened to brim over the edge of her soft gray eyes. Sydney couldn't have that. She despised weepy women who couldn't take life in stride. "Never mind," she said with silken determination. "What I've done, I can undo." She kissed Keith lightly on the cheek. "Go on home, darling. You must be exhausted. We'll have a family powwow tomorrow, when Sean's hangover has faded a little. Say at teatime?"

Keith shook his head. Only his mother would have adopted teatime. "It'll have to be in the morning or the next day. I'll be tied up tomorrow afternoon."

Sean, having found the strength to follow them at last,

leaned against the drawing room's sliding door and began to chuckle weakly. "Going to fetch the lovely Lita when she flies back, are we?" he managed. "Why, we may not see you for days, brother. The last time you took her home, it was forty-eight hours before you were seen again."

Before he could continue, Keith had crossed the distance between them and was hoisting Sean off the floor by his crumpled jacket. "If you so much as mention her name in that kind of context again, you'll be scraping yourself off the nearest wall," Keith threatened him through clenched teeth.

Even in his semidrunken condition, Sean felt the cold anger in his brother's warning. "Hey," he said protestingly, shaking his head in self-defense, "I wouldn't say that about her in front of anyone. But we're all family here, Keith. You know I like Lita."

Keith relaxed his grip and carefully straightened his cuffs. "I'm going home," he said shortly, not trusting himself to stay near his brother much longer without losing his temper completely. "As I said—tomorrow morning. Or I'll be in touch some other time."

He didn't give them time to argue, although neither had any intention of debating with him at that point. Both stared at him in silent surprise as he strode through the big door and took the steps two at a time. As the fading roar of his engine communicated his departure, Sean and Sydney turned to stare at each other in astonishment.

"I'm going to have some coffee," Sean announced, sighing sheepishly. He ran a shaking hand through his tousled hair and walked with still-unsteady steps toward the other wing of the house. Why in the hell did he always have to rile Keith like that? he wondered despondently.

Sydney descended the step she'd been on and followed

after him. "I think I'll join you," she said, attempting to inject a note of cheerfulness into her musical voice. "There are a few things I'd like to ask you, dear."

The planes were landing at Washington National every thirty seconds, like clockwork. Keith pulled smoothly into the complex system of entry ramps as Lita's big jet sailed lower and lower over the Potomac on its final approach. By the time its big wheels began to squeal softly against the concrete runway, he was pulling into a parking space and vaulting out of the car.

He'd been telling himself it was just a case of spring fever. Maybe you got it worse, the older you were. Whatever you wanted to call it, he had quite a case of it.

Ever since he'd dropped her off here a week ago, he'd been plagued by her memory. Lita's soft, seductive voice. Lita's gentle smile. Lita's electrifying kisses and knockout body. Lita's laughter. Lita's cries of passion and sweet kisses of satiation.

"This way, please," the stewardess said, pointing to the exit. "This way, sir. Thank you for flying with us."

Lita held her carry-on luggage in one hand and went with the steady flow of deplaning travelers. She was scared, now that the time had finally come. Suddenly it seemed so long since she had seen Keith. He hadn't called either. That hadn't helped any.

"Excuse me," interrupted a little white-haired lady in a blue print dress, shyly leaning forward to touch Lita's arm. "But aren't you Lita Winslow?"

Lita looked around. Everyone else was too busy gathering their luggage and traveling companions to notice the question. Maybe she wouldn't be held up too long if she admitted it this time. Besides, the lady looked so sweet. "Yes, I am," Lita admitted with a warm smile.

The little old lady's eyes grew round, and her wispy

193

little brows arched in surprise. "Oh, would you sign an autograph for my daughter? She just loves your records."

They stepped onto the escalator and descended to the baggage claim area.

"I'd be happy to."

That was how Keith found her. Standing in the corner with the little old lady, signing an autograph on a stray piece of stationery.

She'd just returned the pen, given the woman her best farewell smile, and was leaning down to pick up her overnight case when she saw him out of the corner of her eye.

He was standing near a ticket counter, his hands jammed in his pockets, staring at her in a dark and moody way as people streamed around him, pushing and pulling luggage in all shapes and forms. It didn't matter. She'd have spotted him anywhere. He stood out in a crowd.

She waved at him as she straightened up, smoothing the slightly rumpled linen skirt of her designer suit. It was a rich shade of chianti and set off her vivid coloring to great effect. From the heat in Keith's eyes as he closed the distance between them, she assumed he had noticed that.

He stopped a foot away from her and electricity suddenly surrounded them both.

"I wondered if you'd really come," she said huskily, her fingers tightening around the handle of her case to keep from losing her nerve.

He took the case from her and smiled slightly. "I told you I would." He gazed at her, drifting slowly over her features as if he were reacquainting himself with her after a long separation.

"That was a long time ago," she replied softly.

Keith put a proprietary arm around her shoulders and steered her toward the conveyor belt, where the luggage was being tossed out in haphazard fashion.

" 'A long time'?" he repeated, a little surprised at her description. He had to admit it had been a long time as far as he was concerned. He hadn't expected her to feel the same way, however. That she did only made him more eager to get her out of the terminal and into his arms. He gave her a wolfish grin and slid his hand under her soft raven hair, letting his thumb caress the back of her neck seductively. "You thought I'd change my mind in a week?" he asked in surprise, guessing her feelings.

She tried to smile it off, but he saw the vulnerability in the blue depths of her eyes. "It did cross my mind," she admitted.

He pressed a quick kiss on her soft lips and reached for her luggage as she pointed it out. "Let's get out of here," he muttered, "and go someplace where I can lay all your fears to rest!"

That sounded intriguing, she thought. And wonderfully safe. There would be no haunting, faceless man threatening her again. Not as long as Keith was near. That unknown madman from her past would do her no harm tonight. She pushed the disturbing memories back into oblivion. The present was too sweet to be warped by fears from the past.

Lita looped her arm through his, and they walked out into the brilliantly clear spring day. It will all be okay, she told herself as her heart beat a little faster and a surge of hope and longing coursed through her. Now that they were together again, everything would be straightened out.

And yet as they raced up the freeway the short hop to Georgetown, she barely saw the beautiful blossoms that painted the city so enchantingly. Some terrible questions had to be asked, and Lita knew it . . .

CHAPTER ELEVEN

The heavy town house door clicked shut. Keith dropped Lita's luggage onto the floor and pulled her into his arms.

She felt the heat rising from his body. Her heart pounded in expectation, and her lips began to tingle in anticipation as he bent his face closer to hers. Storm black eyes were smoldering down at her as his breath brushed tantalizingly across her mouth.

"I'm glad you're back," he muttered huskily as his hands felt the silkiness of her hair and the petal soft texture of her face and neck.

Lita half closed her eyes in rapture as he searched the folds of material, pulling and releasing the necessary parts to give his hands access to her warm, eager skin. Everywhere he touched her she felt alive. Ecstatically, wonderfully alive.

She slid her arms around his solid waist, lingering over the hard masculine contours of his ribs and hips. When his mouth finally came down hard and hungry on hers, she was more than ready for him.

"So am I," she murmured unsteadily as their lips came together. "I missed you." The admission was wrung from her unwilling lips before she could hold it back.

His arms tightened and he pulled her off the floor, holding her up against him. The groan of pleasure deep in his chest made her glad she'd let him know. He slipped an arm under her legs and carried her to the bedroom as he nuzzled her throat provocatively. His black hair slipped through her fingers as she cradled his head in her hands and pulled his mouth back to hers.

Keith's hands traveled over her urgently, loosening her jacket and slipping it from her shoulders, quickly sliding the zipper down her skirt. As each filmy barrier fell away, Lita lost a little of her carefully practiced reserve.

She didn't want any barriers between them. She wanted to belong to him. She wanted him to belong to her. She wanted them to be one in body and in spirit.

A few moments later they were sprawled together on the bed. Keith had shed his jacket and Lita's remaining clothes, but he had lingered over her before going on to remove the rest of his own. His teasing mouth found first one breast, then the other.

"Yes, yes," Lita cried softly, arching her back. His rough, wet tongue was drawing circle after circle of pleasure around the tip of each nipple.

He felt her bare thighs embrace him, and he knew he had to get out of his clothes in a hurry. "Wait," he whispered raggedly, reaching between them to unzip his pants.

But Lita was on fire for him and she wouldn't wait. She slid her hands up under his shirt, raking her nails softly over his back like an eager cat. At the same time, she clenched her legs against the back of his thighs, pulling his hardness against her aching warmth that needed him so desperately. She moved against him in urgently demanding rhythms that catapulted his overheated body into an uncontrollable state.

He gave one violent jerk, freeing his straining flesh from his now-unzipped trousers, and they became one. His arms closed around her back and he pulled her up against his chest, her straining nipples pressing into him through the fine cloth shirt sticking to his dampened chest. He captured her mouth with his as his thrusts became harder and harder, ravaging her with passion. Her eager, wild responses spurred him unmercifully, and he cried out in hoarse protest when the avalanche convulsed them too soon. Afterward, satiated, they lay entwined in a damp, panting tangle.

Weakly Lita ran her affectionate hands down his back, from his shirted shoulders to his still-trousered buttocks. She couldn't help it. She began to giggle.

"What's so funny?" Keith demanded with mock warning. He was enjoying resting his head against her soft naked shoulder and was not about to rouse himself just yet.

"You shouldn't have worn so much clothing to pick me up," she teased, feeling blissfully content. She smiled tenderly against his cheek as she hugged him to her. She felt his ribcage expand and contract as he sighed in resignation.

"Yeah," he agreed, rolling to his side and rearranging his clothing a little more modestly, "I had no idea you'd be in such a hurry that you wouldn't even bother to tear my clothes off," he explained, managing to look astonished at the turn of events.

"Oh!" Lita shrieked, laughing as she sailed a pillow into him.

"Hey! I'm a clean-cut fellow, lady!" he protested, pushing away her gentle projectile with one hand and throwing himself on top of her to prevent any further aggression on her part. He grasped her wrists and held them over her head, staring down at her critically. "I don't go in for any violence in bed," he said severely.

Lita's lips curved impishly and her eyes sparkled seductively. "You could have fooled me," she gently taunted.

His eyes darkened and he bent his lips to the soft skin of her throat. "That wasn't violence," he muttered. "That was being excited beyond human endurance." He kissed her with gentle, lingering kisses then, temporarily putting an end to further conversation.

"Mmm," she replied dubiously as he released her arms and she lovingly slid them back around his neck.

The second time, they managed to get Keith's clothes off. They also managed to take precautions.

"Don't worry about it," she said softly as he returned to the bed after a visit to the bathroom.

The bed sagged under his weight as he lay down next to her. He closed his eyes as if to shut out the names he was calling himself. "What do you mean, 'don't worry'? What if you end up pregnant? What then?"

Lita rolled over on her side and pressed her body against his in a gesture of comfort. She placed one arm protectively across his naked stomach and snuggled against his shoulder. "The odds are against it," she said softly.

He laughed cynically and, sighing, slid an arm around her bare shoulders to hold her protectively. "We'll see," he murmured noncommittally as he brushed a kiss against her damp forehead.

He'd been very careful the last time. There'd been no slipups. And he was very good at it, she'd recalled afterward. He'd protected them from any unplanned complications without interrupting their lovemaking. That had been a little depressing, in a way. She'd wished subconsciously at the time that he had lost a little more of his control than that.

This time, her every desire had been fulfilled. And she was very happy. If she were pregnant . . . She mentally shook her thoughts away from that line of reasoning. It was the wrong time of the month for something like that to happen. She kissed him reassuringly. "It'll be all right, Keith," she assured him softly.

He closed his eyes and exhaled slowly. He'd never

done that. Even as a teenager—even that first time—he'd always taken the few seconds to apply some protection. It was out of character for him to act like he had with her. But then, it had been Lita . . . Beautiful, sun-kissed Lita whose sexy voice, sensuous lyrics, and curvaceous body had been driving him to distraction ever since they'd met.

Maybe he'd wanted nothing between them, he thought with a jolt. Maybe it hadn't been just the all-consuming fires of passion, the loss of control when she'd started teasing him like a fantasy from a dream, he thought. Something in him had wanted to make her his. Completely, utterly his.

How could he tell her that? He didn't have the nerve to. Tough, steely nerved Keith Christophe didn't have the guts to tell her, he privately acknowledged. What was happening to him?

Lita wondered what he was thinking, but she was afraid to ask. What if he told her something she didn't want to hear? Especially after they'd gotten so carried away . . . She didn't want to think about it. It was becoming a dismal train of thought, and she wanted to enjoy her time with him.

Since his eyes were closed, she decided to take the opportunity to look at him. He was stretched out, still naked from head to toe, completely at her service—insofar as looking was concerned!

Her eyes had traveled all the way down his impressive physique once and were halfway back up again when she sensed his eyes weren't closed any longer. Her gaze flew to his face, and a dark coral stained her cheekbones as she saw he had indeed caught her admiring him.

"Look all you like," he told her in amusement, "as long as I can do the same, of course."

She laughed softly and ran a loving hand over the soft pattern of dark hair that curled lightly across his well-muscled chest. Here and there, a scar cut across it and a pale line showed bare skin. "How did you get these?" she asked curiously.

He shrugged as if it didn't matter. "They're diplomas from the School of Hard Knocks," he replied easily, enjoying watching her look at him. Her intense, open curiosity and tender appreciation warmed his soul. And his soul had felt cold for many, many years now.

She gave him a jaundiced look. "What kind of an answer is that?" she asked, giving his solid ribcage a healthy push with the heel of her hand. "Come on, Keith. Please. I'd like to know."

He was giving her that amused look again, and she was afraid he'd make up some silly answer just to put her off. So she decided to take a guess. She ran a slender fingertip gently down the longest scar. It ran from his breastbone across the front left side of his chest, coming to an abrupt stop in a gash just below the ribs. She looked up at him under long, sooty lashes. "This looks like a knife wound," she said after a moment's hesitation, raising her graceful brows as she silently sought his confirmation or denial.

He looked at her for a long, awkwardly silent moment. When she held his gaze without flinching, he relented. "Yeah, a little emergency surgery in a back alley one day."

"It looks like you had more than one visit to that clinic," she pointed out softly, tracing the other scars with her fingertip, one at a time.

He captured her hand and brought it to his mouth, stilling its questing with a tender kiss on her palm. "Yeah," he said unemotionally, "I had lousy surgeons. They wanted to keep at it til they got it right. A persistent bunch of hacks." He turned his head to see her better. Gently he touched her cheek with his hand. "You don't want to hear about it, Lita."

She shook her head stubbornly. "That's where you're wrong, Keith Christophe. I want to know all about you. That includes what's happened to make you the man you are."

He blinked as if touched by her sincerity. The intense, honest caring in her eyes was proving very hard for him to resist. "You melt my insides, damn it," he muttered, fighting the temptation to let her into his past.

"Is that so awful?" she asked tentatively.

He saw the doubt flickering in her eyes and his heart twisted. "Hell, yes," he groaned as he pulled her close, holding her head against his shoulder possessively. "No one's ever done that before. I don't know what to do about it. It's a damned perplexing problem!"

Lita smiled happily at his reluctant confession and wrapped her arms around him in a burst of joy. "Sorry," she murmured unrepentantly.

He laughed at her obvious lie. "I can see that," he retorted sarcastically, smacking her playfully on the bottom in punishment.

That confession was one small nick in his armor, she thought triumphantly. In time, she might get through the rest . . . She pulled away from him, nestling in the crook of his arm where she could still get a view of his face. "Fallon told me you grew up together," she said, treading cautiously since she was unsure of Keith's reaction.

His profile was uncommunicative, as was his tone of voice when he replied. "We were born grown up," he fenced.

"He said you spent a lot of time fighting kids who were picking on you because of your mother," she went on softly.

"Fallon talks too much," Keith muttered.

"Is that where the knife fights came in?"

She wasn't prying out of some kind of prurient interest,

202

and Keith had been around enough to realize it. It was just that he wasn't used to letting his personal life be a topic of conversation. But why was it that he didn't feel his usual instinctive wall going up with Lita? Maybe it was because he was stripped bare and too exhausted and relaxed to bother with the castle walls, he mused. The corners of his mouth curved the tiniest bit in humor. No. It wasn't just because he was as naked as a jaybird. It was because he was willing to have her be close to more than just his naked flesh.

"You're a persistent wench," he said, giving her a glance of amusement. "But in answer to your question, no. They involved a little territorial dispute with a local gang when I was fifteen."

"You were in a gang?" she asked in surprise. She thought of him as a loner.

But Keith was shaking his head. "No. That was part of the problem, though. They didn't think I should walk down their streets without a pass from them. Either get a pass or join the gang, they said. I told them where they could stuff both of those ideas, and they were distinctly lacking in a sense of humor about it."

"How many fights were there?" she asked. She was surprised at the cool sensation of fear that gripped her stomach just thinking about the danger he'd been in all those years ago.

He shrugged dismissingly. "I've forgotten. More than one," he conceded. "They finally decided it wasn't worth it and ditched the pass system altogether. They switched to riding motorcycles around the Virginia countryside instead." He stretched and yawned, then pulled Lita on top of him before she realized what he had in mind. "Now that I've answered all your questions, how about answering one of mine?"

"Sure." Lita felt herself falling into that unseen aura that seemed to surround him. There was something so

203

comforting, so deeply satisfying about being with him like this. She wished it could go on forever.

He was smiling slightly, but his dark eyes were serious. "Don't you even want to know what I'll ask first?" he teased her, searching her eyes as if he would see her soul there.

Warm and secure against his warm, strong chest, she sighed, then said, "No. Ask away."

She was so trusting, he thought. It reminded him once again how seldom anyone had extended that kind of trust. "How long are you staying this time?" he asked.

His voice had been a study in neutrality, but he was lying very still. Since they were in complete contact, Lita found it easy to sense that slight increase in tension in his body. "I don't know," she answered, shutting her eyes and savoring the feel of him against her. She wanted to memorize it, to imprint the sensation of it on her memory forever. "I'm my own woman. I can pretty much come and go as I please."

His lips brushed her ear in a whispery kiss, and his hands traveled slowly up over the satiny curves of her hip and back. "And what do you want now, Lita Winslow?" he asked huskily.

"To stay . . . with . . . you . . ." she struggled to reply between kisses as his hungry mouth once again found hers.

Their arms tightened into a serious preliminary to more lovemaking when the jarring sound of a ringing phone interrupted them.

Amid Keith's sharp protests, Lita scrambled off his aroused body and raced to the phone to stop the incessant shrilling. "Hello?" she said breathlessly.

"Lita? You back?" It was Pete Fallon. "Glad I caught you."

Lita grimaced and raised her eyes to the ceiling at his

embarrassingly accurate choice of words. "What can I do for you, Lieutenant?" she inquired as politely as possible.

Keith, having pulled on his trousers, joined her. When he heard what she said, he sat on the arm of a nearby wing chair and handed her his shirt. Lita gratefully shrugged into it. She had felt distinctly exposed standing in the middle of the room talking on the phone in the buff. The fact that Keith was half dressed had only exacerbated her discomfort.

"I'd like to talk to you about your cousin's death," he explained.

That jerked Lita completely out of her romantic euphoria, and she came crashing back into life's very unpleasant realities. If it weren't for Melanie's death, she wouldn't even be here, she thought. A nauseating wave of guilt rocked her. She forced herself to hang on to the rock until the sensation passed. Unbidden, the memories murmured softly in her head, the soft lilt of Melanie's voice, odd glimpses of their shared girlhood, the silly games they'd played as children.

"Of course," Lita said, somewhat shaken by the strong flush of grief.

"Why don't I drop by in, say, half an hour?" he suggested.

"Half an hour?" she echoed, glancing at Keith to see if he had a problem with that.

He nodded. It was all right with him. Not that he looked particularly thrilled about it, of course.

"Fine. I'll expect you then."

The detective cleared his throat. "Uh . . . I'd like to talk to you alone," he added awkwardly.

"Alone?" she repeated for Keith's benefit. His eyebrows lifted, but he tilted his head, acknowledging that he'd cooperate.

"I just thought you might be seeing Keith," Fallon

explained with an endearingly old-fashioned tone of reticence. "Sorry."

"That's very perceptive, Pete. You don't have to apologize. He's agreed to leave," she dryly assured him. Maybe the man could see through telephones, she thought, suppressing the urge to laugh.

"Yeah, well, tell him it won't take long. I don't want him leaning on me because I'm interfering with his plans," Fallon protested with mock alarm.

"I'll tell him," she promised with a grin. "Bye." Fallon really did care about his old friend, she thought, even if he was laying it on a little thick with that crack about not interfering with Keith's personal life! Lita doubted that Fallon would hesitate to interfere if he thought Keith had broken any laws.

She wandered back into the bedroom and found Keith sitting on the bed and putting on his shoes. He stood up and ran his hands through his tousled hair. It was then she realized he was wearing a T-shirt, since she was still wearing his shirt. She quickly slipped out of it and into her robe.

"This wasn't exactly how I'd envisioned the rest of the day," he said ruefully as he pulled on his shirt and buttoned it up. "How about if I call you in a couple of hours and see if we can't salvage the day after Fallon has left?" he suggested.

She watched in fascination as he tucked in his shirttails and fastened his belt. There was something about watching Keith Christophe get dressed that was absolutely riveting. "Hmm, sure . . ." she murmured.

He chuckled and grabbed her in a tight embrace. "If you keep looking at me like that, Pete's going to be surprised at what he finds when he gets here, believe you me," he threatened her with a gleam in his eyes.

Lita grimaced and saucily looped her arms around his neck. "Yeah. You're right. So go. Go!"

He kissed her until her lips were tingling for more. Then abruptly he released her and gently pulled her arms down. "I'll call you," he promised. His voice was warm with expectation.

Then he was gone.

"So, how was California?" Pete Fallon was asking half an hour later as he shifted awkwardly from one tired foot to the other in the middle of Lita's living room.

Lita, still brushing her hair and freshly showered, waved him toward the couch and the chairs. "Please, Pete, sit down."

He settled on the Queen Anne chair. It looked stiff enough that he figured he wouldn't forget this was business, not a social visit. Looking at the clean-scrubbed beauty in her slacks and lightweight cowl-necked sweater, it was easy to forget.

Her bare feet peeked out gracefully as she paced across the floor to put the brush in the other room.

It didn't take great detective skills to guess that she'd had a midday tryst with his old buddy Keith. Besides the oddly timed shower, there was the telltale glow of her skin and that sparkle in her eyes, both of which became even more noticeable when Keith's name had been mentioned. She wasn't trying to hide the fact, he decided. She was honest about it. Discreet and polite—but honest.

Fallon sighed inaudibly. Keith deserved a girl like that, and she deserved a tough, strong man like Keith. Fallon just hoped that the facts of Melanie's death didn't end up destroying the beautiful music that these two could undoubtedly make together. Right now, he wouldn't care to place a bet on whether they'd get the chance. Frankly he didn't think that things looked very good for them. As a matter of fact, they looked downright bad.

Things looked bad because one's personal loyalties couldn't be ignored, not even in a love affair. And where

207

love was concerned, blood was almost always thicker than water, in Fallon's experience. Keith and Lita might want each other, but how would they feel when they had to choose between their own feelings and their loyalty to their own families? That, as far as Fallon was concerned, was going to be the rub.

Lita returned, sat on the couch, and curled her legs comfortably under her, waiting for the detective to explain the reason for his visit. "Have you found anything new? Any new leads or evidence or anything?" she asked hopefully.

Fallon shook his head. "Not anything new," he said, choosing his words carefully. Then he recalled that to Lita some of it would seem new since she hadn't been privy to the details of the investigation. "Well . . . not new to us," he qualified, clearing his throat. "Although we have fleshed out a few facts here and there, and we've got a pretty fair picture of how your cousin spent the last day and night of her life," he explained as sympathetically as he could.

Lita sat motionless. "Could you tell me what you know so far?" she pleaded, leaning toward him in an unconscious gesture of appeal. "Please, Pete . . ."

He licked his lips and lowered his eyes. He'd expected her to ask and he'd rehearsed his answer. That was part of his lead-in to the questions he wanted to ask her. He just hadn't counted on feeling so sorry for the girl, he realized uncomfortably. She really could tug at a man, he thought. She really could. "As far as we know, she slept late that day. She appears to have left the house for the first time about noon, when she went to a Georgetown café for lunch. A boutique owner places her in a nearby shop shortly afterward, where she ordered a new dress. That dress was delivered here after Ms. King's death."

Lita recalled the box, which the police had opened during their first visit after Melanie's body had been discovered. She hadn't given it any thought at the time. Of course, she hadn't given much thought to any of the things they were looking at. She'd found it painful to watch them going through Melanie's things. It was such a personal invasion, even though Lita knew it was necessary. Lita had answered their questions as best she could, but she'd felt like a stranger answering from some distant planet. Only the shell of her body was sitting in the bustling roomful of investigators.

"Yes," she murmured. It was a little easier to talk about it now. Time was already healing the wound that Melanie's death had made. Now Lita could really take in what was being said.

The detective cupped his hands, his fingertips touching like a bridge, and continued his explanation. "She caught a cab and arrived at the club, where she greeted the regulars and took part in her scheduled rehearsal. There was an argument that day. Apparently it was not the first. It involved Ms. King, Sean Christophe, and Keith Christophe." If he expected much of a reaction from her, he was disappointed. She was staring at him with the steady, wide-eyed stare of a young woman waiting for the rest of a dreaded story. It wasn't the look of a woman suddenly disillusioned about the men she knew. Fallon slowly tapped his fingertips together. "That doesn't come as a surprise to you?" he asked curiously.

Lita looked momentarily confused. "I didn't know they'd argued, if that's what you're wondering," she replied, wondering what lay beneath his simple question. "Should I be surprised?" she asked, cocking her head to one side. "After all, people do argue. All the time. Was there something special about the disagreements? Something that makes them stand out from the usual disagreements people have?"

He shrugged and his face wrinkled into a deprecating smile. "I dunno," he admitted. "I heard they were argu-

209

ing that night about the same thing they had had words over several times in recent weeks—namely, whether Melanie was enjoying life a little too much with Sean and running the risk of getting herself into a jam. You've seen Sean snipe at Keith, and you've seen how Keith runs Sydney's and everything in it—with a steel fist. Add to that your cousin Melanie's personal problems and her tendency to . . ."

Lita knew instinctively that he was searching for polite words. "Her tendency to flirt?" Lita supplied sadly, having long ago accepted that *flirting* didn't begin to cover Melanie's activities and intentions regarding the opposite sex.

Fallon politely accepted the description. "Yes. Her tendency to flirt. To chase men." Beneath his relaxed, slightly embarrassed facade, his savvy eyes fastened on her. "Do you think she could have been flirting with Sean and Keith at the same time? Playing them off against each other? Trying to make one, or both, jealous?"

Lita wanted to protest that that was absurd. She wanted to laugh and tell him no such thing could have been going on. But her mouth was dry and no words came. All she could think of was Melanie's letter—and her thrill at having made "her Greek" jealous. Which Greek? Lita wondered as doubts lacerated her. Which Greek? "I don't know, Pete," she hedged, biting her lower lip in worry. "She seemed to be addicted to men, desperate for a romantic fling every so often to keep her spirits high. She did enjoy the idea that she could make a man jealous. That added to her feeling that she was wanted by him. But of course, since I wasn't here, I don't know what was going on."

She'd been straight with him. She'd wanted to be. But she hadn't told him everything, and she felt guilty about that. If he knew she'd received that letter, he'd want to see it, she was sure. But then, he might misconstrue it.

The words didn't point any real fingers, except for the possibility that there was a third man, of course. "Pete," she began, deciding to tell him about Melanie's letter.

His pager began sounding and he regretfully excused himself to use her phone. After a few curt words to the dispatcher at the other end, he walked quickly through the living room and opened the door. "Sorry," he said apologetically. "Got another case to tend, I'm afraid. When it rains, it pours," he complained good-naturedly.

"But—" she said, following him as he left.

"I'll be in touch. Got a few more things I need to ask you." He was fumbling in the pockets of his wrinkled tan raincoat. Lita had the feeling he wasn't hearing her efforts to get through to him. He grinned as the jingling keys emerged from one tattered pocket seconds later. "And I'll let you know the moment we think we've cracked this one," he was saying in a voice fading away like a man whose thoughts had already left the scene, preceding the rest of him.

"Pete, I got a letter . . ."

The slam of the door of Fallon's unmarked sedan drowned out her voice. The roar of his engine doomed any further effort to relay the news to him.

Lita smiled despondently and waved half heartedly as he pulled away from the curb. His visit had been very unsettling. The cement suddenly felt very cold and hard against her bare feet. Just like the city, she thought. A person could die, and no one would care. I care, she argued back as she trotted inside and waited for Keith to call. And I think Keith does, too.

She fought off a growing sense of fear about Keith's relationship to Melanie. He couldn't be involved in Melanie's death. Lita just couldn't believe her instincts about him could be so wrong. For she surely wouldn't be sleeping with a man who'd directly or indirectly been responsible for her cousin's death!

Stubbornly she kept a stiff, defiant vigil. But the doubts whispered in her ear, all the same. Driving her closer to the distant edge of despair.

CHAPTER TWELVE

The telephone jangled and Lita sprang to her feet.

It was Keith.

"Did Fallon have anything new to report?" he asked a few moments into their conversation.

Lita wound the cord nervously around one forefinger. "Not really. They're still working on it, though. He had to leave before we could finish talking. Something about another case needing his attention."

"That sounds like Fallon," Keith commented wryly. "Could you hold on a minute?" He covered the phone with his hand, but Lita could hear muffled voices. "I'm sorry," he said only a few moments later. "That was Marty. There's a problem with one of our licensing agreements, and the attorney is on the other line. I'm going to have to talk to him."

"That's okay," she said softly. It wasn't. She wanted desperately to talk to him about the night of Melanie's death. She needed to know he wasn't involved in any way. Now, however, was obviously not the time to try to get into that. "I understand."

He muttered something under his breath that she couldn't quite make out. Then he asked, "How about having dinner with me tonight here at Sydney's?"

Lita had been hoping for more privacy, but as soon as he said it she realized that the club would be the perfect spot. There were a few other people she wanted to talk to again, and they all could be found in Keith's nightclub. "I can't think of anything I'd rather do, or anyone I'd rather do it with," she said huskily.

His soft laugh sent a shimmer of longing through her. She could imagine what he was doing as clearly as if she were standing in his office. He'd be leaning back in his well-padded swivel chair behind that broad desk he used like a battleship, a satisfied glint in his eyes.

"You are one provocative woman," he pointed out in a voice roughened by his feelings on the matter. "I only regret I'm not in a position to do anything about that right now. But later . . ."

"Later," she echoed as he said good-bye and hung up. Later. He had said it as a promise. "It's all going to work out in the end," she swore under her breath in an effort to buck up her sagging spirits. And that was a promise as well. One she was making to herself.

Lita drifted into the bedroom and began unpacking. She'd tossed her luggage into a corner after Keith had left and pulled out the clothes she'd donned after her shower, but everything else had been left in her bags.

It was when she opened the closet that the idea came to her. She'd just hung up an elegant sheath and was smoothing it out when her fingers brushed the glossy black cardboard box. Lita glanced down and saw the boutique's name scrawled in big gold letters across the length of it. "The boutique," she mused aloud as the idea formed and then took root. "I wonder if the owner knew why Melanie bought it, or what mood Melanie was in?" Anything to give her a hint about Melanie's personal life just before her death. Perhaps there would be a clue about the identity of the third man Melanie seemed to be alluding to.

Lita dragged the box out of the closet and laid it on top of the cedar chest at the foot of the bed. She lifted the lid and dropped it to one side, curious to see the dress Melanie had bought. The moment her fingers touched the material, she knew it was expensive. It was an original from the spring collection of a small but well-respected European designer.

"After the wardrobe you bought for the tour, why this?" Lita asked. She'd seen Melanie's clothes. The girl, clothes-horse though she may have been, did not need another dress! "How much did you pay for this?" Lita mumbled, searching for a bill of sale in the folds of the knee-length evening dress. There was no bill to be found. "A trip to the boutique manager will put my galloping imagination to rest!" Lita assured herself as she carefully returned the dress to its place in the box and began searching for her shoes.

The boutique manager failed to slow down Lita's runaway imagination. Even worse, she laid sharp spurs into it in the form of a tantalizing new piece of information.

"A man bought the dress for her?" Lita asked, stunned at the totally unexpected news. Pete had said nothing about that, she recalled in surprise. "Who was he?"

The middle-aged manager of the small dress shop was impeccably groomed and beautifully made up. From her neatly coiffured hair to her perfectly matched and stylishly polished nails, she was clearly a woman of breeding as well as commerce. Because discretion was a valuable commodity in society as well as in business, she politely raised a meticulously arched brow and withdrew from the friendly chat they'd been having. "We don't discuss our clients," she said in a regretful tone intended to soothe any irritation her lack of cooperation might produce in her listener. "I do hope you understand . . ."

Lita caught her lower lip between her teeth and tried to think of a ploy to get the woman to make an exception. "I do understand . . ."

As Lita spoke, a speculative look gathered on the

215

lady's porcelain face. Then it turned to one of astonished recognition. "You know," she interrupted genteelly, "you look just like Lita Winslow."

Maybe that would soften her heart, Lita thought as hope began to flicker anew. She hadn't introduced herself yet. She'd merely said she was inquiring about the dress her cousin had bought. Lita gave the woman a small smile. "I'm afraid there's a very simple reason for that . . ."

The manager's eyes lighted up in triumph, and she wagged a sharp-nailed finger enthusiastically in Lita's general direction. "You *are* Lita Winslow!" she exclaimed, her excitement making her latent southern drawl more noticeable.

"I'm afraid so," Lita admitted, hoping the lady was a fan and not a critic of her work. A fan might be sympathetic—a critic, well . . . Lita held her breath.

"I just love your songs. Every last one of them. And I was so excited to hear you were performing again. I wonder, would you give me your autograph?"

Lita let out her breath with a sigh of relief and cheerfully wrote her name across the blank gift card the woman had held out to her. "Of course," she murmured. "I'm glad you've enjoyed my music."

"My favorite is 'Adieu,' " she hurried on enthusiastically, "but then, I loved—"

As she began naming several others, Lita returned the pen and the autograph and listened with polite interest. Finally she had a chance to get back to the subject that she wanted to discuss. "I felt the same way about that song, myself." She paused and moved back to Melanie's boxed dress, which she'd left on the counter. "I do want to thank you for telling me what you could about Melanie's purchase. It means a lot to me, trying to find out who was responsible for her death."

If cold water had suddenly been poured over her head,

the poor manager couldn't have looked more stricken. "Oh, my dear, that's right. She'd be your cousin, wouldn't she? I mean, naturally the police told me that she had died, and since I'd read about it in the paper, as soon as I saw the name I knew it was the same young woman who had been here . . ." She seemed to be wrestling with something. The struggle brought her flow of words to a trickling halt.

You're trying to decide whether to give me what I want, aren't you, Lita guessed silently. Maybe I can give you a little shove in the right direction . . . Lita looked down sadly at the box. "She was a wonderful girl, and she was at the brink of a great career. We grew up together, you know."

"No. I didn't know," murmured the older woman sympathetically.

"And I just can't imagine what possessed her to go down to the canal or the riverfront area in the dead of night. Someone she knew must have taken her there."

The woman leaned forward, distraught. "And you think the man who bought the dress for her may have been involved?" she asked in a hushed, horrified voice.

"Well," Lita shrugged, "I don't know. I'm not a detective, of course. But it obviously interests the police. And no one has stepped forward to admit the purchase, apparently." Lita let the bait dangle in front of her.

The woman blinked uncertainly. "Well, it does seem odd." Then her cheeks rosied. "The police asked the same question you did. About the man's identity, I mean. I had to tell them, of course. But as a rule, we do maintain the confidentiality of our clientele. After all, some of them are in the public eye and value the discretion of the merchants who sell to them," she pointed out diffidently.

"Yes, of course," Lita soothed. Come on! she was screaming all the while inside. His name! His name!

The woman looked a little embarrassed. "In this case,

it probably doesn't matter much. You see, he paid in cash. And, um"—she cleared her throat uncomfortably —"she called him Mr. Wills. Naturally, I thought it odd that she'd call him 'mister' since she threw her arms around his neck to kiss him in thanks when he paid."

Lita was stunned. Wills? Who could that be? And paying in cash? "Yes," Lita murmured distractedly, "that would be confusing. Uh, isn't that unusual—paying in cash for such an expensive item?"

The woman lowered her lashes and produced a knowing, world-weary smile. "Not really. In this town, men do it all the time. It leaves fewer trails for their wives to follow. And throwing around large amounts of cash apparently makes some of them feel big and successful. As a matter of fact, this was really a rather modest purchase in the designer dress class. The price was only"—she wrinkled her brow trying to recall the figure she'd given the police—"three hundred and fifty dollars."

"I see." Lita leaned forward. "Could you describe the man?"

The woman was completely sympathetic, now that she'd finally decided to let the cat out of the bag. "I'll tell you what I told the police. He was about five feet eleven or so . . . average build . . . dark hair . . . reasonably good-looking, I guess. I didn't get a good look at his face, though. He was wearing dark glasses and always turned away. He had on a standard kind of tan raincoat, so I didn't notice his clothes. I remembered him because he was so obviously trying not to be recognized! I actually laughed after they'd left! Compared to some of the people who do that kind of thing all the time, they were like a couple of kids!"

A couple of kids. That was a curious description, Lita thought. She could not imagine Keith's doing anything as silly as that. He wasn't the silly type! Sean . . . perhaps. She could imagine his doing something like that as a joke, or as a way of trying to put something over on his older brother. It was possible that the mysterious Mr. Wills had been Sean, but Lita's gut instinct said no. Perhaps she had stumbled on to the third man. "Thanks!" she said enthusiastically, reaching out to squeeze the woman's hand. "You've been very helpful."

Lita dashed out of the store as the manager, her vivid red mouth agape and her recently squeezed hand still in midair, watched her go in amazement. "Come again," she heard herself automatically call out over the merry tinkle of the bells on the closing door.

Lita didn't hear. She was already thinking hard and fast about what to do next. Somehow she had to find a way to identify the mysterious Mr. Wills. She was beginning to think that he was the missing link to the rest of the puzzle. If only she could find him . . .

"Lita?"

She had been halfway through the door when she'd heard the phone ring. She'd run through the town house to lift the receiver before the caller gave up. When she realized who it was, she slumped against the wall and let the box containing Melanie's dress slide to the floor.

"Hi, Jack." It was pretty anticlimactic. She'd been secretly hoping it was Keith. She'd known Jack for too many years to worry about masking her sense of disappointment.

"Sounds like you were expecting someone else," he said.

There was just a touch of dry humor in the way he said it. Even so, he sounded like the ghost of the Jack Connery she'd known for a decade.

"Sorry, Jack," she apologized. She leaned her head against the wall and closed her eyes, trying to rest while she had a chance. She was planning a long evening, if things went well.

Jack didn't answer at first, as if he were trying to decide what to make of her comments. He cleared his throat. It was a nervous habit he'd had forever. "Anybody in particular?" he inquired curiously.

Lita smiled a secret smile that felt a mile deep. Yes. You'd definitely have to call Keith Christophe someone in particular. There was nothing routine, general, or run-of-the-mill about him. After they made him, they'd broken the mold. "Yes," she replied, "Keith Christophe." The silence this time seemed quieter than the first, she thought. She told herself it was just her overactive imagination, but it was as if he were shocked by her answer.

"Christophe . . ." the agent mused. "From the dreamy smile I hear in your voice, I take it you're not just waiting for a business conversation?"

Lita grinned. "You always were perceptive, Jack," she retorted teasingly.

"I see. Then I don't suppose I could talk you into having dinner with me tonight?" he asked sadly.

Lita's heart went out to him. Poor, loyal, faithful Jack. He was really suffering. "I can't," she said regretfully. "I'm sorry, Jack. I've already made a commitment for this evening. Are you going to be in town?"

"Yeah. I'm flying down on the shuttle from New York. I'm at the airport already, as a matter of fact."

"Could we do it tomorrow?" she offered. "I'd love to see you, Jack. We need to talk . . ." Sometimes the best way to grieve for a dead loved one was to reminisce with someone else who loved that person, too. "I think it would do us both some good," she added softly.

"Yeah. You're probably right, Lita."

He sounded very old and very tired as he said it. He sounded like a man who had no hope that his torture would have an end in this life, she thought. "How about dinner here?" she suggested. "I'll even cook!" she offered, as if that were the ultimate enticement.

220

He laughed shortly. It wasn't a happy laugh. "Fine, Lita. See you then."

"Great."

"Uh, Lita?"

"Yes?"

"Have they . . . Did they . . . Is there any more news about her?" He couldn't say the merciless words.

"No. But they're still working hard. And so am I."

"What?" This time his voice sounded harder and startled.

"I'll tell you all about it when I see you tomorrow night," she promised. She opened her eyes and glanced at her wristwatch. The time made her scramble to her feet. "Look, Jack, I'm sorry, but I've really got to run. See you tomorrow. Okay?"

"Lita!" he practically shouted over the phone. "Don't go digging around! Let the police handle this!"

"We'll talk tomorrow," she promised him. "Gotta go. Bye Jack!"

"Lita!"

She figured the only way to put his arguing to an end was to hang up. So she did. Time to move on to the rest of the evening!

The mood at Sydney's was subdued and intimate.

The band was still scattered to the four corners of the earth, and a well-known jazz pianist was playing soft, evocative melodies on the baby grand. The tables were brimming with silver lamé and coral silk, velvet dinner jackets, and subtle laughter.

Lita followed the pressure of Keith's hand on her back and made her way to a corner table obscured from view by a careful arrangement of three graceful pieces of modern sculpture.

"Isn't this new?" she asked in surprise as she admired the abstract forms in cool white marble.

221

"Yes," Keith replied as he pulled a chair next to hers and sat down. "Sydney's complained for years that the club should have some more private tables. I finally got tired of listening to her point that out."

"They're lovely," Lita said sincerely. "They remind me of Greek statues."

Keith gave her a wicked grin. "That's good. That's exactly what they are. Nude women in an abstract style by a middle-aged Greek sculptor. When he heard I was in the market for some art to serve as a screen, he got in touch with me."

A waiter arrived at their side and attentively took down their order. When he'd gone, Keith rested his arm behind Lita's chair and gave her that faint, heart-wrenching smile she loved.

"In a club named in honor of burlesque queen Sydney Keith, statues of discreetly nude women seemed appropriate," he said wryly.

Lita gazed at him with tender concern. "Has it gotten easier over the years?" she asked gently.

He let a soft strand of her dark hair brush his fingertips. "Yeah. You grow up. You stop trying to make the world something it isn't. You stop hitting your head against a stone wall and start concentrating on working around life's immovable objects instead." He let his gaze wander over her pure and classically lovely features, the half smile still playing gently on his lips. "About the time I was sixteen, I finally realized that it would make more sense to accept it, whether I liked it or not. My mother was a stripper. She was good at it. It made her rich. Those were the facts. Once I stopped trying to twist reality to suit myself, things were a lot easier."

Things were a lot easier . . . She kept hearing his words reverberate in her mind. And yet there had been an undertone of cynical defeat, she thought. The muffled, angry cry of a boy still hurting because the first, dearest

222

person in his young life had been the subject of ridicule. Some wounds go so deeply into the soul of a child that they last a lifetime.

Lita could understand that. She'd had to make her own rationales as a kid. You're the daughter of an actress. Why does she kiss those other men in the movies? Where is your daddy? Why doesn't he live with you? You must think you're better than us . . . The taunting had seemed unrelenting at first.

"Easier?" she murmured, thinking of the hardening his experiences had forced on him. "It sounds more like reality stayed the way it always had been, but you pulled away from it. It didn't get any easier, but you became tougher."

He shrugged. "Maybe," he conceded. "Maybe we're saying the same thing in slightly different ways."

He'd never talked to anyone about this. Not even Marty, Carl, Fallon, or Sean had ever heard him speak about his childhood feelings of anger, outrage, and stoicism. He was so relaxed with Lita that he didn't even feel surprise at how much of himself he was willing tc share with her. Being honest with her was becoming as natural as being honest with himself.

He leaned closer and ran his mouth softly across her ear. "Have I told you how beautiful you look tonight?" he asked huskily. His mouth provocatively brushed the satiny skin of her neck as he spoke.

"No," she whispered. The faint smile had faded now. He was completely serious. And Lita was lost in his captivating stare.

"You are very beautiful, Lita," he said, admiring her with loving eyes.

He was melting her. She felt soft and warm and willing to be molded to his will. Her independence, that thing to which she'd clung with such fierceness all these years, disappeared in the face of his warm and tender onslaught.

She had the wildest urge to throw herself into his arms and tell him she loved him.

And yet she hesitated. A tiny piece of her was afraid to follow her feelings. This "love" she felt for Keith was the passionate kind. And no doubt that would explain his feelings, as well. Yes, she tried to tell herself, their feelings were those of a sexual infatuation. That provided a wonderful foundation for a passionate love affair, but it hardly could sustain something more enduring.

Lita's thoughts brought a shadow of sadness into her velvety eyes. Keith saw it and a frown lined his brow. "Does it make you sad to hear me say I think you're beautiful?" he questioned her softly.

She managed a smile and shook her head quickly. "No. Of course not. I love to hear you say it. It makes me feel beautiful."

"Then why the sad look in your eyes?" he demanded in a low, serious voice, holding her hand as he waited for her to answer.

What could she say? I was just thinking how sad it will be when we have to say good-bye? What could a man say to something like that? Lie to her that there wouldn't be an end? Clear his throat uncomfortably and avoid the issue by changing the subject? God, she felt like a young girl again, tongue-tied and now knowing what to say or how to say it. "I was thinking of how much I missed you while I was in California," she replied, sighing. That was true, and it was also close to the real answer to his question. She'd be feeling that way again in the not-too-distant future, no doubt. She squeezed his hand. "I don't want to dampen our evening," she said on a lighter note. "Let's just concentrate on tonight."

His eyes narrowed thoughtfully and he was about to say something when the waiter arrived with the first course. "To a happy evening," he said a few minutes later as they raised their champagne in a private toast.

"To a happy evening," she returned. May it last forever, she prayed silently.

The evening certainly gave every evidence of being a very happy one, indeed. The chef had outdone himself preparing mouth-watering delicacies from around the globe that complemented one another perfectly. The piano gave just the right sultry touch to the background, and Keith was his customary charming self, serving alternately as fascinating raconteur and interested listener.

They had just finished the frothy lemon mousse when an elegant figure cut a graceful path to their table. Keith looked up and got to his feet, kissing the woman's hand politely.

"Sydney! To what do we owe this honor?" he inquired dryly, giving her a measuring look.

Sydney Keith smiled at him in wide-eyed innocence. She was regally resplendent in a clinging floor-length dress of silvery gray accented with oversized jewel earrings, necklace, and bracelets. She turned her sly gray eyes on Lita. "Why, darling, I hadn't been here in so long that I thought I'd drop in to see what I'd been missing," she purred.

"Would you care to join us?" he asked. He made the invitation with perfunctory politeness. He knew why his mother had dropped in. She wanted to see the woman in his life. For once, he didn't object.

"Of course, dear," Sydney agreed, sitting in the chair her son held out patiently for her. She settled herself comfortably and leaned forward inquisitively as Keith returned to his chair. "Now . . . will you introduce us?" she asked sweetly.

Keith bowed to convention and supplied the formal ritual. "Sydney Keith . . . Lita Winslow. Lita Winslow . . . Sydney Keith."

Lita smiled warmly. Inside that aging beauty lay a will of steel, she thought in amusement.

"I'm so glad to meet you!" Sydney exclaimed. "I've heard such nice things about you," she gushed, giving her son a sideways glance. He didn't rise to the bait by warning her not to carry tales, so she impishly added, "I've been such an admirer of your songs, my dear."

Lita caught the sly verbal teasing, but she pretended it had gone right over her head and murmured a modest thank you.

"Your music has such depth of feeling. Are you writing anything at the moment?" Sydney inquired, apparently fascinated.

"Well, yes, as a matter of fact. But it won't be finished for a while."

Lita was about to ask Sydney about herself, but before she could, Sean joined them. He looked as if someone had just hit him.

"Sorry to interrupt," he said, nodding briefly to his mother and Lita. He turned his full attention to Keith. "I've got to talk to you." This time there was no brotherly animosity, no taunting sneer in Sean's request.

Keith turned to Lita. "Would you excuse me?"

"Of course." She looked worriedly at Sean. There was something about him that made her think that the problem was a personal one. It would have to be something pretty awful for him to come to Keith for help. Sean avoided his older brother's advice and counsel like the plague.

Keith dropped the white linen napkin on the table and pushed back his chair. "I'll be back," he promised her. He dragged his eyes from Lita and shot his mother a warning look. "Don't scare her off, Sydney!"

Sydney stared at him in wide-eyed amazement. "Me?" she protested, her voice liltingly feminine.

"You," he repeated unsympathetically.

The two men left, going in the direction of the offices in the back.

Sydney leaned back in her chair and looked Lita up and down as if the lyricist were a thoroughbred that the former striptease artist was considering buying. She nodded her head approvingly. "I can see why Keith's attracted," she said bluntly.

Lita swirled her ice water in its heavy goblet and studied the woman across the table. She wasn't sure she liked Sydney's almost insultingly frank approach. Lita didn't wish to be hasty, however, so she counted to four and took a sip.

Sydney laughed. "You've got spunk enough to be irritated at that high-handed comment, don't you?" she declared, her gray eyes sparkling with good humor. "I like that," she chuckled. "Not that what I like matters, of course."

Lita smiled her professional smile. Her fur was still standing on end. Sydney might think she was sticking her nose in her son's affair, but from Lita's point of view, she was intruding in Lita's private life.

Sydney's smile softened and she leaned forward in a genuinely friendly gesture. "Do you think we could get acquainted?" the older woman asked, more diffidently. "I have a terrible habit of speaking my mind more plainly than most of the world cares to hear it, but I truly am impressed with you, my dear. And"—her face took on a secretive, knowing look—"I have the feeling we might be seeing more of each other."

Lita wasn't so sure about that, but there was a genuineness underneath Sydney's manner that softened Lita's heart. She put the goblet to one side and decided to take the woman's olive branch. "Where shall we start?"

"How about your mother?" Sydney asked, her eyes alight with enthusiasm. "I've been a tremendous fan of hers for years! Where is she and what's she been doing?"

Lita laughed. She'd been preparing herself for personal inquiries into her relationship with Keith, and the

227

woman turns out to be just like most people—one of her mother's fans!

In Keith's office the mood was quite different.

"Hell! I wish I'd never seen the girl!" Sean exploded. He ran both hands roughly through his hair as he paced back and forth across the room. "I didn't kill her! Damn it. I didn't kill her!"

Keith stood just in front of the closed door, his mouth a straight, grim line.

"Fallon can't do anything about it. The case is being handled by his boss now. He figures there could be some big headlines in it since Melanie comes from such a famous family. All he needs is the okay from the prosecutor and they're going to issue a warrant for my arrest!" Sean stopped in the middle of the elegant office. "I can't believe this is happening, Keith," he said hollowly. "I just can't believe it . . ."

Keith walked across the room and picked up the phone. He punched out a number and left a message. "Our attorney can run rings around anything the prosecutor cares to try," he assured his brother. His voice was granite hard. Sean clung to it like a haven in a storm. "They don't have a case, and leaving it dangling like a knife over your head isn't going to make it any stronger. They're just hoping if you're guilty that the pressure will scare you into doing something foolish. Like running, for example."

Sean watched with hollow eyes. He'd never been in this kind of a spot. Being suspected of murdering a young woman. It was almost enough to make him sick to his stomach. "I've done some stupid things, Keith," he confessed tiredly, "but I've never come close to doing anything like that."

Keith walked closer to his brother and clapped his arm

supportively around his shoulder. "I know, Sean. I know."

Sean threw his arm around his brother in a hard, awkward embrace. A tear threatened and he pulled back, quickly brushing it away. "I wish I knew some Greek," he muttered. "It always sounds like you and Dad are saying something really tough when you swear in Greek."

Keith laughed. "It's never too late to learn."

CHAPTER THIRTEEN

Lita was laughing so hard she thought her seams might burst.

For nearly half an hour Sydney had been regaling her with hilarious, ribald stories of life backstage at a strip-tease joint. After having sized each other up, they'd relaxed and enjoyed becoming better acquainted. Although they worked in different parts of the entertainment industry, it had been easy to relate to each other's amusing anecdotes.

In spite of the difference in their ages, Lita found herself thinking how similar the problems were that they both had faced.

Sydney laughed raucously at the memory of a particularly persistent male who'd made it a point to be in the front row when she'd performed for years. "Men haven't changed much," she observed with a sly chuckle.

"So it seems," Lita agreed.

Sydney's gray eyes narrowed into thoughtful slits. "Keith is just like my husband," Sydney reminisced fondly.

Lita's delicate brows lifted gently as she waited for the rest of the explanation. Sydney clearly had some message she wished to pass on to her about him.

"His father is tough," Sydney said proudly. "He can be arrogantly independent at times, but I never could stay angry at him for that because he has always been so deeply loyal to me. There have been any number of women who wanted him. They didn't care that we were legally married or that he had children," she went on, a hard, angry tone creeping into her voice. "But he—my handsome, sexy, charismatic man—he put us close to his heart and has never let anyone come between us." She shrugged and waved the back of her hand against an imaginary problem as if she were knocking it into oblivion. "So if we live apart much of the time, it's worth it to me. He loves the sea. The sea's his life . . . his job. I knew that, when I married him."

Lita nodded her head in respectful understanding. It would have taken a very strong love to endure those circumstances.

Sydney lowered her eyes briefly, as if hiding for a moment while she decided how to say what she wanted to. "Years ago, it was harder on the boys, of course. They were just children. They didn't understand. And yet they've grown up to be so much like him." A tender glow lighted her softened eyes. "Sean inherited more of my husband's handsomeness," she said, looking steadily at Lita. "But Keith inherited his inner strength and determination. He never runs from trouble. He faces it like a man. All his scars are on his chest." Sydney struck her satin-clad bosom with one tightly clenched fist for emphasis.

Lita vividly recalled some of those scars. Others, no doubt, were not so easily seen. The scars to the psyche and the heart lay hidden within.

Sydney, satisfied for the moment, assumed a sparkling smile and rose elegantly to her feet, ready now to make her grand exit. "Well, my dear, I'm *so* glad to have had the opportunity to meet you. I hope Keith will bring you to the house so we can have a chance to really let our hair down!" She laughed, casting a jaundiced eye on the surrounding bustle, although Lita hadn't noticed that the crowd had dampened Sydney's candor.

As quickly as she'd come, she was gone.

Keith passed her on her way out. "Did you behave?" he asked with a sardonic lift of one dark brow.

Sydney patted him on the cheek and gave him a glittering smile. "Why, darling! How could you doubt me?" she exclaimed. He was not moved by her display. The glitter dissolved and she looked at him with genuine warmth. "We got on famously. I hope you'll bring her with you the next time you flatter me with a visit."

"I can think of other places I'd rather take her," he muttered as Sydney sailed out the door to her waiting limousine. "Sorry," he apologized as he returned to the table. He rested his arm along the back of Lita's chair and turned his full attention back to her. "Now . . . where were we?"

The evening was wonderful but unproductive. It was wonderful because Lita spent it with Keith. To her surprise, and everyone else's, they even spent quite a bit of it on the dance floor.

"I thought you didn't dance here?" she murmured in surprise as he pulled her into his arms the first time.

"I'm turning over a new leaf," he whispered in her ear.

She felt herself melting against him and silently applauded his new rule. Since she'd closed her eyes, she missed the comical looks of utter astonishment on the faces of the nightclub's staff. Carl nearly dropped the drink he was handing to a waiter. Marty forgot what he was saying and stood with his mouth open for several very long seconds.

Only Sean wasn't surprised. He was sitting at the bar nursing a drink while Mitzi and Gloria made do with him.

"I thought he didn't dance with patrons at his own

club!" Gloria complained in outrage, throwing a look in Keith's direction that would have done justice to an assassin's stiletto.

Sean rolled the tumbler of Scotch between his fingertips and grinned wryly. "He still doesn't. She's not a patron," he chuckled. "She is *not* a patron, *believe* me."

Wonderful as being with Keith was, Lita was becoming uncomfortably aware that she wasn't accomplishing her other goal, that of identifying the third man that Melanie had been playing around with. When a tall man carrying a briefcase entered the club later that evening, Lita was actually grateful that Keith excused himself to talk with him. It was icing on the cake when Sean joined them and the three adjourned to Keith's office. With the brothers Christophe tied up, she would finally have a few free moments to make her inquiries.

To her delight, Keith himself unknowingly left her at precisely the spot she'd wanted to be—the bar. "Take care of her for me, Carl," he told the bartender as he helped her onto a stool at the sheltered end of the famed onyx strip.

"Sure thing, Mr. Christophe."

"Can I get you something?" Carl asked diffidently, after the men had gone.

"A brandy alexander would be nice," Lita said with a smile as she slid off the seat where Keith had put her.

She'd pumped the men for information in the past. Tonight she thought she'd try the women. Two women, to be precise. The furious-looking redhead and the slightly embarrassed-looking blond next to her, to be specific. They looked to her as if they were more than ready to be scathingly frank. "Mind if I join you?" Lita asked pleasantly as she sat on the stool between them that Sean had just vacated.

Gloria's eyes widened in amazement, then narrowed in

anticipation. "Not at all, honey," she purred as a dangerous smile slid across her red mouth. "Not at all."

Carl looked anxiously at the three women as he handed Lita her drink. He knew the boss wouldn't like this, but he couldn't think of a single reason to coax Lita into sitting somewhere else. "Just keep your talons sheathed, girls," he muttered.

Gloria shot him a furious glance. Mitzi pretended she hadn't heard. Lita coolly ignored his comment and took her drink from his outstretched hand.

"I don't think we've met," Lita began cordially after she took a fortifying sip of her drink. "I'm Lita Winslow . . ."

Jack Connery paced across his hotel room for the fiftieth time. He lifted the phone and dialed the local number again. There was no answer. He hung up.

Nervously he reached for a pack of cigarettes. With trembling fingers, he lighted one and took a quick drag. He looked at the slim white paper cylinder and closed his eyes in pain. He hadn't smoked in three years. It had been hell quitting. What he was going through now, though, was even worse. He needed the damn things to see the end of this mess without losing his mind.

He clamped the cigarette between his teeth and dragged on his travel-worn raincoat. He grabbed the room key from the glass-topped desk near the door on his way out.

If Lita was gone, maybe he could do a little checking around himself. Maybe luck would be on his side tonight, he thought.

He set off at a brisk pace, heading for a bus stop on a neighboring street. He had to hang on to his nerve for a little longer, just a little longer . . .

* * *

Felice felt Craig's arms gradually loosen and slowly drop down around her hips as they ended their kiss.

They were standing on her parents' porch, discreetly dark since the light was set to go off automatically every night at eleven thirty. Craig had been bringing her back at eleven thirty-five ever since that disturbing evening he'd practically tried to rape her.

Now they did all their farewell kissing standing up on the cement steps. That was entirely Craig's idea, and Felice still couldn't figure out why he was behaving in such a strange way. He seemed to be haunted by something. But what?

"Craig," she whispered tremulously, "are you okay?" Her arms were looped affectionately around his neck, and her eyes gazing up at him were as open and trusting as a puppy's.

Craig rested his forehead against hers and shut his eyes. "Yeah," he replied unconvincingly. "I've just got a case of the prewedding jitters that everyone always talks about."

Felice brushed a chaste, tender kiss against his cheek and leaned her head against his shoulder. Maybe that was it. She felt a little jittery herself. She could understand the feeling. "It is a pretty big step to take. Sort of like jumping into a big, dark unknown, isn't it?" she said softly.

"Yeah."

The dark unknown. Those words conjured up the image of a dark night in the woods, cold fast-running water, and a woman's scream. He trembled and struggled to get a grip on himself. He had to put that all behind him somehow. Before anyone found out. Before Felice found out.

"When can we set a date, Craig?" Felice asked tentatively. "I—I don't want to push us into setting a date before we're ready," she hurried to add. "But, well, peo-

235

ple keep asking, and I thought maybe we should begin thinking in about a month."

Craig felt a cold chill down his back. He didn't want to drag Felice into this disaster. Hell! How could he have asked her to get married before he was certain about . . . He smoothed her hair and bit his lip. Maybe he could find out just what was known about Melanie's death. If no one had connected them . . . "Let's talk about it next Saturday," he suggested, hoping with all his heart he'd be able to do so. "We'll pick a day then. Okay?"

Felice held him tightly, trying to chase away the demons that plagued him. If he wouldn't tell her, she'd try to be patient. But she was deeply disturbed. It wasn't like Craig to be so nervous and preoccupied. Worse still, she was a little frightened of going through with their marriage if he couldn't tell her what was wrong. He had until next Saturday to give her some honest explanation. If he hadn't managed it by then, well, Felice intended to ask for it.

"It's getting late," he said, stepping back from her.

She unlocked the door and went inside.

"I'll see you tomorrow night," he promised.

She blew him a kiss from her fingertips. He waved and ran back down the walk to the driveway.

As Felice was getting ready for bed, however, Craig Wilson was not going home. He was driving toward Georgetown.

It had required an effort, but Lita had been managing to avoid throwing her drink in Gloria's face in spite of exquisite provocation. Mitzi gave every appearance of wanting to sink through the plush red carpeting into the nether world below. Anything would have been preferable to sitting through Gloria's catty remarks.

"Frankly," Lita said easily, "I'm surprised you know

Keith that well. I wouldn't have thought you'd have that much in common."

Gloria's eyes turned a violent shade of green. "And just what do you mean by that crack?" she demanded rather loudly.

Thus far, people had politely pretended to ignore the stinging repartee that the girls were engaging in. Gloria's higher-pitched tone put an end to the charade. Several heads turned, and a few people began to stare at them in open curiosity.

Carl began wiping the bar with unusual vigor and enthusiastically suggesting new drinks all around. If Gloria got much louder, he might even make them on the house! Happily sloshed customers rarely remembered much of anything the next day!

Lita smiled very sweetly at Gloria and stared straight through her. "Why, I'd have thought he preferred someone with some interests in life besides acquiring clothes, jewelry, and a night on the town," she said, widening her eyes innocently. "But then, maybe you haven't spent enough time with him to really have a good old-fashioned conversation and get acquainted," Lita suggested with exaggerated sympathy.

Gloria's face was fast matching the shade of her red hair. "You couldn't be more mistaken," Gloria hissed furiously. "We have spent a great deal of time together." She was so angry she almost forgot herself that nearly all that time had been spent in Sydney's when Keith was working. "Outside of myself, I can't think of anyone I know more intimately," she raged on, aiming now to do as much real damage as she could to any budding relationship between Lita and Keith. She half closed her eyes and let a sensuous expression slide over her face. "He's all man. Those scars . . ." Gloria opened her eyes to see if Lita had gotten the unspoken inference. She saw Lita blink at her mention of the scars and smiled with deep satisfaction. "There are other good old-fashioned activities that a man and a woman can engage in besides verbal conversation, you know," the redhead arrogantly tossed in with a nasty smile.

"I'm sure you're an expert on that," Lita said, giving every appearance of admiring Gloria's prowess.

Gloria, having gotten in over her head, glared at Lita and looked around for a route of escape. She was about to completely lose her temper and create a scene that would no doubt get her banned from Sydney's for life. That she did not want. She spotted an unattached male acquaintance and slipped off the bar stool. "If you'll excuse me," she said icily. Gloria didn't wait to see if she would be excused. She made a straight line from the bar to her quarry, her high heels stabbing the carpet mercilessly each step of the way.

No one would have even considered asking her to stay, of course.

The introductions had barely been made when Lita realized that Gloria's desire to vent her spleen would make it impossible to get any useful information out of her tonight about Melanie's habits. Mitzi, however, had been encouragingly uncomfortable at Gloria's more unpleasant comments. Lita mentally crossed her fingers. Her insight and perseverance were rewarded moments later as Mitzi laid a tentative hand on Lita's arm.

"Gosh, I'm sorry about Gloria," she said unhappily. "She's usually not so . . . Well, she's not like that." Mitzi sighed. "She's a little jealous, I'm afraid."

Lita turned her attention to the little blond. "It's partly my fault," Lita offered, trying to nurture this first real opening in the conversation since she'd approached the women. "I shouldn't have pushed my company onto her. It was rude of me."

"Oh, no! Not at all," Mitzi protested. "It was an

honor. Gloria just wasn't up for it, I'm afraid . . ." Mitzi trailed off lamely.

"Do you come here a lot?" Lita asked, laying the groundwork for her real question.

Mitzi was relieved for the shift in topic and was happy to answer. "Oh, yes. Whenever we can. Sean and Keith have always been very nice to us. They don't mind if we come unescorted, they let us nurse a drink at the bar for as long as we want, and they don't mind if we mingle and make friends with some of the single men that come to Sydney's." She grimaced a little. "And they're nice to us. Sometimes they even take us home if it's late and we can't get a taxi right away."

Lita was scared to let her hopes get too high, but it was hard keeping a rein on them. "You must have seen a lot of the performers that entertain here, then?" she asked casually.

Mitzi nodded. "Oh, sure. Lots. We like to meet them, if we can. It's sort of like"—she struggled for an analogy—"stamp collecting, if you know what I mean," Mitzi explained, a little embarrassed.

"I know what you mean," Lita said reassuringly. "Did you by any chance ever meet Melanie King?" she inquired curiously.

Mitzi caught her lower lip gently between her teeth. "Yes," she admitted uncomfortably. "She spent most of her evenings here after rehearsal. Too bad we never got the chance to see her perform. I, uh, heard that she was your cousin."

Lita nodded and laced her fingers together on her lap to steady herself psychologically. "Yes. She was," Lita said quietly. "Did you have a chance to get to know her?"

Mitzi shook her head. Lita's hopes crumpled. Then came the surprise.

"She was always busy with other people," Mitzi disclosed. "And Keith made certain that she got home every night before it got too late. It was as if she were being chaperoned all the time. Although—" Mitzi lowered her eyes and her cheeks darkened in discomfort.

"Mitzi, whatever it is, I'd like to know." Lita came as close to pleading as her pride would allow. Fortunately, her sincerity and her unthreatening manner loosened Mitzi from her self-imposed reluctance.

"I don't mean to sound critical," Mitzi murmured apologetically.

"Of course not." Lita nodded her head in understanding.

"Gloria had cornered Keith one evening," Mitzi plunged ahead. "And I noticed that for once Melanie was leaving alone. I thought it was strange. And frankly, since they'd made such a fuss about keeping an eye on her, I thought it would be fun to break through their little fence and meet her. It seemed like the perfect chance, so I followed her."

Lita was concentrating so completely on Mitzi's story that she didn't notice the three men emerging from the hallway that led to the offices.

"I thought she was giving them the slip," Mitzi said with a slightly embarrassed shrug. "She looked like a girl trying to escape the dorm before anyone could notice."

That description had a very familiar ring to Lita. It gave immediate credibility to Mitzi's revelations.

"Only she didn't run out into the street and hail a cab," Mitzi continued. "She slipped through the alley to the next street over and stood in the shadows. I had just turned the corner and was all ready to call her name when I realized that she wasn't alone. She was talking with a man. I was so surprised that I just stopped and stared. It was dark and they were absorbed in themselves, so they didn't notice me, but the light from the street in back of them gave just enough contrast that I could see

240

their silhouettes. And I could hear them whispering. Well, it was obvious he wasn't mugging her or anything. She seemed quite happy when he started kissing her." Mitzi sighed. Now that she'd confessed her sin, she felt rather empty. "So I crept back around the corner and into the club. Melanie wandered back in about half an hour. Keith really gave her a dressing down, I think. And his brother, too. Sean was supposed to have been keeping an eye on her then, I guess, but he said Felice had called him to help her with something. She'd been trying to finish up so she could meet her boyfriend for a late dinner or something, I think." Mitzi gave Lita a sad smile. "I wish I could have gotten to know her, though. She seemed like a nice girl. I always did admire girls who didn't let the world tie them down."

Lita managed to return the smile. "Melanie certainly tried to avoid that," Lita admitted. "I bet you would have found quite a bit in common."

Mitzi brightened. "Do you really think so?" To be compared favorably with a glamorous, talented singer certainly was a compliment.

Lita caught her lip between her teeth to keep from letting the pain overwhelm her. Poor, foolish Melanie . . . "Do you have any idea who she met?" Lita asked, trying to keep from sounding like she'd give her eyeteeth to know the answer to that question.

Mitzi frowned. "No. It was too dark and they were too far away. He was a little taller than she was. And he looked like he had an average build, I guess."

That wasn't a lot to go on, Lita thought despondently. "Did she ever talk to him on the phone, that you know of?" Lita asked.

Mitzi looked confused. "I really wouldn't know. She didn't use the public pay phone in the hallway, of course. And even if she had, I wouldn't have known. I certainly don't go around eavesdropping on people's conversations!" She was beginning to feel a little affronted. "I hope you don't think I'm nosey just because I wanted to say hello that night!"

"Oh, no! Not at all," Lita hurried to reassure her. "I was just wondering who the mystery man in her life was. Melanie must have had a reason for keeping his identity so, well, secret."

Mitzi's defensiveness melted and she nodded her head. She'd never really given the singer much thought. But with each question that Lita had asked, Mitzi was beginning to wonder what had really been going on. "It is odd," the little blond said in a hushed voice. "Maybe he would have been recognized here at Sydney's, and he couldn't afford to be seen with her." Mitzi fell silent as the awful possibilities began running through her mind.

Lita gazed around the room. People were beginning to pay their checks. It would be time to close soon. Everyone wanted to go home to their families now. For the time being, they had wearied of the grown-up play.

Could the third man be out there somewhere in the crowd? Lita wondered in mounting frustration. If only she had a face to look for, or a name . . . The name. Lita turned her attention back to Mitzi. "Have you ever met a man by the name of Wills?" she asked.

Mitzi was having trouble making the connection between Lita's question and their previous conversation. "Wills?" Mitzi repeated. "No, I don't know anyone by that name. Why? Was that the man in the alley?"

Lita sighed. Naturally, it couldn't be that easy. "I don't know. I'd heard she'd been seen in the company of a man by that name, and I just wondered if perhaps you might know him. I'd really like to talk to him about all this."

Mitzi was beginning to slide off her stool, clutch in hand. Before she slipped away, Lita had one last, painful question to ask. It had to do with Mitzi's suggestion that the mystery man might not want to be seen being intimate with Melanie by people at the club. "Mitzi, did the man that Melanie met in the alley look like anyone you know?"

Mitzi blanched. She didn't want to get caught in a web that involved the Christophes in any way, shape, or form! "I told you," she said, much more distantly this time, "I couldn't see much. It was dark. That's all I know."

"Thanks, Mitzi," Lita said sincerely.

"That's all right. But I've got to go."

"Of course."

Mitzi hurried up the steps, flying skillfully through the couples like a fluttering bird. Lita stared blindly after her, wondering how she could discover whether it had been Sean in the alley with Melanie that night.

A figure slid into the seat Mitzi had vacated. "You could have asked me." The familiar male voice was low and steely.

Lita stiffened in surprise as she turned her head toward him. "Keith! I didn't realize you were back."

"Obviously."

Lita flinched as if he'd slapped her. The cynical, sarcastic way he'd said it had been totally unexpected.

"I trust you got what you were digging for?" he added, his words sandpapering her as he'd intended.

No longer was he the charming escort of earlier in the evening. Keith had turned into a man of stone. Lita blinked in confusion. All she'd been doing was talking to Mitzi. Was that why he was angry? That was ridiculous!

The last few people began moving away from the bar, leaving them in relative privacy.

"What I was digging for?" she repeated numbly. "I don't understand . . ." She didn't understand why he was suddenly turning against her. She didn't understand why he was lashing out. She lost precious moments in a state of speechless dismay, trying to gather her wits.

243

Keith, having already decided what he wanted to do, suffered no such momentary lapse. He stood up and, firmly grasping her elbow, left her in no doubt that she should do likewise. Without a word of explanation, he hustled her into his office. For the first time, a whisper of fear brushed over her skin. Keith was staring at her as if they were strangers. His black eyes held a cold anger that made her want to flee from his sight.

She clutched her small evening purse and lifted her chin. Her own ire began coming to her rescue. "What do you mean by hustling me in here like this?" she demanded angrily.

A cold smile twisted his mouth, and he strolled over to his broad, heavy desk. He sat on the corner nearest Lita, letting one leg swing free of the floor as he plucked a matchbox from the pocket of his evening jacket and began flipping it open and shut.

It was funny, he thought, how some habits help you think clearly. And right now he wanted to think very, very clearly. He'd had a less-than-uplifting meeting with his attorney and Sean. Then he'd walked out to find Lita pumping one of Sydney's resident gossips for information about Melanie's death. He'd told her to ask him if she wanted to know anything. Why had she gone to someone else? She didn't want him to know she was asking, perhaps?

He hadn't liked it when she'd danced away the better part of a week asking the men in the place to fill her in. But since he and Lita had become more involved, well, he'd expected her to turn to him first. Obviously she'd wanted a source other than him. He concluded that she therefore did not really trust him. And trust was the scale on which everything was weighed in Keith Christophe's personal world. If she didn't trust him, she couldn't love him.

She merely liked to go to bed with him. His cold smile

244

hardened unpleasantly. Maybe she didn't even really like that. Maybe it had been a performance. A primitive male fury began to boil deep in his guts, and he wanted to wring her neck for making him so vulnerable. Lita with her soft skin. Lita with her wet, sweet mouth. Lita with her silken thighs and racehorse legs and the body that he wanted all for himself for as long as they walked the face of the earth.

He stood up and turned his back on her. He had to get a hold of himself before she realized how deeply she had her hooks into him. Sean's life could depend on it, he reminded himself bitterly. He walked over to the expensive stereo system in its smoked-glass-and-chrome cabinet and flicked it on. When he turned to look at Lita, his face had become an impenetrable mask.

"I told you before," he said in a dangerously quiet voice, "if you want to know about Melanie, ask me." He motioned for her to sit in the plush chair in front of him. He sat just across the small coffee table from her. "What do you want to know?"

CHAPTER FOURTEEN

They were only a few feet apart, but to Lita, it seemed like a nearly unbridgeable gulf.

A cold dread began to congeal beneath her anger. *What's happening to us?* She took a deep breath and hung on to her nerve. There had to be a way to work through whatever was eating at Keith without letting it destroy them. There *had* to be. "Who was she seeing while she was here?" Lita asked. There was no sense in beating around the bush. He'd asked her what she wanted to know. That was it.

Keith gave no hint as to how he felt about the question. His reply was direct and to the point. "That depends on what you mean by 'seeing.' If you mean *socializing*—half the men in the club would qualify. If you're referring to privately getting together for a quiet conversation or a little relaxation, the group becomes considerably smaller. As you already know, I spent time with Melanie. So did Sean. So did Marty and Gaius. So did her agent, Jack Connery, when he was in town."

Lita wanted desperately to cross the chasm between them and put her arms around him and plead for him to tell her what was wrong so that they could put it right. Never in her life had she pleaded with a man. Her mother had given her ample proof over the years that pleading only drove a man away. That lesson was too deeply ingrained to overcome. No matter how her heart ached to ignore it now. She swallowed hard and tried not to think about the pain this was causing. "Was there anyone else? Someone she especially liked or tried to see outside, after hours?" Lita asked steadily.

"Not that I know of. We all tried to keep an eye on her. We were trying to protect her." There was a trace of harshness as he said that.

"I know." Lita wanted so badly for him to believe her. She leaned forward, her eyes scanning his anxiously. "I know you were. And it was very good of you to do it."

He hardened against her even more. Her even-tempered patience in the face of his antagonism fanned the fires of his distrust. Only manipulative women could control their feelings so well. If she'd flamed out instead . . . He could feel himself weakening toward her, wanting to believe whatever she told him. Reflexively he snapped the matchbox shut and pushed that idiotic sentiment into oblivion. "Don't mention it. It was business, remember?" he said dismissively. His words were like acid etching metal.

Lita's eyes flashed in anger and she stood up. That snide comment had been the last shot. "Ah, yes, business! Let's not forget about *that!*" she said, her voice shaking with anger. "I, of all people, know how near and dear that can be to your heart!" She paced stiffly back and forth, the motion merely adding fuel to Lita's growing fury. From head to toe, she visually raked the cool-mannered man sitting as relaxed as a sultan in his favorite chaise. "I don't know what's eating at you, Keith," she trampled on in high dudgeon, "but I wish you could have just told me straight out instead of suddenly metamorphosing into a total stranger and criticizing where you have no right to. If I want to ask people about Melanie's activities and her friends, I have as much right as anyone to do it. What's wrong with my asking around? Can you answer me that?"

Keith clenched his fist, crushing the matchbox. "It could be misconstrued," he said angrily. "You don't know what's going on. I told you to come to me!" Her outburst had cracked his steely reserve, and his temper was dangerously close to flaring.

"I *don't* know what's going on!" Lita exclaimed, outraged. "So tell me!"

Keith blinked and stared at her. Memories of making love to her poured into his boiling temper, mellowing it. He rested his elbows on his knees and held his head in his hands. "I don't know whether I'm coming or going anymore," he muttered.

Lita wanted to cry. He looked so defeated. It broke her heart. "Keith," she cried brokenly, "please, I can't stand fighting with you. It hurts too much. I don't want to undermine anything. If there's something I don't know, please, tell me. I don't want to create problems, I swear."

He raised his head and looked at her through tortured eyes. Her eyes were deep blue pools of unhappiness. The silvery shimmer of tears glinted on her lashes. He wanted to drag her into his arms and hold her tight. He needed her to tell him she was his. First, last, and always—that no one had more of a claim on her loyalty than he.

Not even her dead cousin, Melanie.

He was too proud to admit any of it to Lita. There was something besides his pride that was holding him back, too. What if he told her everything and she put her loyalty to someone else first? Putting him in second place. His face darkened, and he leaned back into the lush upholstery. "Let me tell you something you don't know yet," he said coldly. "I left you at the bar this evening because the city prosecutor is playing cat and mouse with someone he suspects of murdering your cousin."

That got Lita's attention.

Keith told himself he didn't give a damn if she looked so vulnerable that a light breeze would knock her over.

She could create problems for Sean that the kid couldn't outlive in a lifetime if she kept digging around on her own, refusing to confide in him. Years of tough negotiating and fighting for what he had gave him the armor plating he needed. But it didn't do a thing for the twisting pain he was feeling inside.

"He doesn't have enough evidence to have the suspect arrested," Keith explained in that same chilling voice. "So he's tailing the kid, calling him in for repeated questioning about the same things over and over again, making an ostentatious show of verifying every detail of the kid's statement, reminding the suspect that he has no alibi and needs to stick around."

Lita stood as if nailed to the spot, riveted by the totally unexpected disclosures Keith was making. Why hadn't he told her if he'd known about this earlier? Surely he owed it to her. They'd been so close. She blinked her eyes, trying to clear the tears from her vision.

An awful thought assailed her. Maybe they hadn't been so close after all. Maybe she'd been falling for him, but he'd just been satisfying a physical urge. She'd never kidded herself that he was in love with her, of course. But she had believed that he truly cared for her . . . She lowered her head as shame overwhelmed her.

Lita turned away, her back rigid with the pain to which she absolutely refused to succumb. She took a deep breath and stared at the oil painting hanging on the wall. The warm gold and red light from the Tiffany lamp on Keith's desk enhanced the rich display. It was a portrait of a woman, done in the abstract, in an impressionist style with hundreds upon hundreds of tiny pinpoints of color forming the graceful, beautiful whole. She repressed a hysterical urge to laugh. She felt just like that. Not a whole woman at all—a woman who had just been turned to a thousand fragments.

The painting blurred a little, and she brushed her hand

quickly against her eyes. "Go on," she said a little shakily. Then, with more determination, "What has this got to do with my creating a problem?"

Her words hit Keith like a blow. All thought of going to her and comforting her evaporated in the white heat of his anger. It was all a superficial facade. The stricken look, the trembling voice. She'd turned her back because, no doubt, she was afraid he'd see through her manipulations and into her heart.

No. He'd heard that note of determination for too many years not to recognize it. Sydney had a patent on it. And she was a woman made of steel. Just like Lita. Bitterness flooded through him. "Every time you question people in this club, it makes them remember. Next, they think about it. They wonder why the beautiful, elusive Lita Winslow would be sniffing around like a bloodhound instead of letting the wheels of justice turn in their own formidable way." Beautiful? Elusive? From the way he'd said them, they sounded like two of the least desirable characteristics a woman could possess.

Keith stood then. He didn't care to say the rest from a seated position. It felt like launching an attack from low ground. Not a recommended procedure in most military manuals. "Then they start remembering who was most often seen taking her home, and who was the last person known to have seen her alive, and who has no alibi because he was dead drunk, sleeping it off in his car all night. They start giving the kid speculative looks when they think he isn't going to notice. Then, pretty soon, he's wondering himself what happened, and he gets the urge to do stupid things like returning to the site of her death to see if he can figure out what happened before someone tries to pin it on him."

Lita turned around slowly, and the pieces of the puzzle began falling into place. With a twinge of despair for Keith she realized why he was behaving so irrationally tonight. He was protecting someone he loved. She wanted to keep him talking now. They had to find a way through this mess.

"You're trying to protect him then?" she said, seeking his confirmation.

"Yes. Not just trying either. They'll get him over my dead body," he declared angrily. "He's innocent, damn it!"

Lita ran her hand tiredly through her shining black hair.

"If he's innocent, the police can't hurt him. And neither can I," she pointed out wearily. Why couldn't this stubborn man make this easier for them, she wondered in exasperation.

"Wrong," he retorted succinctly. "There is always a chance that the scales of justice can make a mistake. All it takes is for a clever prosecutor to weave a convincing enough tale around circumstantial evidence to bring a case like this to trial. This has all the sensational elements in it that make for great press for an ambitious prosecutor with political aspirations. Even if the defendant gets a jury with enough common sense to bring in a finding of not guilty, his reputation has been damaged beyond repair. A man with that kind of blot on his record is never looked at in the same way again. There is no such thing as being found innocent in this country. People would always wonder. . . ."

"Unless the real murderer were caught," Lita pointed out.

She chewed on her lower lip thoughtfully, trying to decide whether or not to ask him straight out whom he was protecting. She knew who he was talking about, but they needed to stop talking in innuendos and be direct with each other. She sighed and took the plunge.

"Keith," she murmured sympathetically. "Whom are you trying to protect?"

His rugged jaw tightened perceptibly as his eyes, unwavering, locked with hers.

"Sean," he said bluntly.

Lita closed her eyes. Hearing it out loud made it so real. As real as it had been for Keith, she thought, as he'd stood by watching the noose gradually tighten around his brother's neck. Slowly she reopened her eyes.

"But why . . . why didn't you tell me?" she asked. Her voice was little more than a broken thread.

"I didn't know what was going on, at first," he reluctantly replied. "When Sean came to me tonight, we finally had to face the fact that this thing isn't going to blow away like a bad dream. The prosecutor means business. He wants a case, whether he's got one or not." Keith clenched his right hand into a fist and slammed it against the open palm of his left. From the expression on his face it was obvious that he'd love to be delivering the blow to the prosecutor's jaw instead.

Lita stared sadly across the distance between them.

"I had our attorney come by tonight to prepare for the prosecutor's next move." His steely gaze returned to Lita. "That's why I left you at the bar."

Lita was truly at a loss to know what to say or do. The delicate tapestry of trust that had been slowly knitting them together had been viciously rent by events over which they had very little control.

Lita pressed her fingertips against her tired eyes. She was very weary. Maybe they both needed a rest, she thought. And a little time. Deep in her heart, she feared that time—and being apart—would turn out to be their worst enemies under the circumstances. They needed to find each other before this awful distance between them became cast in psychological concrete.

Keith couldn't stand it for another minute. She was standing there looking so damned beaten up by it all! It was making him want to forget his distrust and tell her everything would be all right. He'd fix it. *He'd fix it!* And just how in the hell did he think he could do that? he wondered. Sean's problem with the prosecutor was going to require a lot more than a few hours of verbal intimidation. A little sleight of hand or plain old-fashioned magic would come in handy about now. Unfortunately, Keith was fresh out of rabbits and hats! Before he weakened like some green schoolboy, he had to get her out of his sight.

Before he could act on that, the telephone rang. Both of them turned, as if shot, presenting startled faces to the uncaring instrument. The second ring saw Keith jumping across the short distance and jerking the noisy thing off its hook.

"Hello?" he answered harshly. Who in the hell could be calling here at this hour?

"Glad I caught you."

Keith did not look pleased. "Sorry I can't say the same," he snapped. "Why are you calling at this hour, Fallon?"

Lita heard the detective's name and wondered what more could happen. Keith had only been listening for a few seconds when his eyes snapped to her face. Obviously, whatever it was had something to do with her, she thought. What kind of a nightmare have I gotten into? she wondered miserably.

"I see," Keith said.

He was clipped and businesslike now. Butter wouldn't have melted in the man's mouth. Lita could have strangled him.

"Right. We'll be there in ten or fifteen minutes," Keith curtly informed the detective. And then he hung up. "Come on," he ordered. "I'm taking you back to the town house." He walked straight to the office door and held it for her.

"What was that all about?" she asked.

He locked doors and turned on the alarm system as they headed in the direction of his car.

"Someone's broken into your town house . . ." he said grimly, "again."

There was a police car, its lights flashing, in front of the town house when they arrived. Fallon was talking to one of the uniformed officers a few feet away. When he saw them pull up, he came over to join them.

"Sorry, Lita," he said, giving her a sympathetic, rather lopsided grin. "This must be getting pretty old for you, coming back and finding your place broken into."

"I don't see anything humorous about this, Fallon," Keith muttered in annoyance.

Fallon's eyebrows hoisted themselves up. What was eating at Keith? he wondered. He slanted a shrewd glance at Lita. She looked like a woman who'd been through a wringer. "Sorry," the detective mumbled, rubbing his jaw thoughtfully. "I guess I lose my sensitivity some in the wee hours."

"Don't we all," Lita murmured under her breath.

"I beg your pardon?" Fallon said.

Lita waved her hand in the air dismissingly. "Do you know whether anything was taken?" she asked. It had been the first thing that came to her mind. As soon as she'd said it, she realized how odd it sounded. They wouldn't know the contents of the town house. She would.

Fallon, a gentleman at heart, politely refrained from pointing that out. "Uh, we don't think so," he answered. "We don't think he actually got in. It appears that the alarm went off as soon as the window was broken. The perpetrator then fled. We had a car here within ten minutes after the alarm went off."

The three of them walked around to the side of the town house.

"Don't go any closer," Fallon warned them. "We're going to check the ground when it's daylight. We don't want anything disturbed before we've had a chance to go over it with a fine-tooth comb."

"Did anyone get a look at him?" Keith asked sharply.

Fallon was rocking on his heels as he stared at the broken window at one side of the building. "Nope. He was gone too fast." Fallon squinted as if pained.

They went around to the front door and went inside. Police first. Nothing appeared to have been touched. There was no evidence that Lita's town house apartment had been entered.

Lita was standing in the kitchen, staring numbly at the broken window. She really didn't need this, she thought. Sometimes life just didn't give you a break. Fatalistically she surveyed the shattered glass and knelt down to begin cleaning up the mess.

When she did, she saw something. It was a message wrapped around a heavy stone. "Pete!" she called out with less than her usual strength. "I think I found the object he used to break the window."

Instantly the men were around her.

Fallon gently helped her to her feet and examined the missive. He unwrapped it carefully, gingerly holding the smallest pieces of the corners whenever he could. He doubted that they'd get any fingerprints, but you never knew until you tried.

The message was composed of cutout letters from a newspaper. The *Washington Post*, no doubt, Fallon thought. That certainly didn't help narrow down the suspects.

Lita moved to Fallon's side to get a clearer view of the note. The moment she read it, the color drained from her face. She was only vaguely aware of Keith's strong arm coming around her, supporting her as she closed her eyes.

255

The thought of his catching up to her made her feel faint. No, no . . . It couldn't be happening again . . .

Keith quickly read the patched-together message. His eyes were grim as he looked up at Fallon. The words burned in his mind like a brand. " 'It's been five years, baby, but I found you at last. Sorry I had to get your cousin to bring you out of hiding. But it'll be worth it, baby. You'll see.' "

Fallon ran a hand thoughtfully over his chin. "That trouble you had before, Lita—the harassment, the death threat—you never had any more problems with that guy after you quit live performing?"

Lita shook her head. "No." She raised her suffering eyes to Fallon's. "Does this mean that Melanie was murdered by the man who was threatening me?"

Fallon patted her on the shoulder in an awkward gesture of comfort. "It's too soon to say. But, if I recall, no one ever got a look at that guy, right?"

"That's right," Lita said shakily. "That was what made it so frightening. We didn't know who we were looking for. It could have been anyone. And yet it had to be someone I saw all the time. He knew so much about me, my personal schedule, my wardrobe, my travel plans. He had to have been watching or hanging around almost all my performances."

She trembled a little and was grateful for Keith's reassuring closeness. He was warm and solid. In the strong circle of his arms, she felt safe and protected.

"Is it possible that Melanie's Mr. Wills and the man who threatened me five years ago and the man who broke into the town house are one in the same?" Lita asked.

A professional air slid over Fallon. "I don't know yet, but I'm certainly going to try and find out," he promised.

"Who is this Mr. Wills?" Keith asked sharply.

"A guy who bought Melanie a dress." Fallon whipped

his attention back to Lita. "And by the way, how did *you* know that name?"

Lita gave him a weak, apologetic smile. "I was trying to find out how Melanie spent that last day, hoping I might make some sense out of it. Anyway, I went to the dress shop, since I knew she'd bought a dress. And, well, the manager—"

Fallon was grimacing and shaking his head. "Anything else you're doing on your independent investigation?" Fallon asked, almost fearing to hear the answer.

Lita hung her head. She really should have told him earlier. "Well, when I went through my mail, there was a letter from Melanie . . ."

"What!" Fallon and Keith both shouted.

Lita loosened herself from Keith's arm and retrieved the letter from the bedroom. After they'd scanned it, she explained. "I wanted to sit down and talk to you about it, Pete, but we've all been in such a rush. And it didn't point to anyone, didn't offer any direct evidence." She wrapped her arms around herself protectively. She reached deep down and found her courage. With clear eyes and a steady voice, she said, "I've been wondering if the third man that Melanie was seeing was this Mr. Wills, whoever he is."

"Could be," Fallon muttered. All the crimes could be the work of one twisted mind, he thought. But there was something bothering him about all this. It was a little too neat. A little too convenient. Crime wasn't like that. Criminals tended to be messy. Of course, it could be someone trying to get caught. He seemed to enjoy leaving clues. And upping the risk each time. Like going from threatening to kill to actually murdering . . .

Keith stood by grimly, his thoughts virtually identical to Fallon's. By the time he'd reached the same chilling conclusion, it was no longer his brother's safety that commanded his attention. It was Lita's. "Go pack your bags," he ordered her.

If he'd told her to strip, she couldn't have been more taken by surprise. She stared at him in astonishment. He was grim-faced and looking more unrelenting by the second.

"You aren't safe here," he explained curtly. "You're coming with me."

Lita opened her mouth to say thank you, but before she could speak he grabbed her elbow and hustled her into the bedroom. He grabbed a suitcase and threw it on the bed. Then he turned to open drawers and hand her her underclothes.

He'd been sure she was going to argue about it. He could hardly blame her. They weren't exactly on great terms at the moment. Now that it appeared that his brother would have competition for the role of number-one suspect in this case, Keith was remembering how harsh he'd been with Lita. He jerked open the closet door and started going through the hangers. "Is this yours?" he asked gruffly.

Lita raised her eyes to heaven, seeking a long fuse for her temper. Then she calmly walked across the room and took the dress from him. "Look," she said, looking steadily at him, "why don't I do this? It'll only take a few minutes."

He stood there as she walked back to the bed and efficiently proceeded with the packing. At least she wasn't going to argue with him, he realized with a mild sense of relief.

He didn't know how to begin again with her. All the anger he'd thrown at her had disappeared, but the things that had been said couldn't be unsaid. Lita had been right, he thought. He should have told her what was going on. He'd let his distrust of women taint his judgment. Fearing for her safety had freed him to see their conversation at Sydney's from Lita's point of view. How could he make it up to her? "I'll wait for you downstairs," he muttered. "I have a couple of questions for Fallon."

It didn't take long for Lita to finish gathering her things. She was stuffing some notes and music into her bag when she noticed an old airplane ticket among the papers. Out of habit, she opened the long envelope with the airline logo on it and quickly perused the information. Then looked at it again. More slowly. It was a ticket issued to a Mr. J. Smith flying from Reno, Nevada, to San Francisco, California, a month ago. How in the devil had it come into her possession? she wondered. That would have been the night before Jack Connery had unexpectedly dropped in on her in California to tell her that Melanie was missing. Lita frowned in concentration.

Maybe when she and Jack had flown back to the East Coast, she'd somehow accidentally picked up someone else's used ticket. That was really peculiar, though. She couldn't imagine how she could have done that.

And then she saw what had happened as clearly as if she were seeing it again. Jack had taken Melanie's ticket when the agent had issued it. He'd given both of their tickets to the cabin attendant when they'd entered the plane, and then he'd slipped them into his jacket. He'd handed her ticket back to her just before they picked up their luggage. That had to be it, she thought. But how had Jack come by the ticket?

Keith strode into the room. "Let's go," he said, reaching for the waiting suitcase.

There wasn't time to think about it anymore, so Lita shook it out of her mind. But she couldn't quite bring herself to throw the ticket away, so she slipped it into her purse and grabbed her coat. "I'm ready," she said, marshaling her nerve.

She didn't need a program to know where Keith was taking her. Under other circumstances, she'd have been very happy to spend what little remained of the night at his apartment. Considering how strained the atmosphere was between them at the moment, however, she was afraid that this would not end up being a cherished memory.

Fallon watched them go. He'd been afraid this would happen to them. It was obvious they were both taking it hard.

Fallon wanted to break this case. He wanted that badly. If he could solve it, he'd feel he'd made a small repayment on a debt he'd owed Keith Christophe for over twenty years. It was a debt that he'd never be able to pay in full. How could you repay a man who'd stepped in front of you in an alley fight and taken a knife in the belly that had been aimed for you?

Blood is thicker than water, Fallon told himself. It was one of his favorite observations on life. Only this time, he didn't just mean the blood of common parentage.

Lita had been lying on the bed, staring at the ceiling in the pitch dark for an eternity. She'd tried multiplication tables in French and long division in Spanish. Nothing helped. She simply could not fall asleep.

It was Keith, of course. The strain between them was tough for her to take. They'd driven to Crystal City in a silence so thick you could have cut it with a knife. Then he had carried her bags into his bedroom, told her to help herself to the contents of his refrigerator, and disappeared into his study. It was obvious he didn't want her company.

Tears began to burn and well up against her lashes. He might not be eager for her company, but she was certainly longing for his, she thought miserably. The longing just kept getting worse and worse, too. The worse it got, the harder it was to resist the temptation to go to him and try to find a way to patch up their problems.

Finally, she couldn't stand it anymore. She tossed the covers off and slipped out of bed. She almost lost her nerve when she got to the study. The door was closed. She stood there wondering if she were making a big mistake. You probably are, she admitted. But if you don't try, you'll always regret it. You'll always wonder if it could have made a difference.

The brass handle felt cold against her palm as she rallied her courage and opened the door. At first, she didn't see him in the dark. But when her eyes became accustomed to the gloom, she made out Keith's form in the far corner of the room. He was stretched out on a corner of a long sofa, a glass in his hand and a tall clear bottle on the table nearby. He was half sitting, half lying. And he gave no sign that he was aware she had entered.

Slowly Lita crossed the room. "Keith?" she whispered when she was about three or four feet away from him.

His eyes opened and he struggled to sit up a little more. "Yes?" His speech was slurred.

Lita took a step nearer and picked up the bottle to see what he was drinking. Ouzo. She had no idea how much had been in it when he'd started, but there was less than a third of a bottle now. She put it back down and sank to her knees beside him. "It's not good to drink alone," she whispered. Now that she was here, she still couldn't find the words to tell him what was in her heart. And the ache to burrow against him, to hold him, to be held in his arms, was almost unbearable. She felt the tears threatening again and bit her lip.

Keith was looking at her strangely. He reached out tentatively and touched her cheek with the fingertips of one hand. "It's not good to be alone," he murmured.

She leaned forward, putting her arms around him as best she could, and lay her head against his firmly muscled stomach. The tears she'd held at bay for so long finally began to fall. "Please let me stay with you," she whispered unsteadily. It was the voice of a child pleading. She felt his hand on her head, and the tenderness of it broke the last thread of her control. Softly she began to sob in his arms.

"Don't cry," he begged her. He grasped her just below the arms and pulled her up a little higher on his chest. "Lita . . ." He pulled her chin up so that he could see her. "Lita," he whispered hoarsely. He kissed her tear-dampened eyes and cheeks, groaning softly as if a man in pain. "Don't cry," he implored. His lips caressed her cheek as he spoke. "I'm sorry. I'm sorry." He was drying her cheeks with his hand and stroking her hair and back as he spoke.

They resettled themselves on the couch, Keith rolling Lita fully on top of him, Lita with her arms secured around him.

"Can we start over again?" Lita asked, holding him tightly, as if to ward off the answer.

He sighed and rubbed his hands slowly up and down her back. "Can anyone ever start over?" There was an uncharacteristic note of painful doubt in his rich, masculine voice. He'd had a lot to drink, and it had lowered his inhibitions. The gate to his heart was wide open, and Keith laid it all in plain view for the first time in his life. "I learned as a kid not to trust people too easily," he said, his words still slurring now and again from the ouzo. "Even Sydney used my weaknesses for her own purposes. I was a pawn in a game she played with my old man. She thought by getting pregnant that he'd give up the sea and stay with her." He gave a soft, bitter laugh. "She didn't know him very well then. By the time she realized he wasn't going to change, I was half grown and Sean was about to arrive. So I got to substitute as the father. Whether I liked it or not."

Lita's tears sprang up anew, and she slid her hands into his hair, kissing him tenderly on the jaw.

His arms tightened around her gratefully. "She's a warm, loving woman," he rambled on, rather sleepily, "but she likes to dominate everyone. She hates to share, hates to give in, hates not to have her way." He sighed in recollection of the unrelenting struggle for independence that had been his childhood. "I guess I learned to be the same way. Partly in self-defense. Then, hanging around this town—well, you get a belly full of strong-willed people who don't give a damn about anything but themselves and who take an expedient view of friendship: You make friends with people who can be useful to you. You kiss them good-bye when they cease to be."

He grasped her face in both his hands and held her so their lips were just inches apart. His longing for her was plain to see. The hunger of a man who needed a woman had left its hard stamp on him. With a heart suddenly full of joy, Lita saw it.

"I don't make friends that way," he said roughly, searching her eyes. "That's why there are very few people I truly consider my friends." His fingers tightened in the tangle of her soft black hair, and he closed his eyes. "And I never considered you a candidate for friendship, Lita Winslow," he raggedly admitted. "My beautiful, soft-hearted, silken-voiced witch. You . . . you created a category of your own."

His mouth covered hers in a poignant, tender kiss. Reluctantly he broke away, smoothing her hair and kissing her brow. "If I could take back what I said to you at Sydney's, I would," he murmured. "I regretted most of it as soon as I'd said it."

Lita blinked the last of her tears away and gazed at him through glistening lashes. Her heart was so full that she thought it might burst. "It doesn't matter," she whispered, kissing him softly in reassurance. "I understand."

263

And she did. She saw the old wounds in his heart, the scars of disillusionment and cynicism. But most of all, she saw the strong and tender spirit that flourished in spite of those old battles.

He squeezed her so tightly she could not breathe, but she didn't care. She didn't care at all. If she never took another sweet breath of air, it would be worth it. Because in that rib-crushing embrace, she felt how much he truly did care for her, and that knowledge gave her heart wings to soar.

"If I ever get my hands on the bastard who's been threatening you . . ." he said harshly, his voice suddenly gone stone-cold. He didn't finish the sentence. He didn't have to.

Lita's fingertips brushed his lips. "Shh. Let's not talk about it."

Keith slid his hands over her satin pajamas, then began loosening the fastenings. "You're mine, Lita Winslow," he said, almost harshly. His eyes burned into hers as his conquering hands began handling her in a more serious way.

Lita pressed lingering kisses on his eyes, his ears, his neck. Desire began to lick at her everywhere he touched her—along her arms, her sides, her breasts, down her belly and the insides of her thighs. She began twisting slowly against him, caressing him with her entire body as he freed them of their clothing.

Be mine, she was silently pleading as he loosened his belt and she helped him out of his trousers. The soft scattering of hair on his chest pressed into the soft, sensitive flesh of her breasts and belly. His hot mouth ravaged hers as their naked bodies captured one another like prisoners of love.

"Ah, yes," he groaned in satisfaction as she ran her hands over him. "Yes . . . yesss . . ."

Their mouths locked in an urgent frenzy, and they were convulsed by a great, scalding tide of release.

But when that primitive storm surge had passed and washed gently away from the shore once more, it was only Lita who murmured, "I love you."

CHAPTER FIFTEEN

The song was finished.

It had taken longer than most of the songs that Lita wrote, but then, she'd learned more about herself in writing this one. She'd been standing in front of Keith's panoramic view of the Potomac and Washington, searching one last time for a title.

"It's too quiet to think," she said, sighing. "No sound of the waves on the rocks, or the flapping of wings and cries of seabirds. It's like being entombed . . ." She bit her lip.

It didn't feel that way when Keith was near. It hadn't felt that way last night when he'd made love to her. Nor when he'd carried her into his bedroom afterward. It hadn't felt that way until she'd gradually awakened this morning. She'd found herself alone in his bed, with a note at the bedside, occupying an apartment that had suddenly gone cold and sterile.

"The Shadow of a Dream," Lita murmured, trying the sound of it on for size again. Yes. That definitely was going to be the song's title. That's what she'd been calling it for the past month, and nothing else really fitted.

Lita picked up her purse and went toward the door. By the time she reached the glass-walled foyer of the high rise, the taxi she'd called was waiting for her. The driver swiftly dodged through the heavy traffic, and she arrived at the town house in Georgetown in record time.

"Thanks," she said as she paid him and got out. She needed to use her tape recorder and the piano. Then she could move on to the next item of business for the day.

While Keith was down at the police station trying to sort things out for Sean, she was going to take one last shot at finding that third man. There was one person she realized she had never really talked to about Melanie. A person who came to Sydney's every business day. A person who, as the owner's secretary, might have noticed the comings and goings of such a man.

A person by the name of Felice Moore.

"I'm sorry, Mr. Christophe isn't in the office at the moment . . . May I take a message?" Felice hugged the receiver between her head and her shoulder as she reached for the message pad and a pencil. "Yes. I'll be sure to tell him as soon as he comes in, Mr. Remington," she promised. "Good-bye."

She hung up the phone and swiveled her chair away from the desk, grabbing a sheaf of papers. She hurried into her boss's office and placed them neatly on the center of his desk, where he couldn't fail to see them. The ones marked Urgent were on the top. She wracked her brain trying to remember if she'd forgotten anything. No. The most important things had been taken care of.

She tried dialing Craig's number again. The receptionist intercepted the call, just as she had the previous three tries that Felice had made during the past hour. Felice chewed on her lip in agitation. She didn't want to stand him up, but she didn't have a choice. She couldn't meet him as she'd promised to. She had to hand deliver the contracts to Mr. Christophe's attorney immediately. "Well . . . thanks anyway," she said unhappily.

"I'm going to lunch myself," the receptionist said, not sounding too concerned about the hitch in her coworker's meal plans. "But I'll drop the messages on his desk before I go. If he checks in, he'll get the message."

"Thanks," Felice replied.

She grabbed her sweater and keys and picked up the envelope containing the contracts.

Craig Wilson folded the torn and tattered menu for the tenth time and placed it on the table beside him. Felice had stood him up and he couldn't believe it.

The waitress who'd been eyeing him cheerlessly for the forty-five minutes he'd been sitting in the corner booth approached him for the third time. "Ready to order yet?" she asked skeptically, tapping her pencil in irritation on the pad in her hand.

Craig had been starved when he'd walked into the place. It was Felice's favorite Italian restaurant. If the bustling noontime crush were any measure, it was a lot of other people's favorite, too. The four hungry people standing in the front of the line waiting to be seated had been watching him with growing annoyance for the past fifteen minutes. Between their looks, the waitress's increasing coolness, and his growing agitation over Felice's absence, he'd pretty much lost his appetite.

"Uh, no," he said, embarrassed. "I think I'll check and see how much longer it will be before my fiancée can join me." There was no answer at Felice's work number. As an afterthought, he called his own office.

The typist who had been pressed into covering the phones during the lunch hour was busy with two other calls and couldn't work up much concern over his problem. "I don't see any messages here," she announced crisply as she glanced quickly over the profusion of notes on top of the receptionist's desk. "Sorry."

Craig was left with the cold sound of a dial tone. And no Felice.

"My fiancée's been held up," he muttered to the wait-

268

ress as he hurried past her and brushed through the crowd of people waiting to get in.

Lita and Carl Dietrick, the bartender, arrived at Sydney's back door at the same time.

"Afraid nobody's here," he told her apologetically.

"That's okay," she reassured him with a friendly smile. "I can wait."

He unlocked the door and they went inside—Carl toward the bar to check supplies and Lita toward Keith's office to kill some time.

She went over to his tape deck and rather disinterestedly perused the selections. She'd heard so many tapes over the years that it wasn't usually a big thrill to listen to them anymore. Some were obviously for listening pleasure, but most were demos of people wanting to be hired for one thing or another. One caught her eye, and she reached out and touched it.

It was Melanie King's.

Craig Wilson had made it a point not to hang around Sydney's. Until recently he couldn't have afforded a drink of water in the posh night spot, let alone the cover charge. When he'd picked Felice up after work, he'd parked on the street out in front.

And then, when he'd met Melanie . . . Well, it had obviously been smart for them to meet as far from the club as possible. Neither of them wanted any complications in their lives. They'd only slipped once. That night in the alley when she'd needed to see him about their last-minute change in plans. Thinking about it still made him break out in a cold sweat. What if someone had seen them together? Especially now that Melanie was dead.

He parked the car one block away from the club and walked through that same alley. If he weren't so worried about why Felice hadn't showed up, he wouldn't have had the nerve to do this. His hands were cold and damp as he tried the back door. They left it unlocked sometimes if people were inside. To his relief, and increased anxiety, it was open.

Damn it, Felice, he thought in a flash of anger. If you're in here without a good excuse, I'll . . .

He walked cautiously down the hall. The lights were off in Felice's office. He was about to leave as unobtrusively as possible when he heard a voice, singing a cappella, floating from another office nearby. He was frozen in shock at first. Then, like a man in a trance, he moved in the direction from which the song was coming. His hand trembled as he gripped the doorknob. The door was already ajar. He pushed it open a little wider.

She was partially obscured by the large chair just in front of her, so he could see only her upper back. But that voluptuously styled black hair, that elusive figure, that sweet songbird voice . . . It could be only one person.

"Melanie?" he whispered in a disbelieving, tortured voice.

Part of him was shouting that it couldn't be true. Melanie was dead. And there was something odd about her voice. He stepped forward shakily, reaching out a hand as if to dispel a ghost.

It is strange how the mind sometimes sees what it expects to see. A form and voice like Melanie's added to the heavy weight of guilt that had been gnawing at him for so long combined to make him see what in all the world he most feared to see: Melanie King.

Lita heard his strangled voice, and startled, she turned sharply. He was a stranger to her, frozen in the doorway in the act of stepping into the room. There was an expression of utter horror on his face.

She'd been stunned to hear her dead cousin's name on the lips of a stranger, coming as it had in such a totally

270

unexpected way. The man had thought that she was Melanie, she realized uneasily. And he'd been terrified. Not just shocked. Terrified. It was a very peculiar reaction indeed, and one that aroused her own defensive instincts. There was an odor of danger about this man, about this situation, and she went on guard.

They stared at each other warily. As Lita took in his appearance, the man blinked and nervously wiped a hand across his eyes, as if to clear his vision.

"You're not . . ." he mumbled, his voice trailing off in a whisper.

A chill of anticipation cloaked her. Her midnight eyes narrowed in shrewd, reckless determination as she decided to take a gamble.

"Mr. Wills?" she ventured in a calculating guess.

His hand dropped from his face and he turned as white as a sheet. She watched him back away, as if caught in a bad dream and unable to move with any speed. A look of shock replaced the horror on his face.

"How did you know . . . ?" he choked.

How could she have known? What, exactly, did she know? All his worst nightmares were suddenly becoming a reality. He felt the awful panic rise up in him. His brittle nerves, worn and frayed from night after night of fear of discovery, began to shatter.

His world toppled around him like a house of cards, and he turned and ran into the hall.

Carl Dietrick had been hearing the sound of voices from his position behind the bar. That had worried him. It wouldn't be the first time that someone had tried to sneak into Sydney's when it was closed. He tossed the pencil down on the pad of paper. He'd get back to his list of supplies to order after he'd checked to make sure that everything was all right.

The bartender had just walked down the hall to investigate when Craig hurtled by. Dietrick took the younger man's full weight in his chest. He grunted in surprise, and his big arms automatically closed around the fleeing figure.

Lita dashed across the room as Craig fell back and tried urgently to get away.

"Stop!" she cried out.

Carl's big hand closed over Craig's shoulder. Craig knew then that he'd lost. All the fight drained out of him, and he stood limply waiting for the curtain to fall on his future.

Lita braced herself with a hand on the doorway molding.

"Please . . . don't leave yet, Mr. Wills," she urged a little sarcastically as she looked him over with greater care. "There are a few things I'd like to ask you."

Carl, who'd taken a closer look at his captive by now, gazed from Lita to Craig in surprise.

"Mr. Wills?" Carl repeated, baffled. "This is Craig Wilson. Felice's fiancé. What the devil is going on?"

Lita saw Craig blush at the mention of Felice's name, and she guessed that Felice had been another innocent victim of this whole disastrous mess. No matter what he'd done, Craig wasn't very good at concealing his feelings of guilt or humiliation.

Lita forced herself to think of Melanie, and she hardened her heart against sympathy for Felice. She wanted to find out what Craig had to do with Melanie. And whether he was responsible for her death.

Since she still didn't know exactly what had transpired between Craig and Melanie, Lita decided to take another shot in the dark, just to see what she might accidentally shoot down. After all, "Mr. Wills" was up to his neck in this; it was about time he felt the urgent need to explain his role if he were innocent.

"Mr. Wilson?" Lita tried the name on for size, marveling at the way her desire to avenge her cousin gave her

272

the cool, calculating nerve that she needed. "Mr. Wilson, I'd like to know why you killed Melanie King."

It had taken a conscious effort, but Lita was as convincing as a police interrogator, so much so that both Carl and Craig Wilson gaped at her in astonishment. Carl's hand loosened and Craig stumbled back into Keith's office. He slumped into a chair, his face falling forward into his hands and his shoulders shaking from the sobs that were wrenching upward from his stomach.

"I didn't kill her!" he cried out, his voice muffled by his hands. "I swear! I didn't!"

He raised his tortured face and looked from Lita to Carl and back to Lita again, as if pleading to be believed.

"We'd been seeing each other . . . after hours . . . during breaks a couple of times . . . once on the weekend. It was a whirlwind, unexpected thing. It just . . . happened. I met her the day before she was to start rehearsals. She was checking Sydney's over and I had just dropped Felice off for work. It was raining and we both ran into the coffee shop across the street to get a bite to eat." He closed his eyes in bitter recrimination. "I was feeling like the world was closing in on me. I knew that Felice wanted to get married and start a family. But I—I kept thinking of all the women I'd be missing out on if I settled down. Melanie was like a fantasy. She was beautiful and effervescent and wild and free. She was a nightclub entertainer. What man would have let the chance to go out with her slip through his fingers?"

He shot them each the same desperate, challenging look. Carl was too aghast to react. Lita, however, knew Melanie well enough to follow what Craig was talking about.

"Go on," she ordered unsympathetically.

Craig seemed to wilt against the chair. "Well . . . she found it exciting, too. She was playing this little game of keep away with the Christophes and the various chaperones they kept sending home with her. I was her forbidden toy!" He shook his head in disbelief. "God! You can't know how that swelled my ego! I was the plaything, the secret lover of a glamorous singer!"

Carl had moved into the room, as had Lita. No one noticed the slight figure that came down the hall, stopping as if shot as he said the word *lover*.

"The night she was killed," he whispered, still horrified by the thought of it, "we had been planning to get together. I had dropped Felice off at her house and had driven by Melanie's town house just as Sean was bringing her home. She sent him away, and when he was out of sight I went up to the house."

Lita tensely awaited the rest. She was so close now, so close . . .

Craig leaned forward intently, a man suddenly possessed with the need to be believed. "She sent me away," he told them matter-of-factly, a note of desperation creeping into his voice. "She told me she'd been having a problem with an old friend and she was going to talk to him in half an hour and settle it permanently. Then she'd be free to do as she pleased. And we could"—his voice cracked—"we could pick up where we left off the following night."

A painful silence filled the room. Then a slender figure emerged from the shadowed hallway. It was Felice.

"I kept telling myself it was just prewedding jitters," she said, completely stunned by what she had just heard.

Her wounded eyes said it all. She twisted her engagement ring off her finger and, with shaking hands, held it out to Craig. Without thinking, he took it from her. He was so shocked to see her there that he didn't really realize what they were doing.

"I knew, deep inside, that it was more serious than that," she went on shakily. "But I kept thinking if I give Craig enough time, he'll tell me what it is and we can work it out." She lifted cold, trembling fingers to her cheek. "I had no idea—I didn't think—" She couldn't go on. With a choked sob, she turned and ran from the office as hot, bitter tears of betrayal spilled down her cheeks.

"Felice!" Craig cried out hoarsely. He sprang up, suddenly comprehending what was happening. "Please! Felice! Let me explain!"

"Do you want him stopped?" Carl asked sharply as Craig rushed past.

Lita shook her head. "No . . . thanks, Carl." She stood in the middle of Keith's elegant office and tried to concentrate. What had Craig said? Melanie had been having a problem with an old friend, and she was going to settle it permanently. An old friend. "An old Washington friend?" Lita mused aloud. It didn't make any sense.

The cassette clicked off. Melanie's tape had run its course. Lita removed it and stared at it as if hoping she would see the name of the old friend on it. What old friend was in Washington? And causing a problem?

Lita paled and the cassette slipped from her fingers, falling to the plush carpeting. "Oh, no! It can't be . . ." she whispered in agonizing disbelief. "It can't be . . ." But it *had* to be. And in her heart, Lita knew it. "Carl, do me a favor."

"Sure thing, Lita."

She scribbled a message on a notepad she found on Keith's desk. Then she ripped it off and thrust it into Carl's hand. "Could you give this to Keith when he comes in? He should be here any minute."

"No problem."

"Thanks, Carl."

Before he could ask where she was going, she was gone.

Half an hour later she was in a hotel lobby telephone booth, dialing a number.

275

"Hello?" came the tired answer.

Her fingers tightened around the hard, cool plastic. "Jack?" she said as naturally as she could. "It's Lita."

"Lita?" He sounded a little confused. "Uh, am I late? I thought we were getting together for dinner?"

"Yes, you're right. But something's come up, and I wanted to talk to you about it. I was wondering if I could see you?" Her heart was pounding. The world had tilted on its side and nothing was the same.

He hesitated. "I have a couple of appointments this afternoon," he said slowly. "An aspiring recording artist in an hour, and a local songwriter who thinks he's got some material one of my clients could use."

Lita squeezed her eyes shut to hold back the pain. "This is important, Jack." Her control began to slip. "It has to do with Melanie . . ."

The silence this time was different. It hung between them like an invisible sword, sharp and threatening and heavy with danger.

"All right," he reluctantly agreed. "Give me a few minutes to call them and cancel out. Where shall I meet you?"

Where indeed? She'd been wondering that herself. A public setting might be safer, but she just couldn't do what she had to do there. With total strangers all around. Watching as she and a man she'd known for years confronted the awful truth about Melanie's death.

No. This was a private conversation. Between two people who'd known each other in good times and in bad, who'd leaned on each other more times than she could count, who'd cared for each other as friends and trusted each other as business partners. You didn't have a conversation like this in the eye of the world, for all to behold. Theirs should be a private meeting, Lita had decided. A very private meeting.

When she'd walked into the hotel lobby, she'd wondered whether she might be making a mistake in seeing him alone. But she'd known Jack Connery for too many years to be truly afraid of him. The act he had committed must have been done in a fit of passion. She just couldn't conceive of him hurting her.

"I'm downstairs, Jack," she told him. She knew he would hear the pain in her voice. He always had. Jack had a sensitive ear for things like that. "If you don't mind, I'd like to come up to your room."

If there had been any doubt in his mind about the direction their conversation would be taking, her request removed it. It was a defeated, resigned man who replied to her suggestion.

"Okay, Lita. Five minutes . . . Give me five minutes?"

"Sure, Jack. Five minutes."

Keith was standing next to Pete Fallon's desk, preparing to use the detective's telephone to call Lita at the club. He'd asked her to meet him there for a late lunch if she didn't have anything pressing to take care of. He was looking forward to it with rather mixed feelings at the moment.

He had some bad news for Lita, and he wanted to break it to her personally, before she read about it in the papers. Fallon had enough evidence to make an arrest. It wouldn't be long now before the police had Melanie's murderer in custody.

"Why did you start checking the airline schedules?" Keith asked curiously.

Fallon rocked back in his chair and propped his feet on top of his battered desk. "Well, the murder had all the earmarks of a crime of passion. She hadn't been brutalized in any way. There were no marks of attack or attempted rape or even of a major struggle. She hadn't been robbed. We found her purse nearby with everything in it." The detective laced his hands behind his head. "I never thought Sean had anything to do with it." He gave Keith a lopsided grin. "I've known him too long. He wouldn't do something like that."

Keith shrugged. Now that Sean was clear of this mess, he could engage in a little arguing over that point.

"You never know what a man will do over a woman, Fallon," he argued.

Fallon nodded in agreement. "True. But Sean barely knew Melanie King. He may have a temper when he's crossed, but he couldn't have gotten that intensely involved with her in such a short time."

That made sense to Keith. But then, he'd never doubted his brother's innocence.

"No," Fallon mused, recalling his reasoning. "It had to be someone who knew her well enough to lure her out late at night. It had to be someone who was deeply, intensely involved with her—a boyfriend or a lover, or someone aspiring for those positions. The only problem was finding a candidate and proving he had access to her. Considering how closely you were keeping tabs on her, the pool of candidates at first appeared to be zero." Fallon's face took on an air of grim satisfaction. "And then I looked at the facts one more time," he explained. "Who else besides the boys at the club had access to her? We never could identify Mr. Wills, but as sure as God made little green apples, we could come up with one other man."

"Jack Connery," Keith filled in, his voice hardening.

Fallon nodded. "So I started doing the groundwork to prove it. I checked airline records. I can prove he flew under an alias to the West Coast. I assume he went out there prepared to kill Lita if Melanie had given her any hint that he was becoming a problem. If he'd had to do that, he could have flown back, claiming to have been on the East Coast."

Keith's face darkened with a deep rage at the thought of what Connery had been considering doing to Lita.

Fallon stuffed a piece of gum in his mouth. "He may be responsible for a few other of the convenient coincidences in this case," the detective suggested. "There were just too many neatly wrapped-up loose ends in the wrong places to suit me."

Keith dialed the club and got Carl Dietrick. As Carl talked, Keith tensed. "She's gone *where?*" he roared, then uttered an expletive.

"I can't wait for your legal paperwork, Fallon," Keith announced abruptly as he slammed down the receiver and ran to the door. "Lita's gone to see Connery at his hotel."

"What!" Fallon nearly choked on his gum as he stumbled to his feet to follow Keith. "Get in my car! We'll use the lights and the siren!"

Lita knocked on Jack's door. After a few moments it slowly swung open.

"Hi, Lita," he said tiredly.

"Hi, Jack," she murmured, feeling very awkward and not knowing how to begin. How *do* you begin a conversation like this? she wondered in despair.

They stared at each other for a long moment, then Jack stepped back and motioned uneasily for her to enter. He followed her in silence. It certainly didn't look as if he intended to run away, she thought. He was wearing a T-shirt and casual slacks with a wrinkled, slept-in look. There were no shoes on his feet, just black socks.

And he looked like a man who had lost everything, including the hope of forgiveness.

"You know about Melanie, then . . ." he murmured in a thin, flat voice.

His arms were hanging limply at his sides. Then he turned and sat down in the lone chair in the corner of the nondescript hotel room. He searched her face in a brief, anguished way, as if hoping to find some comfort there. All he found was shock and a deep, deep regret.

Lita stood next to the simple dresser, leaning against it for support.

"I guessed . . ." she admitted. She shook her head and closed her eyes. "How could it have happened, Jack?" she pleaded, furious and totally shattered by his act of betrayal. "How could you . . ."

He leaned back in his chair, his face seeming as pale as the sand-colored fabric.

"I don't know," he whispered, then, more forcefully, "I just don't know!"

His hands lay limply on his thighs. He was the image of a beaten man.

"I loved her . . ." he said as if the words had been wrenched from him in torture. "I loved her." He opened his eyes and stared at Lita as if she were a thousand miles away from him. "And she never saw it. Never. In all those years."

He drew in a ragged breath and ran his hand weakly across his brow.

"This is a hell of a way for it to end, isn't it?" he murmured. The bitter, humorless laugh died half-voiced on his lips.

Lita took in the disheveled setting and sadly had to agree. His briefcase lay open on a small table. A couple of demo tapes were scattered carelessly about.

He turned his head with an effort and squinted his eyes to focus on what she was looking at.

"I've been so blown away," he said, speaking rather slowly now, "that I haven't been able to listen to the demos . . . or . . ." He turned his head slowly back and his voice trailed off. "It doesn't really matter any-more."

Lita's hands were clenched around the strap on her

purse. Her fingernails were biting into her palms from the tension. Tears welled up in her eyes, and she bit her lip to keep from falling apart.

"Jack," she said in a tear-choked voice. "How could it have happened?"

She felt like a wounded person asking for salt to be thrown on her sores, but she had to know. If for no other reason than to stop the agonizing wondering that would otherwise plague her for the rest of her life.

He drew in a ragged, shallow breath.

"All . . . those years . . . I tracked her down and pulled her out of drunken binges . . . I pulled strings to keep her working . . . I worshiped her . . . from afar . . . and she was grateful . . . but that was all. She thought I did it out of friendship!" His eyes shut tightly and a tear squeezed out of each corner, sliding down his face. "Friendship! She thought it was just a business interest in her that kept me going, kept me planning for her future. . . ." More tears trickled down his cheeks, and he grimaced in deep suffering. "I slaved for her . . . because I loved her."

Lita suffered with him in spite of it all. She vividly recalled Melanie's last letter and the unfeeling way that she'd described poor Jack. Who'd want him? she'd flung out, not thinking how those terrible words would wound her faithful, adoring friend.

Jack lay against the chair, breathing shallowly.

Lita still did not have the answer she'd sought. Now she feared that Jack was so lost in his own misery that he would not willingly tell her what had finally been the last straw and ignited the fatal struggle.

Lita wet her lips and asked.

"But Jack, how could you have . . ." She flinched and stopped, unable to say the awful words aloud.

It didn't matter. He knew what she meant, and he made no effort to pretend otherwise.

"Through all the men she played with over the years . . . I waited." He seemed to be concentrating all his energies on forming the words now. "I kept hoping . . . that finally . . . she'd give it all up . . . the men . . . I kept praying . . . that one day she'd see . . . me . . . want me . . . like I wanted her all those years."

Lita found she couldn't watch him as he bared the dreaded fact to her, and she looked at the dresser. His dobb kit was open, its contents overflowing. On top lay an empty bottle of prescription medication. Something to help him sleep.

"That night . . . I was waiting for her . . . when Sean brought her home," Jack was saying in strange, distant tones. "She'd given me a key. But . . . when she saw me . . . she was . . . furious. She said . . . she had a busy night planned. She was going out with Craig Wilson." Jack's face contorted weakly into a sneer. "How could she have let . . . that self-serving kid . . . near her?" he asked.

Jack stared vacantly into space, as if seeing the scene again.

His breathing seemed shallower and slower and his eyes were very dark, as if the pupils were very dilated. Lita began to feel an uneasy twinge of fear. He didn't look just afraid or overwhelmed with remorse or deeply depressed and guilty because of the crime he'd committed. He looked like a man going into a medical emergency.

Her purse slipped from her fingers and she came a step closer.

"Jack . . . are you all right?" she whispered fearfully.

He didn't seem to hear her. He continued what he had been saying instead.

"I told her to call it quits. I ordered her to concentrate on her career . . . I shouted at her to stop humiliating herself with every man who came sniffing around." He half-blinked his eyes, as if flinching in recollection. The rest of his body lay slack in the chair. "She slapped me . . . that . . . that was when . . . I just seemed to snap . . . I didn't care anymore . . . I grabbed her . . . and I . . . I kissed her . . . I kissed her just the way I'd wanted to for years and years . . . and once I got so close to her like that . . . I couldn't let her go."

In his hoarsely whispered admission Jack sounded both profoundly ashamed and bitterly triumphant.

Lita could imagine the shock that Melanie had had then, never having thought of Jack that way. It would have been especially hard for her since she had always made it a point to have her love affairs with men who were basically strangers. And for Jack to love her and want her like that . . . Jack, who knew more about her than anyone who walked the face of the earth. Except for Lita, perhaps.

Jack's pallor was even more pronounced, and his words sounded slurred. With growing trepidation Lita drew closer to him.

"Jack, have you taken something?" she asked anxiously, recalling the empty container on the dresser.

Jack made a great effort to finish what he had to say.

"Then . . . that jerk . . . Wilson . . . showed up on her . . . doorstep. . . . She told him to go away . . . she told him . . ." Jack's voice cracked poignantly. "She told him . . . she had a problem . . . with an old friend . . . and she was going to take care of it first . . . and then they could go out. . . ."

Lita sank down next to him on limbs numb with fear and shock.

"Something broke inside. I . . . grabbed her . . . arm . . . forced her outside. We walked a long way until there was . . . only . . . darkness . . . and woods . . . and the sound . . . of running water. I begged her.

283

I begged her. But she said . . . she didn't . . . love . . . me."

Lita felt his brow. It was cold. His breathing was very strange. In terror she jumped up and grabbed the phone. It rang and rang and rang.

"I . . . was . . . the . . . one . . . who . . . broke . . . in," he said, his breathing becoming labored and irregular. "I . . . wanted . . . them . . . to . . . think . . . that . . . guy . . . we . . . never . . . caught . . . did . . . it. Killed . . . her."

"Hold please," the operator said into the earpiece before Lita could scream no.

Lita dragged the phone closer to Jack and knelt in front of him.

"Jack," she said urgently, grabbing his cold limp hand in hers. "What did you take?"

He blinked very slowly. All his reflexes seemed to be gone. It was becoming very hard to see her. He couldn't focus anymore. The effort took almost everything he had left. Somehow he managed to raise his fingertips slightly in a last effort to touch her face. Tears swam in his sad, tragic eyes.

"I'm . . . sorry . . . Lita. Forgive . . ."

He never finished. The breath slid out of him, and his fingers sank back limply onto his lap.

Lita grabbed his shoulders and shook him.

"Jack! Jack! What have you done to yourself!" she shouted at him brokenly through her own tears.

There was a great banging on the door, and Lita sprang across the room to fling it open. Fallon and Keith crashed inside as she broke into an immediate plea for help.

"Call an ambulance! He's taken something!"

She grabbed the empty medication container and thrust it toward the detective.

And then there was organized pandemonium as the

call was placed and the police tried artificial resuscitation. The paramedics were there in a matter of minutes, and Jack was taken to the D.C. General emergency room a short time later.

It was all for naught.

Jack Connery was dead on arrival.

Keith put a comforting arm around Lita as she cried for Melanie, for Jack . . . for their wasted lives . . .

The stars were shimmering like white diamonds in a velvet sky, but Lita didn't see a one.

She was standing in the middle of her living room with her eyes shut and her arms positioned as if dancing with a man who wasn't there. The soft light of a candle cast a warm glow around the soft cushions and hardwood floors, striking out into the darkness through the huge glass windows that had been fitted into every wall.

The tape she'd pushed into the stereo system began to play, and softly she sang along. The guys had done a great job on the orchestration. She still felt like crying whenever she heard it.

> I'd lived an empty illusion of life.
> A dreamer of dreams unmet . . .
> Each year they'd faded into regret.
>
> For years, no one had reached me at all.
> Men came and went without knowing how.
> There wasn't one for whom I could fall.
>
> Til you . . . You touched the soul of my heart.
> You warmed the fires of love.
> You taught me all, only to depart.
>
> Come back! Come back and love me again!
> We two were meant to be . . .
> One flesh, one heart, one eternity.